ROOIKAT

BY THE SAME AUTHOR

SA Flyfishing Clinic
Fishing the Margins
Fishing Wider Margins

(With Jonathan Boulton and others)
SA Yellowfish Clinic
SA Saltwater Clinic
SA Flyfishing Clinic (revised)

(With Bruce Black)
Bait, Lure & Drop Shot Clinic

ROOIKAT

By

PAUL CURTIS

PLATANNA
PRESS

Rooikat
by Paul Curtis

First published by Platanna Press, 2017

ISBN 978-0-9814255-6-6

Platanna Press
www.platannapress.co.za

10 9 8 7 6 5 4 3 2 1

23:00 SUNDAY, SEPTEMBER 10, 1989

Pelindaba Nuclear Research Centre

SECURITY WAS SLACK at Pelindaba that night – unusually so for such an important facility. But the guards had become used to it since production had stopped. Except for checking-in the odd mysterious comings and goings late at night, the job was one long, empty, hour after hour. It was also the last hour of the graveyard shift and rumour had it they were all soon to be out of work anyway. So when the camouflage-painted South African Defence Force Unimog recovery vehicle pulled up at the gate, loaded with the large coffin-shaped metal box in the back, it was waved through with the briefest, most cursory inspection. Half-an-hour later, the same Unimog, still loaded with the box, left the facility by the same gate – the guards not even giving it a second glance.

It wasn't always so. Especially in the early days, when the programme began, and security checks had been stringent to the point of paranoia. And doubly so around the aircraft-hanger-like Building 5000, the most secret of secret places. You couldn't even get near it unless you'd been thoroughly vetted and all foreigners were especially forbidden. You had to be a natural-born, white South African to work there – of solid Afrikaans stock preferably.

Now all the work had come to an end. The seven, 1.8m high, 65cm wide, 118 kiloton bombs, each named after a heroic Boer general, lying in their lead-lined vaults were to be finally taken out, made safe, dismantled and then, their highly enriched uranium hearts harvested and put aside, melted-down into scrap metal. The seven locally-made Israeli Jericho ballistic missiles in the armoury nearby were to suffer the same fate. Originally there had been eight bombs and missiles manufactured at Pelindaba. But the first completed, code-named General Botha had, over the South Atlantic on 22 September, 1979, exploded in a blaze of worldwide intelligence agency chatter and media interest.

* * *

The operation was carried out with military precision, which was not surprising as the four ex-SADF Special Forces members were once part of a battle-hardened forward unit that was sometimes called in to re-arm the Olifant Mk1 tanks that had penetrated, or been cut-off, deep inside Angola during South African 'border war' excursions. They knew how to move dangerous munitions long distances, and load and offload heavy ordnance as quickly as safety or circumstances permitted, and how to fight their way out again under fire from Cuban troops, sometimes with Russian Migs circling overhead. This mission would be nothing – at worse they might have to knock a couple of half-awake guards on the head, but probably not even that.

The seven great Boer generals – Meijer, Kruitzinger, Hertzog, de Wet, Joubert, Cronje and de la Rey, lay silent in their vaults. The men worked almost reverentially. The main building was, as promised, unlocked, and the freshly-oiled doors slid noiselessly apart. They reversed the Unimog back to a row of bays against the back wall. Vault 7, with its heavy, lead-lined steel door was also unlocked, the trolley inside cradling the 1.8m bomb code named de la Rey.

Now came the tricky part. Muscling the trolley up alongside the Unimog, they first opened the metal box on the back and, using the truck's 1.5 tonne hoist, lifted out and lowered to the floor what appeared to be de la Rey's twin brother. Next they hoisted the genuine bomb off the cradle and into the box and replaced it with the fake. Box closed, and cradle back into Vault 7, they drove out of the hanger, closed the doors and headed back towards the gate. The bored guard gave a half-hearted salute and raised the boom. They were nearly home and dry, just a long drive on deserted Sunday night roads. Piece of cake.

* * *

At exactly 07:00 Monday morning, Jan Coetsee, Commandant of Guards, pulled into the main gate of Pelindaba. The day shift had been on for an hour. Calling one of the guards he asked to see the night book. As expected, not very busy. Nothing the whole night until the early morning when there was a single entry: Army utility vehicle DTD365M, *four military personnel including driver, in 04:45, out 05:12.*

So no problems then. Coetsee drove on to Building 5000, parked in his bay and walked across to the doors – pleased that they looked exactly as he had left them when he locked up. He opened them and strode across to Vault 7 – locked too. He opened it and checked that de la Rey was safe and secure. Locked up again and walked across to his office, sat down and smiled. Everything looked okay. It was going to be a busy day – his staff would be in around eight, the IAEA were coming for their first inspection at 12:00 sharp. His thoughts were interrupted by the phone.

'Good morning, Coetsee speaking …'

'*Môre* Jan. I just wanted to let you know de la Rey is back home, safe and sound.'

'Thank you Colonel, I'm happy to have been of service. We'll speak soon, *totsiens*.'

'*Totsiens* Commandant.'

Coetsee put the phone down and lit the first Peter Stuyvesant of the day. Sucking hard, he took the smoke deep into his lungs and exhaled, giving a long sigh of relief.

* * *

The four inspectors of the International Atomic Energy were on time and presented their credentials at the main gate at Pelindaba. The inspectors were accompanied by officials from State President de Klerk's office and the chief atomic scientist from Armscor, Dr. Henri du Plessis. Coetsee, who had himself seen the delegation through the security proceedures, welcomed them and asked what they would like to see first.

'They want to see the bombs first, Commandant. The six finished and the seventh unarmed one,' replied one of the officials.

'We won't take up too much of your time today Commandant, but over the next few months you're going to get sick of us,' added Dr. du Plessis.

Coetsee, thinking that at least he was in a job for a few more months, led them over to the first vault and opened it.

'I'm happy to help. Meet General Meijer.'

The rest of the inspection went well. Each general was introduced in turn, and when Vault 7 was opened one of the inspectors asked:

'And this is the one that is under construction, yes?'

'That's correct, code name de la Rey.'

Dr. du Plessis cut in: 'We were going to arm it when the State President called a halt to the programme. The HEU is still in the main stockpile, we haven't processed it yet.'

Coetsee thought that he caught the slightest wink from du Plessis as he turned towards him but he could have been mistaken. The inspector seemed satisfied.

'Okay, let's go see these Israeli rockets you claim to have souped-up.'

* * *

It was the final inspection. The whole rigmarole had taken a lot longer than Coetsee had thought – closer to three-and-a-half years than the couple of months first anticipated. Dozens of inspections were made by several different teams to Pelindaba and Building 5000, to the nearby Armscor facility, Advena Labs, to the old testing site in the Kalahari, and to the nuclear waste facility nearby. All the documents and blueprints for the design of the bombs were destroyed by order of State President de Klerk – all that remained was the destruction of the bombs themselves.

This was finally carried out in April, 1993. The inspectors accompanied by Hazmat suited-up technicians from Armscor.

It took less than a week to dismantle the bombs. Their explosive heads made safe, their HE uranium cores removed and put into lead-lined canisters to be stored in a separate concrete bunker next to other nuclear waste from the Koeberg reactor. This waste facility was deep underground at dry, dusty Vaalputs in the Northern Cape hinterland. The metal bomb casings were then unceremoniously dumped outside the building, to be taken later to the smelter at Iscor iron foundry at Vanderbjilpark, south of Johannesburg.

When the process was complete, Coetsee shook hands with the inspectors, half of whom left to oversee the cores on the long trip to the waste storage facility, half to escort the casings on the much shorter trip to Iscor. As the heavy-duty vehicles with armed outriders left the main gate, the Commandant gave an uncharacteristic skip of delight. They'd actually got away with it. *Magtig!*

THIS YEAR

ONE

Pa

PA WAS DEAD. I caught the Mango red-eye from Cape Town to Lanseria – the puke-orange colour of the 737 and the graphics that went out with bell-bottoms mixed with the smell of aviation fuel nearly bringing up the brandies I'd thought I'd slept off the night before. I was feeling my age. The girl at the Tempest car hire counter didn't help – bubbly and efficient, all teeth and tits – where do they find them? Especially those who are happy to be behind a desk at sparrow's fart. Didn't take long and I was pointing their basic-but-cheap Toyota bakkie back towards Jo'burg and the turn-off to the highway west. It was mid-morning now and you could feel the heat building already. But I'm not a complete *doos*, the bakkie did have aircon and I hadn't forgotten my Polaroids.

The traffic was heavy as I skirted Sandton, then Krugersdorp, stop-start driving through the inevitable roadworks that they promised would be finished back in 2014 and three years later were as bad as ever. But thankfully the roadworks thinned out a little where the dual carriageway petered out. I began to settle into long distance driving mode, hunched down in the seat, aircon on full blast, elbow out the window – one eye on the potholes, the other looking out for stray cattle, goats, the occasional mangy dog. I set my brain into neutral for the next six or seven, maybe even eight hours – through seemingly endless mielie fields, then cattle country due west to Ventersdorp, Sannieshof, Delareyville and Vryburg. Then into dry bushveld north past Tosca, Pomfret and west again through semi-desert to Terre'Blanche and home. The drive, as it always is in these parts, was interminable. I tried the radio but couldn't find anything other than incessant talkshow chat, township jive or sqeezebox-heavy *boeremusiek*. And that's when I could get reception.

You count the distances in hours – hour after mind-numbing hour, the road endlessly straight as an arrow in the heat-stunned distance. You only stop when your stomach says you have to, or your bladder. I stopped at Vryburg, an old Boer settlement, grown fat on the best beef raised in Africa. I had a piece of one at the Durado Steers, flame-grilled, washed down with a Castle Lager. I filled-up the bakkie and, leaving the highway, turned north – nearly half-way.

I was in that semi-comatose state that most South African drivers slip into when the road is endless and straight when, with a blast of horns, a heavy-duty truck with *Venison Meat Supply* in big letters on the back ripped past me from behind. It woke me up, which was a pretty good thing as the road had deteriorated to the extent where you couldn't tell whether there was more tar or more potholes. Didn't bother me too much though; after all I was in a hired Toyota and, as everyone knows, hire vehicles are indestructible. So I began to think of Pa and what arrangements I'd have to make for the funeral.

Oom Mackie had phoned last night to tell me that Pa had died in a car crash and I felt next to *fokol*. We'd grown apart over the years, especially the last ten after Ma had passed on.

To be sure, we'd never been that close. He'd never been home much when I was growing up – his duties in the army kept him busy and, later, his job heading up security at the atomic energy research facility at Pelindaba, near Pretoria. He wouldn't talk about either. What happened in special ops often wasn't fit conversation for the family dinner table and the security job came under the Official Secrets Act of 1959 and breaking it could end up with a late night visit and a non-return trip to a John Vorster Square holding cell.

Life, from my earliest memories, up to when I went to live with my grandparents at the farm, was a series of army pre-fab houses – married quarters on various bases scattered around the country. Tempe, Heidelburg, Kimberley, Phalaborwa, Middelburg, Oudtshoorn, Potch and, once, even Durban. We'd move every couple of years – new house, new school, new friends, never really settled, always the outsider. The townie kids always made it hard for us army *braks.* But we coped. We had to, and anyway most of us were tough, brought up by tough fathers who wouldn't have it any other way. Also I had rugby. I was quick, and once I'd filled out my lanky frame, stronger than most of the other kids. In the small town schools I went to I was an automatic pick for the first team in my age group, and often in the next group up. A fearsome schoolboy eighth man – one day I was sure to be a Springbok. Of course, once I got to big city university there were six bigger, tougher, faster, more fearsome number eights ahead of me. And I got sorted out quickly.

Pa, now he *was* a rugby star – played for Griquas in the Sixties, a little before their legendary Currie Cup champion heydays. In Kimberley they still talk about Buddy Swartz's two tries in the final against the mighty Blue Bulls of 1970. The few pictures of Pa at the time in the family album show a tall, rangy man, with blue eyes and hair cropped short. He was good-looking in a severe sort of way. (People say that I look a lot like him, but with almost white hair and Ma's grey eyes.) Ma, a farm girl, fell head over heels – the wedding pictures show her holding on to his arm as if he was about to bolt for it. It might have been better for her in the long run if he had.

I remember fleeting images from the sporadic times Pa was at home – usually he'd be on border patrol (or 'shooting communists' as he called it) for three to six months at a stretch with a month home R&R. These short breaks home always started with two weeks of family time. Ma would fuss about a lot and we'd visit either her parents back at the farm near Terre'Blanche, or we'd camp at a nearby, usually inland, holiday resort. Fish and braai, braai and fish. These were good times, but never lasted. Once we were back, Pa would get together with his mates, other officers and a couple of long-term NCOs, to swop yarns over braaivleis about what they'd been up to on the Caprivi or inside Angola. These get-togethers were always beer and brandy-fuelled and usually degenerated into raucousness, ending in a state of morose, drunken comradeship. After a week or so of this, Pa would go into his shell. He'd stop socialising, stop even talking to us. He'd spend time in the gym, running, or on the shooting range, getting himself back to his fighting-fit self. For the few days before shipping out he'd be wound up like a spring, itching to get back to what really drove him – war. Neither Ma nor I could compete with that sort of pull.

One furlough though, Pa came back from a shorter than usual deployment looking as if he'd seen a ghost. He was a shadow of himself, just sat for days in a room with the shades drawn. Even Ma couldn't get what had happened out of him. The pals as usual came round to braai and drink. But they were also pale imitations of themselves. They still drank, but now with the quiet seriousness as if at a funeral.

I only realised much later that it was indeed something of a death. They were drinking because what had died was their belief in their own invincibility.

It was kept very quiet at the time, and even today nobody knows what really happened – like most history it depends on which side is writing it. But in March 1988, the South African army retreated from Angola after the bloody battle of Cuito Cuanavale. Where, in the middle of the fight and after virtually destroying the Angolan and Cuban forces, they were ordered by their political masters in Pretoria not to take the town which had been the main objective of the battle. To the soldiers involved it was a betrayal they never got over. To those that died there, well, they didn't give a fuck one way or another.

A few weeks later Pa announced that he was resigning his commission and leaving the army. He was being seconded to a new security service and we were moving to Pretoria.

The country began to change as I drove west. The typical South African grassveld that once fed vast herds of zebra and wildebeest and now grew out prime beef, changed almost imperceptibly into semi-desert thornveld, with game farms and canned lion hunting, which 800 kilometres further on became Kalahari desert sand which grew out *fokol*, except sidewinder snakes and thirst-crazed jackals. But fortunately I wasn't going that far – I was nearly at my destination. I was feeling pretty thirsty myself by this time. Almost hungry for a beer. A cold, cold, *cold* beer.

Terre'Blanche

The new South Africa broom has barely swept away the cobwebs, hardly scratched the surface of the old South African town of Terre'Blanche. Granted the signs that had ordered where whites could piss and blacks should shit, and vice versa, had been long ago taken down. And the dozen or so fast food joints and watering holes, two sex shops and the local massage parlour-cum lap-dancing club on what the townsfolk called the *boerewors* strip, were also colour blind. It was the colour of your money that was their sole concern. But the dust devils still blew down the hard-packed, potholed main street and devilment, if not the devil himself, lurked behind the dark curtained windows of the corrugated iron-fronted houses.

Terre'Blanche was named after a Boer hunter who, legend has it, had fallen off his horse and ended up spending a couple of weeks in the shade of the nearby koppie recovering. It began life as a trading outpost for passing hunters and trekker stock farmers, who were too foot and heart sore to carry on. Later, these early settlers were joined by unreconstructed Boer fighters who wanted to live as far away as possible from the crowds of Brits and chancers from the Cape who had moved into the vacuum of the conquered Boer republics – especially into the rich goldfields of Johannesburg and the Eastern

Transvaal. The town grew to the west of the koppie, the major landmark in the area – a large round-bouldered carbuncle that poked its way out of the surrounding white sand scrubland. At a couple of hundred metres higher than the surrounding flat and dry country, and marking the place of springs that had never been known to dry completely, it was an important beacon for the early Bushman and Khoikhoi wanderers long before the later hunters and trekkers. The hunters who were in search of elephants; the trekkers, greener pastures, which they never found.

The town grew like many South African backveld towns – in fits and starts. And depending on its prosperity and the styles of the times, with buildings that could range from badly-copied Cape Dutch to poorly-built examples of what was thought to be modern or classy. A hotchpotch of mainly square or rectangular houses, some with curvaceous gables and a stoep, large wooden front doors and sash windows with tin roofs instead of the original thatch. Then a big stone church was built, towering over the townspeople. Later there was a spurt of 1950s-ugly during the wool boom – more cement box buildings.

In the 1960s and 1970s, the growth spurts became a flood when the platinum mines opened with, if possible, even uglier buildings – so-called Boere Bauhaus – heavy cement, glass and steel civic monstrosities. And with new suburbs mushrooming that were pure mining town – tin and *broekie* lace. Even the so-called Location, a mile or so out of town, with its wood and iron shacks that itinerant Coloured and Northern Sotho workers called home, was modernised. The shacks torn down and replaced by street after street of concrete boxes with outdoor privies and that were given one of those poetic Afrikaans or vernacular African names that meant Beautiful View or Sunrise, but which seldom lived up to the name. The locals called it the Township.

But all this was overshadowed by the work that was commissioned to celebrate South Africa's twentieth anniversary of becoming a republic – a giant head of assassinated Prime Minister, H.F. Verwoerd, 'the architect of Apartheid', carved out of the great boulder topping the landmark koppie that overlooked the town. Mount Rushmore in the thornveld.

I hadn't been in Terre'Blanche since I'd been kicked out of the police force. Or, more politically correctly, taken my package. Most of my pale male colleagues had done the same – early retirement with a large lump sum and nothing to do with it except buy a bar or bottle store. Most of them did just that and sat around all day in various stages of happiness waiting for the cirrhosis to carry them off. I, of course, was a lot more stupid. I didn't just take my package, but I took my sergeant, Chesney Cook, with me and opened the Rainbow Nation's first, and probably still only, multiracial private detective agency – Koekemoer & Cook, or Cook & Koekemoer depending if we were touting for BEE business. We had cards printed for both eventualities. And up to now both of us had spent most of the time sitting around.

I parked in front of the Royal Hotel which had been my drinking hole in my varsity holidays and sporadic visits home. The place hadn't changed much. At three in the afternoon almost deserted – a couple of locals at the bar, a miner passed out at a table, lying with arms stretched out, one big hand clutching a glass that had contained the last of a string of double spook and diesels. The other hand holding onto the edge of the tabletop as if it were flotsam from a shipwreck. Let go and he'd surely drown.

The first Castle didn't touch sides. They still kept them ice-cold at the Royal. The second began to revive me. I felt almost normal again as I asked the barman for a third. He was fat faced with a ponytail and looked like a middle-aged refugee from a Jo'burg advertising agency. I didn't know him, but that wasn't unusual – country pub barmen come and go. I said thanks for the beer and asked him if he was from these parts. Now, anyone who's spent a lot of their life sitting on a bar counter knows there are only two types of barmen. The talkative ones, and those that say nothing. Fat Face was the former.

'Naw, been here eighteen months, feels like eighteen years.'

'Where from?' I asked.

'Cape Town.'

'Cape Town, *fok*, you're a long way from home, what happened, take a wrong turn at the Bellville flyover?'

He laughed, and said, 'Naw, followed my chick here, she's working as a hostess at the Slipped Disc.'

I assumed this was one of establishments on the strip and nodded.

'Anything happening here?' And nodding towards the comatose miner, 'Or is it as sleepy as the oke over there?'

Now he really got into the swing of things, probably hadn't had an ear to bend since he'd arrived.

'We still have our moments but it's pretty quiet these days, everyone's shit-scared over what's going to happen at the mine. They say prices are so low it's hardly worth mining anymore. The company's already moved their head office from Jo'burg to overseas. The owners have fucked off too … they're more interested in mining London property than holes in the veld they say. I hear though that a curry muncher company is interested in buying them out here and that there's going to be a new mine opening and lots of cash floating around. But it's probably just bullshit. Naw, I think we're going to have to split … I hear good things about Botswana. They've got diamonds coming out of their ears there. There'll be lots of thirsty miners there and plenty looking for a *pomp* … shit, a fucking gold mine for me and the chick or a diamond mine … *Ja*, Botswana here we come …'

Fok. Once I'd turned on his tap it was impossible to switch it off. I paid the bill and chucked another twenty down on the counter and told my new best friend to have one on me. I couldn't put it off any longer, it was time to head out to the old place.

Klein Drinkwater

The farm was named *Klein Drinkwater* by the Boer trekker that first settled there and who had come from a rock-strewn dot on the map called *Onder Klein Drinkwater*, about half-way between Adelaide and Cradock in the Eastern Cape. He was Petrus de Jager and was my mother's great-grandfather. He was considered somewhat eccentric, if not mad, especially for the times he lived in. Instead of clearing out the Khoikhoi families he found on 'his' new property, he offered them a deal. They could continue to live on the land and come and go as they pleased so long as one family stayed on permanently to work as herdsmen. Over the next hundred and fifty years this worked surprising well. The Khoikhoi who lived on the farm eventually even taking a version of the de Jager family name, first as *'die swart de Jagers'* as the Boer neighbours mockingly called them. By the 1900s they were known as *'swart Jagers'*, eventually simply called *Swartjagter* – which for a people with a couple of thousand years heritage of hunting the land around is not a bad name I reckon.

Although there was, especially in the Apartheid years after 1950, a racial chasm between the de Jagers and the Swartjagters, there was a close symbiotic relationship. The Swartjagters prospered as the de Jagers prospered. But not to the same extent. The relationship fell apart eventually when the pull of jobs on the mines and in town became irresistible. Still, remnants of the Swartjagter clan remained on *Klein Drinkwater*.

I'd always thought of the farm as my second home. Besides the family visits on Pa's short R&Rs from the army, I spent most school holidays there with my grandparents, especially after the family move to Pretoria. And for the last two years of my high school education it really was home to me. Ma and Pa were going through bad times and Ma thought I'd be better off out of the line of fire. I didn't mind – school in Pretoria was not much fun. So it was quite a relief to get away. Of course I never would have agreed if I'd known how ill Ma was. I guess she thought it better for me not to know. Oupa and Ouma were old school Afrikaners – church every Sunday and brandy reserved for special occasions – christenings, weddings, funerals and at the annual big hunt where half the district turned out to shoot Oupa's *spingbokke*.

Ouma baked thick crusty farm bread, *koeksisters*, *melktert*, *roosterkoek*, jam tarts, apricot, apple and lemon meringue pies, and cakes of endless variety. Oupa chain-smoked Lexingtons. They put up with Pa because he was married to their favourite daughter but they didn't like him much. I was the son they'd never had and while Ouma tried her best to feed me up, Oupa taught me the things important to him. Man's things, like cleaning the rifle after using it, how to whistle in dog language, and to never trust a man whose eyes are too close together.

The drive was, even after so many years away, familiar. The never-forgotten landmarks: a rocky outcrop home to countless generations of dassies, the old cement reservoir with the remnants of a long-broken *windpomp*, the gully where I'd laid-up waiting for the springbok to pour past, chased by herdsmen on the nimble Basuto ponies used for rounding up the sheep in the backveld. I shot my first buck there – I remember Pa making me eat the heart raw as his pals laughed and shouted encouragement.

'Eat boy you're a *jagter* now.'

I remember too, how pissed they all got at the braai after the hunt. And my first taste of the brandy I necked from the bottle when they were too far gone to notice. I spat it out then … *sies.* Pity I got a taste for it just a few years later.

The farmhouse hadn't changed. A solid, thick-walled rectangle with big windows and heavy wooden shutters and a shady reed-ceilinged stoep around all four sides, backing on to a rocky, round-bouldered koppie like the many others that every here and there poked their heads out of the flat dry thornveld of the district. The tall gables promised an indoors of spacious rooms and high ceilings, with plenty of dark attic space under the Karroo-red painted corrugated iron roof. The sort of house that was at once at home in Africa whilst daring the elements to throw everything it could at it. Blistering, unrelenting heat much of the year … bitter cold winter nights … high winds and dust storms sand-blasting across the thousand kilometres of highveld … torrential rain and flash flood, thunder and lightning heralding hailstones the size of guineafowl eggs drumming on the roof like stampeding wildebeest. The house had survived them all.

I pulled up under the straggly pin oak which Ouma had nurtured and cherished for fifty years and which had grudgingly responded by merely surviving. I got out of the car, alone with my thoughts, when I was interrupted.

'*Kleinbaas* Jaco! Ai, ai, such sorry times bring you home.'

It was Annetjie, matriarch of the Swartjagter family, and housekeeper for as long as I can remember. Once almost a mahogany carbon copy of Ouma, but now wizened, face furrowed and concerned.

'I have cleaned the house and made up the bed in your old room, I knew you'd be coming. I asked the Lord and he said yes, Annetjie, he'll be sure to come.'

Grabbing my travel bag and laptop, I followed her into the house, a pace or two behind, bowing my head so she couldn't see the tears that had suddenly filled my eyes. As I surreptitiously brushed them away, I saw in the gloom all the familiar things. The precious *wakis* that old Petrus De Jager had carried on the back of his wagon all the way from the Eastern Cape in the 1830s, the later-added stinkwood tallboy and dining table, the big Aga stove bought after an especially good wool cheque, the fly-proof mesh section of the stoep where the biltong was cured in the cold dry winter air. The recipe was an old family one that was followed religiously. The meat, fat on, cut lengthways into strips. The secret marinade rubbed into each strip. The day's soaking. The careful hanging to make sure no single strip touches another. And then the wait, the impatient testing, cutting small slivers until it is just how wet or dry you like it best.

I dropped the bag in the room and followed Annetjie back to the kitchen. She had a sandwich of fresh farm bread and cold mutton with home-made apricot chutney waiting for me.

When I finished eating I went outside again, where Annetjie's son Carolus was waiting, hat held before him, quiet, solemn-featured.

'Evening Boss,' he greeted me.

Carolus was the last Swartjagter man left on the farm. The rest had drifted off to work in the mines or to follow one dream or another in the city. There was little enough to keep anyone here now Pa was gone, and anyway he'd never been much of one for farming. So he more or less gave Carolus the run of the place to do what he wanted. This worked out well for Carolus as he'd always hated the thought of mining. From boyhood he'd had great affinity for animals – sheep would follow him as if he was the Messiah. Which to the sheep, especially when he broke out the bales of lucerne in winter, he was.

I asked Carolus to show me around, not expecting much. He had anticipated me and already had a couple of horses saddled. Boerperds – that mixed breed of Arab, thoroughbred and Flemish horses that ran the British troops ragged in the Anglo-Boer War for three years. Boerperds are known for their stamina and ability to get by on meagre rations and just veld grass if necessary. The Brits had thoroughbreds shipped out from England that needed to be grain-fed and pampered.

I couldn't remember when last I'd ridden but was happy not to embarrass myself getting on. It took a while before I felt fully in control again and then, slowly, that surge of enjoyment when you become almost part of the horse.

We didn't have much time to look around though, dusk was fast approaching. But what I saw was good. The fences were strung tight as guitar-strings and the stock – mainly sheep but with some goats and a herd of Nguni cattle, cows with calves at foot looked good too. The Ngunis were a testament to Oupa's insistence years ago that to thrive as a cattle farmer in African veld you needed African cattle. I could see Carolus thought the same from the light in his eyes as he pointed out his favourites, telling me the names of each one. One a brown and white bull with horns that wouldn't be out of place in Texas was called, surprisingly, Shortie.

We got home just as night fell. I helped Carolus unsaddle and turn the horses into the stock pen. I told him I thought he'd done a fine job and I'd like to see more tomorrow. He said that would be fine. He wasn't going anywhere in a hurry.

It had been a long day. That night I slept like the dead.

Oom Mackie

I woke up with a clear head – clean air and sleep without the aid of brandy will do that. I smelled coffee – *moer koffie*, a potent blend of pulverised coffee and chicory simmered in a blue enamel coffee pot on the Aga; no filters, just the grounds in water bubbling away, thick and strong with a layer of sediment at the bottom of the pot. I washed quickly and headed for the kitchen.

'How many eggs, boss Jaco?' Was old Annetjie's greeting.

'Three please, but first coffee.'

It was a while since I'd had moer koffie and I scorched my hand grabbing the pot off the stove. I used a tea cloth and was more successful, pouring the steaming black liquid through a strainer into a matching enamel mug. I added a big dollop of sweetened condensed milk straight from the can into the coffee, then stirred and watched as it turned a perfect golden-brown. I blew on it and took a sip … it was still much too hot, but delicious.

After breakfast I phoned Oom Mackie and said I'd arrived. He farmed about thirty kilometres away, close to the Botswana border. He said he was glad I'd made it alright and he was on his way – be about an hour as he had to stop in town first.

To kill time, I decided to begin to sort through Pa's office. It had a large roll top desk and an old swivel leather chair, a four-drawer metal filing cabinet, a gun safe, three bookcases filled with what looked like books on war and the military, and a small table with a surprisingly expensive desktop computer, and a brand new scanner-printer. I wanted to see if he had left any instructions about what he wanted in the way of a funeral. Check if there were any outstanding bills to pay – all the things some sad person in the family was always left to do after a death. I began with the desk. It was unlocked but I felt like a burglar going though Pa's stuff. Of course I'd rifled through plenty of people's possessions as a cop without any thought. This was different. I thought the old man was going to walk in any moment and catch me at it.

The desk looked like it was on inspection – a place for everything and everything in its place. Pens in the left drawer, paperclips and stapler in the right. There was a stack of bills all marked 'paid', and a batch of letters with a rubber band round them. His identity documents, passport, army pension card, marriage certificate and Ma's death certificate were in a clear plastic envelope. Other plastic envelopes contained property deeds and mortgage certificates, livestock sale invoices and statements, life insurance certificates and a funeral plan, South African Revenue Service tax returns for ten years, Absa bank statements and one with a label that said 'miscellaneous correspondence' which mainly contained notifications of stock sales, and junk mail selling farm equipment and life insurance. There was one interesting letter though, which Pa had scored through with a red pen – a letter from local lawyers Eloff en Seun, with a firm offer to buy 'the farm known as Klein Drinkwater, District of Terre'Blanche, North-West Province'. This I took out of the pile and put aside, as well as the Avbob funeral insurance document – I figured I'd need both.

The rest of the papers were nothing out of the ordinary. I left them in the desk more or less where they'd been. There were also three sets of keys, one labelled 'gun safe', one labelled 'bakkie spares' and the third, 'spare farm keys'. First I opened the gun safe. There was a shotgun and four rifles in it, and a 9mm pistol – an army issue Star Parabellum. The shotgun was a battered Greener 12 bore; the rifles an old full-stock Mannlicher; Oupa's 'sporterised' second world war .303 Lee-Enfield; a nice Remington model 70 in 30-06 which I assumed was Pa's; and a full-on FN R1 assault rifle, also Pa's. I locked the safe again and turned to the filing cabinet. It was locked and none of the keys in the three sets fitted it. It looked like I'd have to force the lock, but holding my impatience in check, I searched the desk again. The key was taped to the underside of the left-hand drawer. I was about to open the cabinet when I heard a vehicle coming up the farm road,. I slipped the key into my pocket and went out to greet Mackie.

It was good to see him again – Koos 'Mackie' McNaughton (an offshoot from the Scots family who'd settled in and near Graaff-Reinet back in the 1820s) was almost sixty but could pass for ten years less. He was a long drink of water with a craggy face and short-cropped grey hair and a faraway look in his eyes – the sort you get when you're used to shooting running springbok over open sights, four hundred metres away. He had inherited a small farm from his father and through hard work and some inherited Scots canniness had built it into one of the most productive cattle spreads in the Terre'Blanche district. He'd married Ma's much younger sister, Hester, who had been on a tighter rein than Ma and was kept away from anyone Ouma and Oupa thought unsuitable, and had produced five sons, their personal small clan of McNaughtons. The eldest, Stefan, was my age and farming with his dad, the other four, like many South African sons, had spread around the world with families of their own.

We shook hands and Mackie said:

'Jaco, I'm so sorry. Your father was a good friend and I'll miss him. Anything I can do to help, just ask.'

I invited him into the house and we sat down in the front room where Annetjie had laid out more coffee and rusks. He had pain in his eyes that you can't fake. It was strange, but out of everyone I knew who knew Pa, either in the army or later, Mackie was the only one that he'd had a genuine bond of friendship with.

Mackie told me that Pa had died three days ago, that he'd been killed instantly when his bakkie left the road at the sharp bend outside town and rolled. He hadn't been wearing a seat belt and had been thrown clear, head first into a rock. He hadn't stood a chance.

He said that the cops had tried several times to phone me in Cape Town, but couldn't get a reply, so had informed him instead.

'Where's his body?' I asked. 'I suppose they'll need me to identify it.'

Mackie said, 'No, I've already done that, and I got hold of Avbob to arrange things.'

Avbob, of course, is the ubiquitous Afrikaans funeral company – there's a branch in just about every town and city in South Africa. Terre'Blanche was no exception and as the old joke went, Afrikaners wouldn't be caught dead using anyone else.

I said, 'Thanks, I'll get hold of them in the morning. And also the local police – I'd like to check out the accident report. Who's the station commander, still that prick van Schalkwyk?'

'No, van Scalkwyk was given his marching orders quite a while back. He's a big shot now – in business, in Pretoria. We've had a few chiefs since and the new man's a Zulu. He's a full captain. Nathi Mpanza he's called.'

I said, 'They're all full captains now. Shit, the local Boere must be pissed off.'

'They were at first. But Mpanza's actually been quite jacked up. He's polite and surprisingly efficient. So, so far, so good.'

We talked a bit about farming things, the price of cattle, and what Mackie's sons were up to overseas and, of course, as is inevitable when *Boere* get together, rugby. Oom Mackie for the hundredth time telling me that I'd had the talent to go much further than I had. And me responding with my usual story about it was my hair that prevented it. My hair was a shock of nearly white blonde – a throwback to some long ago *kaaskop* Hollander forebear no doubt. My bloody hair. It made me a marked man, especially for selectors. They noticed me more often. Which was fine if I played well but if, as more often happened, I knocked on, dropped the ball, or missed a tackle, the hair gave it away. In truth, I was never good enough and knew it.

Just before Oom Mackie left he asked me how things were going in the Cape and had I thought about what I was going to do with the farm? I told him I hadn't given it any thought at all but that I knew I'd have to.

'Whatever you decide to do, you should look after that foreman of your Pa's. Carolus – he's a diamond and the best stockman I know. I'll hire him like a shot if you decide to sell up,' he said.

We shook hands again and I waited as he drove off, watching the plume of dust kicked up as his vehicle receded into the distance. I turned back into the house. Time had flown, lunch was waiting I hadn't had it so good in years.

Later that afternoon Carolus and I headed out on horseback again. I was stiff from yesterday's short ride. We took the same route as we did previously but instead of stopping where we'd seen the Nguni cattle grazing we carried on a kilometre or so. Carolus wanted to show me something. We stopped next to a small koppie and dismounted. Carolus led me on a short climb about halfway up the slope and said:

'Boss, last week I was checking the cattle when I heard hammering sounds coming from this direction. I was worried it could be poachers so I rode over this way and saw this young guy with a small pickaxe working on rocks up there. He got a big fright when he saw me.'

'What did you do?'

'Well I thought that maybe he was doing something for *oubaas* Jaco, so I asked him if I could help. He said, no, he was finished. And he picked up a heavy rucksack, got on a motorbike and rode away.'

I could just make out thin tyre tracks heading towards our boundary. The ground was hard and dry and they hardly showed.

'That's strange, Carolus, what did the oubaas say?'

'He said ignore it. It was nothing important, just someone he'd hired to do some testing for water.'

'Hmph,' I grunted, and we rode on.

We spent the rest of the afternoon crisscrossing the thornbush veld. It was looking lush – the rains last month had been good. We saw lots of buck – mainly springbuck. But there were also kudu and hartebeest and a small group of zebras and, as always, plenty of warthogs. One big old boar that been sleeping in a hollow next to the track was kicked up by my horse. I don't know who got a bigger fright, me or the warthog. Carolus thought it was very funny and, after a bit, so did I. I told him I hadn't seen so much game ever on the farm and he said, 'It's been a good couple of years, but it brings its problems.'

And added as he spat on the ground, 'Poachers.'

It was dark by the time we got back. I hit the sack early.

Avbob, Eloff en Seun, Royal Hotel

It was early, the sun was just over the horizon and the air still cool and crisp. I stretched and looked out of the bedroom window – two duikers were nibbling at buds growing on the remnants of what had once been Ma's rose garden gone wild. I felt the sudden urge for a smoke. I'd given up five years before, but isn't it amazing how you can't ever shake off the need. I had a shower instead. I'd just finished getting dressed when I heard Annetjie opening the back door and then the rattle of the coffee pot on the iron stove top. It drew me like a magnet to the kitchen.

I was just about to leave after breakfast when the phone rang. It was a woman who said she was with Eloff en Seun the lawyers, and they were representing my father's estate, and was it possible that I could come in to their offices as soon as possible. I said I was on the way into town and could probably see them around midday. She said that would be perfect, and gave me the address.

I drove into town and turned into the Avbob parking lot. The funeral parlour itself was a low slung, Sixties-style building painted railway station brown and cream, with a small stone chapel attached. I walked into the front office, and asked the pretty, blonde receptionist, who looked all of fourteen years old, if I could talk to someone about arranging my father's funeral and that Mr. McNaughton had already told them that I'd be coming.

'Oh yes, Oom Mackie. You must be his nephew, Jaco. So sorry about your father. I'll just call Mrs. Nienaber.'

With this she picked up the phone and said, 'Mrs. Nienaber, I have Oom Mackie's nephew Jaco in reception Mister ... ?' Looking up at me.

'Koekemoer.'

She repeated this into the mouthpiece, turned to me and said that Mrs. Nienaber would be with me in a moment, would I like to take a seat, coffee? I said no, I'd just had some and sat down. I had expected to see a man – probably a long, thin, cadaverous specimen with a soft handshake and an unctuous manner. What sort of woman could Mrs. Nienaber be? Morticia Adams?

I was nearly right about the name, not the rest. This good-looking, dark-haired woman in an expensive suit walked up and said:

'Mr. Koekemoer? Welcome, I'm Mauretia Nienaber, please come with me.'

I followed her, trying not to stare at her legs. I reckon she guessed, as I think I caught a wisp of a smile when we had a little awkward moment as she opened the office door and gestured me to go in before her and we did a quick two-step when I said, 'No, ladies first.'

She led me to a couple of comfortable-looking two-seater sofas either side of a coffee table with a laptop on it and said, 'Lets sit here.'

She sat down and crossed her legs, I did the same. Again the smile, this time a little wider.

She had green eyes and fine high cheekbones. And she wasn't wearing a wedding ring. I wondered why? Shit, Koekemoer, I thought, stop it, this is a funeral parlour and you've come to bury your father you idiot. I realised she was speaking.

'Sorry? What did you say?'

She smiled again: 'Would you like some coffee?'

I said no thanks, the girl at the front had already asked me, then I handed her the Avbob funeral insurance document I'd found last night and said I'd never buried anyone before and where did we begin?

Again that fleeting smile. 'Well the funeral plan's a good place to start.'

She looked at the papers and tapped into the laptop.

'It's all fine and paid up to date. What sort of funeral do you think your father would have wanted, did he say in his will?'

Stupid me, the will.

'I didn't even think of that,' I said.

'Be easier if you could find out. Have you done the other formalities? Identified the body? Got the death certificate?'

'My uncle, Koos McNaughton, has done the I.D. Where do I get the death certificate?'

'I can do it for you if you like, we deal with the coroner all the time. You'll just have to sign a waiver and fill in your details and cell phone number.'

I filled-in and signed the paper she put in front of me and got up to leave. She got up too and put out her hand. For one crazy moment I considered kissing it, but shook it instead. She said she'd call me in the morning.

I got to the lawyers with time to spare.

Twenty-seven Fanie Viljoen was a couple of streets behind what was formerly Paul Kruger, now Nelson Mandela Avenue, the main street of Terre'Blanche. Eloff en Seun Attorneys at Law were, like most rural South African law practices, in an old house converted into offices. They were a new firm though, that must have opened in the last few years – the paint on the sign hadn't yet been bleached away by the sun. The receptionist, who looked like an advertisement for Pep Stores and had big hair that wouldn't have been out of place in *Mad Men*, looked up from examining her nails and greeted me.

'Good morning Oom.' Then seeing my frown, began again with 'Can I help you, Sir?'

I told her I was Jaco Koekemoer and that I had an appointment at twelve. She said, 'Oh yes, I phoned. It's about your father's will.'

I wondered how they knew so quickly I was in town, but put it down to the local grapevine. Miss Pep Stores asked me if I wanted coffee and that Mr. Eloff had just stepped out but would be back in a minute or two. I said no to the coffee and that I'd wait.

A few minutes later Mr. Eloff arrived. I assumed it was Mr. Eloff senior and not the son. It wasn't a great feat of detection – he was around seventy-years-old. He ushered me into his office, this time I had no interest in legs.

Eloff dressed like an old-school, Apartheid-era civil servant – black suit, white shirt, grey tie, matching grey shoes. The tufts of hair that sprouted from his ears and round-rim glasses gave him an owlish expression which was enhanced by his habit of looking straight at you and slowly blinking his eyes as punctuation to almost every sentence. He offered me his condolences on my loss and got down to business. It didn't take long. He told me that Pa had appointed him executor of his estate and that he had left me the farm, all the equipment and livestock, a sum of R200 000 from a Sanlam annuity and another R150K in an Absa account. In addition he had provided legacies of R10K each to Annetjie and Carolus Swartjagter and his antique full-stock Mannlicher-Schoenauer 6.5 x 54 rifle, to Mr. Jacobus (Koos) McNaughton. Pa used to boast it was the same as the gun the famous *rooinek* hunter, Karamojo Bell shot all his elephants with in East Africa.

I wasn't surprised to get the farm or about the legacies to

Annetjie, Carolus and Oom Mackie, but I was surprised at the amount of money Pa had left me. The army never paid much and I know Ma's illness had cost plenty. Maybe the Pelindaba security job was a bigger earner than I realised, but I had my doubts.

I asked Eloff what the next step was. He said that everything would have to go through probate, but he didn't expect any hold-ups, the estate was quite straightforward – perhaps six months at the most. I said that sounded a long time, he snorted and said, 'Mr. Koekemoer this is the new South Africa, six months is short. I've known some estates take over six *years* to be wound up. It's not like the old days. The courts are jammed-up and nobody wants to work anymore.'

I nodded, and said I was sure he'd do his best.

I had planned to show him the letter he'd sent Pa about buying the farm and that Pa had scratched through in red pen, but something held me back. So I made a move to get up and leave when he asked me if he could take up a bit more of my time as there was something else he wanted to talk to me about.

I said, 'Go ahead...'

He said: 'I don't know if your father told you that he was planning to sell the farm and had, in fact, been made a very fine offer which he was carefully considering.'

(So carefully that he'd crossed through it with a red pen, I thought) and answered: 'No. He never said anything to me.'

'Well there has been a good offer and now you're the owner, or at least will be once everything's settled. Maybe you'd be interested?'

I said: 'How much?'

'Over two million … but they could go more.'

I told him it was tempting but that I didn't think I would be interested, *Klein Drinkwater* had been in the family for generations. Then I stupidly said, 'Anyway, I was planning to maybe farm it from long distance. Make the foreman, Carolus Swartjagter, who was the real farmer there, not Pa, a partner, and see if it would work. In fact, here's a plan. Why don't you draw up a partnership agreement for me and Carolus. Just leave the percentages part blank for the moment. I must give it a little more thought.'

Eloff looked somewhat startled by this and said he'd draw something up if that was really what I wanted, but he's still like to see if he could get me a better offer for the farm. I said: 'No, just draw up the partnership, forget any further offers.'

I got up and left, the girl at reception was still filing her nails. Little did I know my parting shot to Eloff was going to stir up a hornet's nest.

Business with the lawyer had left a bad taste in my mouth. So I headed to the Royal for some mouthwash – the kind that's got a label that reads 'Castle Lager'. Parked outside was a dust and graffiti encrusted bus with Western Province number plates. A banner across the rear window said '#VerwoerdMustFall!' As I walked up the stairs to the stoep and the front doors, and adjusted my eyes from the outside glare to inside semi-darkness, I could hear loud voices and the pukka-pukka-puk of a bongo drum. What the fuck? I nearly turned around and left, but the thirst for a cold one won out.

At the bar counter was a multi-ethnic group of, what I later discovered, were students from the University of Cape Town. Seated nearby at two tables which they'd pushed together, were several more students, the guys shaven-headed or with pony tails or those weird bun things that Japanese sumo wrestlers wear to keep their hair up and made popular by overseas soccer stars. The girls were dressed in the flowing, eastern printed, beaded, laid-back look that hasn't changed much since the Sixties. The bongo player was predictably dreadlocked and stoned.

The group at the bar was dominated by a large young black guy, pissed as a rat, haranguing Fat Face, the barman.

'Yes, we're going to make him fall. But first, we're going to shit on his head.'

I was sure I'd seen the black guy before, and then realised Of course – on TV. Thabo Mkhize. He was one of the #RhodesMustFall leaders who'd forced Cape Town university to pull down the statue of Cecil John Rhodes, their greatest benefactor. Taking a good pull of the icy bottle Fat Face had placed in front of me, I addressed Thabo Mkhize in my best ex-cop voice.

'Who are you going to make fall, Mr. Mkhize?'

Mkhize blinked a couple of times.

'Verwoerd.'

'Verwoerd? But he's already fallen. A short fat Greek with a long knife did for him in parliament fifty years ago.'

'No … not Verwoerd, Verwoerd … Verwoerd the face on the mountain. That giant piece of racist shit just out of town.'

'*Ja*? Well good luck with that. You're going to need a ton of dynamite.'

I turned away and asked Fat Face for another Castle. He told me the students had been in since opening time and had, except for Mkhize's occasional ranting, been no trouble at all. I asked him how the plans were going for Botswana and he said he'd decided to stick around a while longer and that it seemed likely that the Indian company was indeed going to buy the mine, or so he'd heard. I told him good luck with that and left for the farm.

TWO

Secrets

HELL, I COULD GET USED TO this waking up with eggs, sausages and *roosterkoek* ready and waiting. And coffee of course, strong moer koffie. Only problem, I'd be fifty kilos heavier in months, if not weeks. I'd better talk to Annetjie about provisions though. I never checked how much Pa had in and we'd certainly need to replenish them if I was going to stay a while longer and sort out the funeral. Annie said she'd make a list but there was no hurry, we had enough in the larder and deep freeze to feed an army.

So forgetting town, I decided I'd spend the day properly sifting through Pa's filing cabinet. I opened it and saw that, except for some empty folders in the back of the bottom drawer, it was stuffed chock-a-block with plastic folders. I decided that slow and methodical was the way forward. So I started with the top drawer, from front to back, and worked my way to the bottom of the four-drawer cabinet.

It was a long, laborious job – but at the same time fascinating. If you wanted a history of one man's role in the Apartheid-era wars, this was it. It gave me a much deeper insight into Pa's army career than I'd had before and, at the same time, the devious ways of governments and diplomacy. He had made a serious study of the Angolan war, but there was also a lot on Mozambique and Rhodesia. Each folder contained files of official army papers, many of which he probably had no right to have, or that were copied from back issues of the official military history society magazines or downloaded from the Internet. All had been carefully referenced with a label and a number – 3A 11 Ch6 or 1B 3 Ch7, etcetera. I couldn't work out what this code meant until I found one that read 2A 7 Ch2 Steenkamp, Border War, when I realised they were book references and on examining the bookcases, that they referenced the books in the collection. So 2A 7 Ch2 was the book in the second bookcase, the A was the top shelf (of three), the 7 was that it was the seventh book along and the Ch2 was the chapter in the book that expanded on the paper. Some of the papers had several codes on them meaning that there were various differing interpretations of the actions or orders the papers described. Once I got used to it was easy. Read the paper – find out what various authorities had to say about it. The official South African position differing widely from the Cuban or even from allies like the USA.

Attached to many of the papers were notes in Pa's handwriting with comments like: 'Bullshit, I was there – it wasn't like that at all'. Or: 'Bloody politicians let us down, again'. Or: 'Cubans half-starved and badly equipped'.

After many, many, hours I realised that to get access to, especially the official secret documents, Pa must have been more than an officer in the regular army and more likely to have been in military intelligence. Also that he was planning to maybe write a book on it all – and what a book it would have made.

It was only when I'd almost reached the end of the cabinet that I realised that I hadn't found anything on Pa's life after the army. Nothing about his hush-hush job at Pelindaba.

It was in the very last plastic folder I opened, labelled 'de la Rey', that I found the letter and the memory stick. They were in an envelope addressed to me. The letter was from Pa and it began:

Son, if you're reading this I am already dead. Please don't judge me for what you find on the memory stick. Times were very different then. I made certain decisions that I thought were necessary for the safety of our country. There are no hard copies left of the documents I scanned onto the stick, I've burnt them all. Do what you think is best, but be careful who you talk to. Pa.

I pocketed the stick, grabbed a sandwich and a coffee, fetched my laptop from the bedroom and sat down on the sofa in the sitting room. I plugged the blade into my Mac and started to open the files. There were four in total. The first said 'History'. The second: 'The Politics of the SA Atomic Programme'. The third: 'Dismantling the Project'. And the fourth: 'Project de la Rey'. I wondered what the hell the old man had been up to. Several hours later I knew. And I didn't like it at all.

You can get the gist of the first three files by some careful reading on the Internet. You just have to balance out the facts from the conspiracy theories and the South Africa propaganda from the left-wing politically correct bullshit. Somewhere in the middle is the truth.

The history is well recorded. Originally it was thought that nuclear explosives could play a role in deep gold and platinum mining operations, and in the early 1970s South Africa joined the USA's 'Peaceful Nuclear Explosions' programme. This proved to be a cover for building nuclear weapons and by the mid-Seventies South Africa had two test sites built in the Kalahari Desert and nuclear devices ready to test. The first test was aborted when the site was discovered through Soviet espionage and pressure was put on South Africa by America to stop proceedings. The site was then abandoned but, two years later, a US military satellite recorded 'a double flash' over the South Atlantic – suspected to be a joint SA-Israeli test. This was denied by both parties. The programme was accelerated through the 1980s with the testing and building of delivery systems – with rockets that were supposedly developed by the South African 'space programme' but were essentially enhanced Israeli Jericho missiles with intercontinental capabilities.

South Africa now had a viable nuclear deterrent, which was, in the paranoia of the P.W. Botha regime, scary to contemplate. Everything changed, however, when F.W. de Klerk took over and the talks with the ANC began. The world was allowed to take a look behind the gates at Pelindaba and the nearby Armscor Nuclear Research facilities. This was in preparation for the announcement that South Africa was, in the spirit of reconciliation, to give up its nuclear arsenal. By the time of the referendum in 1992, the nuclear arsenal had been inspected and the six finished and one half-completed Hiroshima-sized bombs were dismantled under the supervision of the International Atomic Energy Agency and all plans and technical drawings destroyed. But not the pictures of the bombs lying in their purpose-built cradles at Pelindaba.

Personally I think that for 'spirit of reconciliation' you should read: 'We don't want the bombs to fall in the hands of a black government'. But call me cynical.

You'll also find carefully thought-out political reasons on the Internet and in books about why South Africa wanted a nuclear deterrent in the first place. Most will hypothesize that it was designed as a last resort if the Angolan adventure proved to be a total disaster and the Russian/Cuban armies swept across the border – but take that with a large pinch of salt. It was much more likely that it was simply a matter of boy's toys. The military wanted to play in the big league and, in paranoid Apartheid South Africa, what the military wanted, it got.

The fourth, 'de la Rey' file you won't find on the Net. This was Pa's doing, and Pa's alone. It was all laid out in a perfectly reasoned plan, how he, and a very small group of fellow 'patriots', had stolen one of the bombs and replaced it with a dummy two weeks before the first IAEA inspection. And that this bomb was now hidden where no one would think of looking for it.

His reasons for doing this were laid out logically and in a reasonable tone. I'd thought his doubts about the army had begun after the Cuito Cuanavale debacle, but realised they had been brewing for much longer. In fact, they had begun fifteen years earlier during the first Angolan incursion which was taken at the behest of the Americans who had asked for help to support the pro-Western liberation group, Unita, against the pro-Soviet Union MPLA. Both groups had been involved in the liberation war against Portugal, but neither accepted sharing political power. The South Africans responded to this call for help from the Americans seriously and went in boots and all.

There was possibly a bad misreading by the CIA or American politicians about how capable the South African army actually was. Certainly things happened much faster than anyone expected. On the big push into Angola in 1975 the SADF forces reached the outskirts of the capital, Luanda, in less than a week and were waiting for orders to take it, when the Yanks, fearing a face-off against Russia, panicked and said pull back – we didn't really *mean* for you to beat them so quickly. Or maybe it was wishful thinking by the Apartheid government that the US had ever given them a full go-ahead to take Angola.

The dossier (because that was what it was) went on to illustrate dozens of further mistakes, in Pa's mind anyway, that the army chiefs and the politicians had made during the following years, culminating with the failure to use one of the A-bombs when the troops were bogged down at Cuito

Cuanavale.

He then gave a summary (and this is when I realised how deluded Pa had actually been) of what he expected to happen in the new South Africa – 'the traitor de Klerk's pipe dream' he called it. And how the Afrikaner nation would need the A-bomb he had stolen, or at least the deterrent of using it, when they'd had enough of the new South Africa and would take their rightful place running the country they had built on the blood of their ancestors.

This was followed by a precise description of how the bomb was stolen. That they were code-named after Afrikaner Boer War generals and that a dummy bomb casing had been secretly manufactured. There was a purchasing order to a Johannesburg industrial boiler making company with detailed engineering drawings attached of the 'boiler for display purposed only'. This order had specific instructions of the materials to be used, sizes to the millimetre and a delivery address: *Klein Drinkwater*, Terre'Blanche District, and a map how to get there. I compared the engineering drawings with the photographs of the bombs lying in their cradles, and the 'boiler' was identical to the bomb casings.

There was also official correspondence between the director general of the Pelindaba facility and State President de Klerk's office, confirming that there were six completed bombs and one that still had to be armed. Most of this counter-signed by Col. J. Koekemoer, Chief of Security. There were diagrams of alarm systems and precise timetables of movements of guards. And finally, a short list of names – Jan Pieter Coetsee, Gerhardus Tertius van Niekerk, Danie Pienaar, Derrick Smit, Carel (Boet) Bezuidenhout – and written on the bottom of this was a somewhat cryptic inscription in my father's hand: 'de la Rey is under Verwoerd – PAL code:1847'.

I spent half the night thinking about what I'd found on the

memory stick and especially the final message Who were these names? Why was de la Rey under Verwoerd? And what was PAL code: 1847? A bank pin number? Key to a combination lock? A grave site?

Just before I fell asleep I remembered that Mauretia Nienaber from Avbob hadn't phoned me about the funeral. Later I dreamt about her and Pa and A-bombs and del la Rey riding through the veld, his horse wild and black with nostrils snorting fire. All to the soundtrack of Bok van Blerk singing: '*De la Rey, de la Rey …*'

Mpanza

It took me two mugs of Annetjie's moer koffie to shake off the restless night. I was just about to pick up the phone and call Mauretia Nienaber when she called me. Talk about great minds thinking alike. She said she was really sorry she hadn't got hold of me yesterday but that there was something of a problem, which she'd thought she could sort out, but wasn't able to. I asked what problem?

'They won't release your father's body yet.'

I said, 'Why not?'

'It's the police. The coroner wouldn't tell me why, but maybe you can pull some strings being part of the force. Or ex-part of the force.'

I said I'd talk to the local cops and see what the problem was and I'd get hold of her shortly.

The police station was much as I remembered it when I was posted there for my first job as a newly-minted detective constable thinking I knew it all having finished my degree and passed out of the police academy in Pretoria. Only instead of a fat white sergeant with a droopy moustache manning the charge office desk, who pretended to be busy when you approached and wouldn't look up, there was a plump black lady sergeant who, deep in a book, ignored me. Also the picture of the State President had changed from a smug F.W. de Klerk to an even smugger Jacob Zuma.

I'd done the lady sergeant a disservice. When she noticed me she leapt up and said: 'Sorry Sir, I'm Sergeant Gugu Mayisela, I'm studying for exams, I was lost in my book.'

'What book?' I asked.

She said: 'You probably won't know it. Snyman's Criminal Law Casebook.'

I laughed, 'I studied Snyman when I was doing Criminology at Tukkies twenty years ago'.

She said: 'I'm doing my degree online, through Unisa. Are you a lawyer, sir?'

I laughed again. 'No, I was like you. Police. Is it possible to see Captain Mpanza?'

'I'll see if he's available, what's your name?'

'Jaco Koekemoer .'

'Captain? Major?'

'No. Now I'm just plain mister.'

She rang through to her superior and said: 'Captain, there's an ex-police officer Koekemoer here to see you.'

I could hear Mpanza ask her something. She looked up from the phone:

'Are you Colonel J. Koekemoer's son?'

'Yes.'

'The captain wants to see you immediately. Let me show you the way.'

I told her it wasn't necessary, I knew where the station commander's office was – two doors down the corridor to the right – and she should get back to her studies. She said thanks, she would.

Nathi Mpanza was a large, handsome Zulu, not quite my height but with even broader shoulders. He shook my hand with the gentle handshake typical of his people. The soft grip, not a sign of weakness, as some fools have found out to their cost, but one of respect. He said that he was very sorry about my father and that it was a terrible thing. I said: 'Yes, to die that way, alone in a motor accident …'

He looked up at me and said, 'I'm sorry to have to tell you this, but we're not treating it as an accident.'

'What then? Suicide? I can't believe it … he'd never …'

'No. We think homicide. The evidence points to him being deliberately run off the road or hit and run at the very least.'

'Homicide … but who would want to kill … what happened?'

I could see that Mpanza was sizing me up, wondering how much he should tell me. He gave a little nod to himself, got up and said: 'Come with me.'

As we walked towards the station's vehicle impoundment yard, I thought that now I know why they won't release the body. If it had been a road accident, the autopsy would have been done by the duty pathologist, with the minimum of fuss and the body probably already released. But in a case of suspicious death, a competent investigating officer would want as thorough a medical examination as possible by a senior pathologist. Sometimes this could add days onto the releasing of the body.

Mpanza was saying something. I said: 'Sorry, my mind was elsewhere.'

He passed me a pair of blue latex gloves and said: 'Here is the vehicle your father was driving. I'm only showing you this as a courtesy to an ex-police officer, and I know you were in Serious Crimes so you know what to do and what not to.'

Naturally he'd checked up on me, I would have done the same in his shoes. I'd been in Serious Crimes in Jo'burg and Cape Town before I'd set out in the wonderful world of private-eyeing. I guess the report he got about me was a pass mark, or I wouldn't be here with him.

The vehicle, a white Toyota Hi-lux double-cab about ten years older than the bakkie I'd hired from Tempest, was a wreck. It had obviously rolled a dozen or more times down a rocky incline and was so smashed up it looked like it had been attacked by multiple sledgehammers. The roof was slanted at forty five degrees, the driver's side pillars had caved in and both front and back had concertinaed. Three of the tyres had burst and the front bumper had bent almost in two. This was probably caused by the tow-truck pulling it out of the donga. Shit, no-one could have survived a crash like this.

'What am I looking for?' I asked Mpanza.

He lead me round to the back of bakkie: 'See this? The black stripe. Like a scar on white skin.'

'Yes.'

'That's where it got hit. The other vehicle came up from behind, fast, and knocked him off the road. Probably had bull bars on the front. You see how the dent of the impact is rounded?'

'Must have been a big vehicle to knock a double-cab off the road.'

'Yes, my thoughts exactly.'

'You sure that black scar wasn't caused by the tow truck pulling the double cab back onto the highway?'

'No, I checked that first off. The tow truck had a bull bar, but a stainless steel one. No black anywhere.'

'Did you find anything else at the scene?'

'Some broken glass, probably from your father's bakkie but we can't be sure that some of it wasn't from another vehicle. I've sent all we collected to forensics and a sample of the paint from the black stripe. There was also the normal rubbish people throw out of their car windows, but nothing else relevant to the investigation.'

'Do you mind if I go have a look?'

Captain Mpanza shrugged, 'Be my guest. I doubt we've

missed anything, but if we have, I ask you please to contact us immediately.'

'Promise.'

Mpanza told me to follow him back to the office where he'd give me a copy of the official diagram of the scene of the crime. This was highly irregular but, I'd begun to realise, so was Mpanza. When we got back to the charge office he asked me to wait while he got the copy. The sergeant was head down, nose stuck in her book. Mpanza smiled her way and left. He was back shortly and handed me an envelope with his police business card stapled to it. He also told me that while he was in his office the coroner had phoned and said that the autopsy would be carried out that afternoon and the body would be released first thing in the morning. I suspected that Captain Mpanza had put a little pressure on them to hurry up, and thanked him.

'*Ngiyabonga* Captain. You've been a great help.'

I drove round to Avbob to give Mauretia the news about Pa's body being released in the morning. But she wasn't there so I left a note with the fourteen-year-old blonde to say the body could be picked up in the morning and I was sorry I'd missed her. Really romantic stuff.

A beer was calling me loudly but I decided I'd head out to the scene of the crime instead. I poked around in the heat for a bit but Mpanza was right, I found nothing. So I headed to the Royal – I had to make some calls to my business partner, Chesney Cook, for one. I needed to put him in the picture about what was up and also to ask him to check out a few people. Cook, besides being one of the best Google detectives I've ever met, also seemed to have a girlfriend in every official records office in the country and I guess the cool of the Royal bar would be as good a place as anywhere to call from.

We had a long chat – he filled me in about the case we'd

been working on before I was called away to Terre'Blanche. It had a lot to do with fishing permits, illegal fishing, Chinese trawlers and great white sharks, and he seemed to have things under control. Rather him than me, I thought. I quickly filled him in on what I'd been up to and gave him my list. First the names at the end of Pa's 'Pelindaba' folder – Coetsee, van Niekerk, Pienaar, Smit, Bezuidenhout – who were they? Also I asked him to find out what he could about the lawyer Eloff and, lastly, Captain Nathi Mpanza of the Terre'Blanche police. Cook said he'd get on to it right away.

The bar was cool, and this time, a lot quieter. Fat Face the barman told me that I should have been in last night. The gang of UCT students had been joined by another bunch from Wits and things had got pretty raucous. He said they'd told him they were planning to stick around a while and were going to set up camp at the koppie. I told him that they'd better watch out for snakes.

After another couple of beers I headed to the farm.

I hadn't been back home more than a couple of minutes when I noticed the dust of two vehicles that had turned off the tar road and were coming towards the farm. I waited for them on the front stoep. They pulled up under Ouma's pin oak. I wasn't that surprised when the lawyer, Eloff, got out of the first car – a five-year-old Merc that looked like it had a couple of hundred thousand kilometres on the clock but probably only had a few thousand, the local roads will do that. The second vehicle was brand new – a Toyota Land Cruiser Station Wagon, which cost nearly four times the average police captain's annual salary. Ex-police captain Wouter van Schalkwyk stepped out of the Cruiser and smiled up at me. A crocodile's would have been warmer.

Bastards

Wouter van Schalkwyk was a genuine two-time bastard. Not only through paternity but by inclination also.

He was brought up by Oom Swart Danie van Schalkwyk his grandfather who, by hook or by crook, ended up owning just about half of the buildings and businesses in town. Swart Danie had arrived in the district in last days of WWII having trekked with his herd of sheep up the National road from Cookhouse in the Eastern Cape nearly eight hundred kilometres to the south, grazing them on the sides of the road. It took almost two years to get to Terre'Blanche and why he finally stopped there nobody knows – maybe he felt at home with the jackal buzzards flying above. Somewhere along the long road north he'd picked up a woman – a long, gaunt, heavy-boned, haunted-eyed woman who he drove north alongside the sheep.

But two years of living and sleeping among sheep on the side of the National road cured Swart Danie of any affinity with sheep and instead of setting up as a stock farmer, he sold the lot, bought a pub and a greasy spoon restaurant, and set out to shear the people of Terre'Blanche instead.

Swart Danie and the gaunt woman had produced only one child, Petronella, who had fled home for Johannesburg and had only came back once to drop off her own child, Wouter.

She told them she didn't know who the father was, and didn't care. She never returned to pick him up.

Wouter was, for a short time, my boss. He made life difficult for me. A few years older than me, he'd left the local high school before I got to Terre'Blanche. And went on to study, of all things, Divinity, at Potchefstroom University. I'd played rugby for Tukkies against him once in a grudge inter-varsity game. I don't think he ever forgave me the dummy I sold him to set up the winning try. But he treated Pa with great respect. He knew that Pa, while not that active in right wing politics, had connections at the very top of the movement. Van Schalkwyk, if the old Apartheid regime had continued, would have no doubt risen to high rank in the police. Maybe even the top job. When I worked for him he was head of the local detective division and already building a power base in the west of Transvaal. Later, as chief of police he was an important figure in the district with important Party affiliations. He knew where most of the bodies were buried – but then he'd buried many of them himself. He'd clearly done well in the new South Africa though – he was looking seal-sleek and prosperous.

We shook hands – we're polite people, us Afrikaners. I counted my fingers to see if they were all still there and invited van Schalkwyk and Eloff into the house.

We got down to business right away, van Schalkwyk opening with: 'Jaco, Eloff here told me that you've rejected, out of hand, the offer I made on the farm.'

'*You* made the offer?'

'Yes, if it wasn't enough, I apologise, I can go higher.'

'It's not the money, Wouter. This place was Ma's family's farm and I want to keep it so. Anyway since when did you become a farmer?'

He laughed, showing a fine set of freshly-capped teeth.

'No, I want it as a game farm. For entertaining customers.'

'Business must be good.'

'It's more than good. Van Schalkwyk Makatini Investments is one of the fastest growing corporations in South Africa.'

'Makatini? Who's that?'

I'm surprised you haven't heard of them. They're the big Jo'burg mining company. Bought out half of Anglo. They're my partners.'

Then van Schalkwyk wrote something brief on a piece of paper, folded it and gave it to me, saying: 'We've got things to discuss in town, but when we're gone, please look at the number on this and get hold of me through Eloff .'

I walked them to their vehicles, we shook hands and again I counted my fingers. Van Schakwyk drove off first, Eloff hung back, eating his dust. I walked back to the stoep and stopping, took a look at the note van Schalkwyk had given me. There was a three on it followed by six zeroes. Three million rands. I went inside and sat down.

Jesus.

My daydreams of what I could do with three million bucks were interrupted by the ring of the landline. It was Mauretia. She told me that she'd got my message and that Pa's body was on its way to the funeral parlour, and could I come into town and discuss the funeral plans.

I said, 'Sure, what time?' We agreed on ten a.m. the next day.

A little later I got another call. It was from a young guy with an English accent. He said his name was Jack Bolton.

'Can I speak with Colonel Koekemoer, please?'

I said, 'Sorry. That's not possible.'

'When would it be convenient, then?'

'I'm afraid the Colonel is dead. A car accident.'

'Oh. I am sorry to hear that. Who's speaking?'

I told him.

He said, 'Then you're probably the right person to send my report to. Can I have your e-mail address?'

I asked, 'What report?'

'The geological report the Colonel wanted.'

'Oh that one. Yes, e-mail it to me please, and your details, my address is …'

A few minutes later my Mac went 'ping'. There was something waiting in the inbox and it was indeed the report from a company called Geo Logical. It took me a while to get through it. To put it plainly I didn't know my late Archean from my early Proterozoic or my hornfels from my leptites. There was, however, a semi-understandable summary at the end which essentially said that the underground platinum reef that geologists had years ago determined petered out just west of Terre'Blanche, did indeed end there, but there was 'strong evidence' that the reef re-emerged on the farm *Klein Drinkwater* two kilometres to the west. My farm. And that further exploration and prospecting was needed to confirm this.

So much for van Schalkwyk's 'game farm'. What he was hunting went much deeper. Bastard.

I thought I'd better get hold of Chesney Cook again and ask him to make a few additions to the list I'd given him. Such as Makatini Investments, Geo Logical and ex-police captain Wouter van Schalkwyk.

Cook said he'd get on to it right away, but meantime he had tracked down some info on the earlier names I'd given him. He told me that Coetsee, van Niekerk, Pienaar, Smit and Bezuidenhout were all ex-army. But whereas Coetsee had been in weapons procurement and had been in charge of security at the main weapons depot at Kimberley, the other four were hard-core fighting men.

'I smell ex-Special Forces,' he told me. 'Maybe even Koevoet or the Recces. I'm waiting for their files.'

I said, 'Can you try to track down where they are now? Also Coetsee.'

'Will do.'

'Anything on Captain Mpanza?'

'Now there's an interesting oke. He comes from a small village near Kamberg in the Drakensberg and his father's a labourer on a dairy farm. He was educated at a local farm school but obviously had brains because he got matric and then a B.A. in Criminology from the University of KwaZulu-Natal and finished top of his class at the Chatsworth Police Academy. He made captain in the Durban detective squad faster than anyone ever in the police, even you Koekie, and he'd just got a promotion to Pretoria headquarters when the shit hit the fan and he was posted to Terre'Blanche instead.'

'*Fok*, what happened?'

'Apparently, he was heading back to Durban from a trip to his family kraal up in Kamberg when, on the highway near 'Maritzburg there was a traffic accident just in front of him and he stopped to see if he could help. It wasn't that major a prang, but a small car had been shunted in the back by a BMW 4x4. Apparently, as Mpanza approached the two cars, this very angry, very *dronk* Zulu gets out of the Beemer and starts shooting at the whiteys in the car he'd pranged, Bam! Bam!, Bam!, Bam! Bam! Glass exploding everywhere. It was by sheer luck he didn't kill anyone. He was so pissed he didn't even see Mpanza walk up on him – one klap on the back of his head and it was lights out.'

'Shit, and then?'

'Well Mpanza called the local station and when they arrived, he identified himself and told them to arrest and cuff the Zulu who'd now woken up, and then to take a statement from the whiteys. The sergeant in the squad car said he wouldn't do it and asked Mpanza if he realised who the man was he was arresting. Mpanza apparently said that he didn't care if it was the Honourable State President himself. 'Arrest this man or I'll put you under arrest.'

'And then?'

'Well it obviously wasn't the President, but it was a nephew. And he had the cheek to lay a charge of assault against Mpanza himself.'

'Christ, and I suppose the people in the other car wouldn't back him up?'

'No, they'd been got at. Shit scared, said they saw nothing.'

'So that's how Mpanza ended up here. Transferred as far away as possible from the shit-storm. Typical police management. Bastards.'

THREE

Trouble brewing

THERE WAS A LOT on my mind as I blew on the morning's first cup of coffee to cool it down.

Who'd want Pa dead? Was it connected to the offer on the farm? The possible riches underground? Or was it something more sinister from his past? And Mpanza. Now that was another story. Must be difficult for him trying to run the station in Terre'Blanche of all places. No Zulu spoken, little English. Mainly Afrikaans and Setswana. The local Tswana's were leery of their Zulu brothers – the stories of Shaka Zulu's renegade chieftain Mzilikazi and the slaughter and suffering he brought to the Tswana people on his journey to create the Matabele kingdom in the north, still haunted their folklore. 'The Path of Blood' as it was known. They would not welcome his presence amongst them and in return he would treat them with the total disdain Zulus have for lesser people. Which in most Zulu eyes was everyone – white, black, purple or green.

I got to the funeral parlour at ten sharp. Mauretia had a folder prepared for me. It contained a brochure of a selection of coffins, a sample order of service of the Dutch Reformed Church funeral, and a long list of services that the funeral insurance that Pa had taken out entitled him to. Avbob could primp him up, dress him up, bury him, cremate him, organise the service, organise flowers and cars for the mourners. They would hire pall-bearers, grave diggers, caterers, chairs and graveside tents, notify the papers, hire the minister. And coffins? You could choose from the Ambassador, Royal, Executive, Superior, Traditional, Dignity, Luxury, Presidential, Standard, Sovereign, Jewish, Monarch, Little Angel and Ash. And that was just the Avbob house range.

In the end we settled for a standard coffin, a Dutch Reform Church service (Pa didn't believe in heaven and hell, but I thought, why take the risk?) and decided we'd bury him on the farm with Ma and her forebears, and for afterwards coffee, finger food and brandy on the stoep.

It was lunchtime when we were done – it's amazing how time flies when you're having fun. I asked Mauretia if there was anywhere good in town for a bite and if she would like to join me. She said the local Steers was still about the best place, they made great flame-grilled chicken. I reckoned the rack of ribs would do for me.

When I got back to the farm Annetjie was waiting for me. She had fear in her eyes. 'Boss Jaco, there's been trouble. Carolus heard shots from the direction of the cattle grazing, he's ridden out to see what's going on.'

I ran to the gun cabinet and, ignoring the pistol and the three hunting rifles, took out Pa's R1 and two full 20 round clips of 7.62 x 51mm ammo. It wasn't the most modern South African military assault rifle but was more accurate than the new, small calibre, R5. It was one of the special accuratised FNs for designated marksmen – semi-automatic and fitted with telescopic sights. Pa had probably neglected to hand it in to the armoury when he'd left – a lot of old regime servicemen managed to hang on to some serious weaponry on the changeover to the new SADF. I had a quick check and, as expected, saw that the gun was clean as a whistle and lubricated. Pa, being ex-army, would be manic about looking after his weapons.

I jumped in to the hired Toyata Hi-lux and flew down the track to where we'd last seen the cattle. I stopped, turned the ignition off and got out. I listened carefully. No shots, just the sound of painful bellowing from the thorn trees two hundred metres away. I hurried toward it, as quick as possible but keeping low, the crouched run we were taught at training school, expecting a bullet in the back at any moment as I crab-ran towards the thicket. The bellowing had stopped. I saw Shortie, the brown and white bull with the long horns, lying in the shade, dead. He'd been gut shot. Two cows were also down. From the bullet wounds I surmised that the shots had probably come from the direction of the koppie we'd scouted a few days back. Shit. A long shot from there, five hundred metres at least. I hunkered down behind a dead thorn tree – it offered some protection, but not much. I called softly:

'Carolus … Carolus …'

I didn't expect to hear any reply but tried again.

'Carolus …'

I heard a low groan to the left. And scurried towards it, head down. It was Carolus. It looked bad. He was on his back, the side of his head and neck covered in blood. I scrabbled on my knees next to him and took a close look. I hadn't yet found an entry or exit wound, when he groaned again, this time a little louder. Then he shook his head and rolled over. He tried to get to his feet, but I stopped him.

'No, stay down. The shooter could still be in the area.'

We waited. The bleeding had stopped and I could see a ragged strip in Carolus's scalp where the bullet had torn through. We waited some more. A little later I heard the sound of a vehicle starting up and then saw a dust cloud from behind the koppie – he was heading for the back road to town. I helped Carolus to his feet and supporting him on my shoulder headed for the Hilux.

'We need to have that wound seen to, it looks ugly.'

Carolus grunted. 'My head feels like a *pampoen*.'

On the drive over the veld back to the farm house I tried hard not to jar Carolus and his sore head too much, but by the time we got there I could see he was nearly out on his feet.

His ma, Annetjie, took one look and him and told him to sit on the *riempie* bench on the stoep. She had a basin of hot water prepared and the farm first aid kit next to it. She carefully cleaned around the wound. Thankfully it all looked a million times worse than it actually was – the shot had only grazed the left ear and then the fleshy bit at the back of it. A couple of centimetres to the right though …

I left Carolus to his mother's care and called the ambulance service. Then I called Nathi Mpanza. I was put through right away.

'Captain, it's Jaco Koekemoer. We've had a shooting out at the farm. My foreman's been shot. I've called the ambulance but maybe you should get out here as soon as you can.'

Mpanza said he was on his way and put the phone down.

He was true to his word, in fact he beat the ambulance by ten minutes. He brought two of his sidekicks with him, one the young female sergeant, Gugu Mayisela, and the other a much older man – a constable in police camouflage. Mpanza asked me where the wounded man was and if he was conscious. I told him yes, the wound didn't seem too bad. He said let's talk to him then.

Carolus told him the same story he'd told me. He was at the farmhouse for the midday meal when he heard some shots in the far distance and rode out to see what was happening

Mpanza asked if he was armed.

'No, I know most of the poachers in the area and I don't think they'd shoot me but I don't want to give them an excuse to either.'

'Did you see who did?'

'No, all I saw were the dead cows and the big bull. He was down but struggling hard to get to his feet. Then nothing until Boss Jaco shook me awake.'

The ambulance came and took Carolus to the small hospital in town, Annetjie accompanied him. I told her I'd be in as soon as I could and that I was sure Carolus would be fine, but that the doctor should check him over. Mpanza told Sergeant Gugu she should go with them and make sure Carolus got attended as soon as possible, then called the constable over and turned to me:

'Let's go see where this all happened.'

I grabbed the FN and spoke as I saw his eyes widen when he saw the assault rifle.

'I don't think it was poachers' I told him and pointing to his 9mm parabellum service sidearm,

'And I don't think that pea-shooter would be much use either if he's come back. Whoever shot Carolus was a long, long, way off and armed with something with long distance capability.'

Mpanza said: 'A professional?'

'Yes. Or army. But hopefully they're long gone by now.'

'Okay.' Mpanza said. 'Let's go. You can tell me why you think this was more than just poachers on the ride out.'

We hopped in the police vehicle. Like most it was a Toyota Hilux bakkie with a wire meshed steel cage on the back and, because this was farming country issue, a bull bar on the front. Mpanza drove, I sat in front next to him and the constable, who Mpanza introduced as Witbooi, rode standing on the bull bar on the front. It didn't take long to get to where I'd found the cows. We got out next to the dead bull. Mpanza shook his head sorrowfully, clucking his tongue in the universal Zulu sign of sorrow and disapproval. I could feel his thoughts. 'What a waste of a magnificent animal.' Zulus love cattle more than just about anything in life. We walked over to the two dead cows. I could see Mpanza doing the same mental calculation that I did. He grunted.

'And where did you find your foreman?'

'Just over there, near the withaak tree'.

We walked to where I'd found Carolus. Mpanza frowned.

'You're right. This wasn't poachers. They might shoot you if you stumble on top of them, but not likely from so far away. They'd rather run.'

And pointing to the distant koppie,

'The shots came from way over there. From a single rifle. Each cow head shot, the bull gut shot, whoever the shooter was, he wanted the bull to suffer and maybe draw in another target like Carolus. It was deliberate. This is really someone very bad. A stone cold killer. I reckon a trained sniper.'

He turned to his constable:

'Witbooi, come, it's your turn now. The shots came from that koppie, check around and see if you can find anything.'

The three of us walked in single file to the koppie half a kilometre away. It was hot, the heat radiating upwards from the dust under foot. When we got to the base of the koppie, Mpanza told Witbooi to see if he could find exactly where the bushwacker had shot from.

'If anyone can find something, Witbooi can. He was Koevoet before he joined the police.'

He didn't have to give any further explanation. Koevoet was the shadowy, counter-insurgency arm of the SADF that reigned terror on enemies of the Apartheid state in their border wars. They were drawn from SADF special services, but were in the main Ovambo and Bushman recruits from South West Africa.

Most fled to South Africa when the South Africans withdrew, fearing reprisals from the new governments in Namibia and Angola. Many of the Ovambo and Bushmen were resettled in Pomfret, not far from Terre-Blanche, and lived there in some hardship – the new South African government not happy about their presence. Witbooi must have had special qualities or friends with influence to get a job in the police force.

A short while later we heard a low whistle – it was Witbooi summonsing us. We scrambled upward to where he was squatting on his haunches. He pointed.

'One man Captain. He spat on the ground here.'

In the dust at the base of a tree that had long ago been struck by lightning there was a gobbet of tobacco-stained saliva. Mpanza took a sample envelope out of his bullet-proof vest and with a twig, brushed the sputum into the bag, sealed it and tucked it into his pocket.

'If he's on record, this will have enough DNA to identify him. Well spotted Witbooi.'

Witbooi nodded and rising, pointed to a side branch of the dead tree.

'He rested the gun here.'

And then moving a couple of feet away, 'He picked up the shells here, here, here and here. Four shots only.'

I said, 'Four shots, four hits. At five hundred metres that's some shooting.'

Witbooi replied: 'Yes Captain, but not as good as the best I've seen. He missed the last shot. Your foreman would be dead otherwise.'

Witbooi showed us the path up the koppie the shooter had taken and then followed the trail when he left, taking us all the way to where his vehicle had been parked. Broad 4x4 sand tyres led to the fence line, where he had cut the wire with clippers. The tracks only went a few metres on before turning right on the back road that led past the township outside

Terre'Blanche, and on to wherever.

We drove back to the farmhouse, Witbooi again guiding Mpanza over the worst bits of the track. When we arrived, Mpanza said he had to get back to the station and get the saliva sample to Pretoria, but he would send Witbooi back later with the forensics officer – maybe it would be possible to find one of the bullets in one of the dead cows, or perhaps the one that had grazed Carolus's head. Witbooi walked round the bakkie to the passenger door, but just before he climbed in, said to me quietly:

'I knew your father, I see you carry his rifle, I was his point man once in the bush war many years ago. He was a good man in a fight – that gun killed many, many enemies.'

As they drove off I marvelled again at what Pa had got up to in the army – and now Koevoet. My God, he'd been involved in some shady, dangerous things. I realised that I never really knew him at all. Then I thought that I had better get into town and see how Carolus was.

The killer

'Fuck, how did I miss, I had a bead straight on the centre of the Hotnot's forehead. Must have been a dud bullet. But how that could be? I load myself. Each stage done with meticulous attention to detail. Maybe I'm getting careless.'

The killer had always been a natural shot. Years of killing small animals and birds on the farm with an air rifle and later a .22 had made him ever more deadly. The army had taken this raw talent and honed it into professionalism. He had been awarded his chrome rifle with laurel wreath snipers badge and represented the SADF at the South African Bisley, winning the long-distance F Class on his first attempt. But this time he had missed. An easy shot from barely five hundred metres away – not a great distance for a shooter of his ability. He wasn't happy.

He sat at his workbench reloading cartridges for the .243 rifle, a much-used, always cared-for, Sako Forrester bolt action rifle with the 23" Bofors steel barrel in a 1 in 10 twist. He had a long-time work routine which he tried never to vary – whether he was loading 60-grain bullets for the jackals he shot at extreme range; 80-grain bullets for springbok, with full metal jackets so as not to ruin the meat; or what he was loading right now – heavier 110-grain with expanding points that mushroomed for bigger buck like bushbuck, or sometimes kudu. Or deadlier game … like men. He didn't like shooting kudu with the .243 though. The 30-06 or even the .375 with much heavier bullets were more effective, but men weren't as tough and he'd rather have the long-range accuracy the .243 guaranteed because sometimes they shot back.

He had been loading his bullets from scratch for forty years – years of trial and error – until he fixed on the loads that suited him best. He rarely changed to something new and never just for the sake of it. He had been forced, through international arms sanctions, to hoard some of his supplies – Winchester gunpowder for one – but found the local arms industry soon had effective substitutes, Somchem 355 for example. And anyway, there were always sanctions busters, and supplies of anything, legal or illegal, were always available in South Africa, no matter what resolution was passed in the United Nations. He remembered a mission once to Rhodesia when he was seconded to the South African police helping the BSAP guard the Zambian border at Kariba – his job was to take out a headman who was said to be collaborating with the local insurgents – Terrs as the Rhodies called them. He'd expected to find a country with empty shelves and nothing to eat – someone had even told him before he went to take his own toilet paper. What he found was a country of plenty. What they couldn't smuggle in they made themselves, from motor cars to machine guns, whiskey to headache pills. They even had TV! He'd been told that the UK programme he 'd been watching had aired the night before in England.

So he didn't mind using local if he had to – a man shot with a bullet propelled by 40-grains of Somchem was just as dead as if you'd measured the same amount of genuine Win 760 into the brass cartridge. But now, in the new South Africa, it was easy to get the best again, so he used it. For man hunting, the choice of gunpowder was IMR 4064. The brass, factory Winchester, the primer, Federal 210m, and the bullet the 100 grain Sierra Spitzer boat tail. He'd been thinking of moving to an even heavier round – the new 115 grain DTAC had received some good press – but until he range-tested it, he'd stick with what he knew worked. No-one had ever got up before today. But one thing was for sure, he no longer trusted the last batch of cartridges he'd handloaded, so he unloaded the Sako's magazine and chucked the remaining bullets into the steel box where he kept all the rejects.

Reloading was, for the killer, a ritual. Nothing was allowed to disturb him. His woman, the kid, or the various part-time nannies his woman hired to look after the kid when she was working on her tan or just too lazy to clean the house herself. All walked in quiet steps and spoke, if necessary at all, in whispers whenever he retired to the gun room. Once, when a bokmakierie's shrill call in the distance interrupted his calm, measured, process, he made it disappear in a cloud of blood and yellow feathers.

Everything had gone to plan so far. All so easy. He'd eliminated all the others. The heroes of the new Boer Republic the Colonel had called them – Coetsee, Pienaar, Bezuidenhout and Smit. And of course, himself. He reckoned they should have looked after him better. They should have known him better. They should never have given up on the dream. Or the meetings. They'd promised to meet regularly at the Colonel's farm to decide if and when it was time to overthrow the bastard new government. And, for the first few years they kept to it, and met every four months. But then this became maybe once a year, and then some years back, stopped altogether. It was all over. They were just sad middle-aged men with a lost country they'd never find again. He'd nearly given up then, too, but decided if he couldn't help the nation, then maybe he should help himself.

It had been surprisingly easy, only Smit had recognised

him immediately. All of them except the Colonel had put on weight, they'd lost that lean and mean look you get when your life depends on tracking men and killing them before they kill you. Even he had. When he had first met his comrades he was just out of basic training. He'd been a fit, tough *boerseun* then. A farm boy sick of how his father treated him as an extra unpaid labourer on his deadend sheep farm. Only nineteen but already nearly two years in. He'd signed up in the permanent force the day he'd turned eighteen, hitchhiking down the N1 to Cape Town and the nearest big army base. Why wait to be called-up for two years national service like his school mates he thought. Why wait to leave home? Nobody could treat him worse than his piss-cat father did, he reckoned. And he was right. He took to the army like he'd always belonged there. Didn't even mind the harshness of the basic training, the learning of automatic responses to orders they required of him. He'd understood what they were doing. Honing his response times – forcing him to react to whatever situation with the correct, immediate solution. The army also recognised in him something that neither school teachers nor parents had – an ability for meticulous planning and then the rare talent to act quickly, decisively and even brutally when necessary to carry out the plan. The army didn't mind that he showed a little too much keenness to spill blood. It was what they needed at the time and they passed him on to Special Forces where his blood lust could be properly channeled.

Ja, killing his ex-comrades-in-arms had been easy. Even as out of shape as he himself was these days. They'd all lost that edge that active duty on the border gave you. Except Coetsee of course – he'd never actually ever had it, had never really been one of them, just a desk jockey.

Bezuidenhout and Smit were first and second on the list. He did them in that order because it was convenient – they both lived in the Jo'burg area. And also because that was the way the plan he came up with said he should. The killer spent a week monitoring both target's movements. He'd checked into a rundown motel in Jeppe; it was a fleapit but central, and once he'd paid the week up front he knew he could come and go as he pleased, no-one would hassle him.

The surveillance of Bezuidenhout and Smit wasn't difficult. Both had simple routines. Bezuidenhout worked nights as a guard for Strike First Security and his shift was from nine at night to six in the morning. He lived in a boarding house in the run-down part of Mayfair and would be dropped back home by the company van at 06:15. At around two in the afternoon he'd surface and head out for food and a couple of beers at a pub a hundred metres walk down the road. He'd stay there until early evening and then go home for a quick kip and to change into his uniform before he was picked up at 20:30 by the company van. Only once in three days had his routine changed and then it was only to walk another few hundred metres to a bottle store to buy a couple of half-jacks of liquor and a carton of cigarettes. Bezuidenhout had gone completely to seed – fat beer gut hanging over his khaki uniform trousers. The area they'd given him to patrol couldn't have helped either – Louis Botha Avenue and the side streets in the immediate vicinity of the Radium Beerhall in Orange Grove. The Radium was not only the most popular bar in Jo'burg but coupled with a host of nearby late night fast-food joints, would be a hard place for anyone to stay in shape even if you wanted to.

Bezuidenhout didn't take his job very seriously. But then it wasn't much of a job. The killer had been watching him for the past few nights and it seemed all Bezuidenout did was to patrol up and down as a deterrent to any would-be thieves interested in the Radium's customers' cars parked in the streets. And also to chase off any beggars who hassled them as they got out of their cars. Only when the bar shut for the night and its customers left in their cars (some of the drunker ones tipping him quite handsomely), would he knock off for a break. Then he'd take himself and his tips across the road where he'd be the final trick for the hooker that worked out of Vangelia Court, the flats across the street.

The killer was waiting for Bezuidenhout fifty metres from the front entrance of the Radium, outside the laundry on 9th Street. It was around three in the morning when everyone was long gone home after the music and drinking were over. Bezuidenhout had finished his visit with the hooker and come out of her building to go back on patrol He took a swig from his hip-flask and lit a cigarette and then wheezed his way towards where the killer was hidden in the shadows.

It took a couple of whacks on the head with a wheel spanner to put him down. One on the back of his head and the other on his right temple as he was falling. Poetic justice, a *koevoet* to kill an ex-member of Koevoet. There was the crack of glass breaking when he hit the ground and then what looked like a pool of piss spreading out from under his trousers. It wasn't piss though, The killer could smell brandy from the half-jack Bezuidenhout had carried in his back pocket and which had broken when he hit the pavement. He felt for the pulse at Bezuidenhout's neck to check whether he was still alive but the wheel spanner had done its job. He was *morsdood.* Looking at him lying there with his fat gut and no prospects, the killer reckoned he'd done him a favour. He took Bezuidenhout's wallet, his security guard I.D. with his picture on it and his pistol, and melted back into the shadows.

He took Smit out the very next morning, before the newspaper or local radio alerted him that his pal Bezuidenhout had been murdered. Although that was unlikely. Murder, unless extremely brutal or involving high profile people, seldom made the South African news these days, so many were there.

Smit had become a recluse since he'd left the army. It happened with some ex-combatants, particularly special services operatives. And especially if they had been involved in serious dirty tricks like Smit and were paranoid about either retribution from the State, ghosts, or God. Smit had barred himself into a jail of his own making. A townhouse in an armed patrolled, electric fenced, gated complex just off Ferndale Main Street. He stayed in his townhouse day and night behind a direct response alarm system, burglar bars, steel security doors and automatic lights that switched on if a mouse scurried past their sensors. None of it helped when the killer came calling.

He gained entrance to the main gate of the complex the easy way – by bribing the bored-looking security guard at the gate. The killer was in overalls with dark glasses, cotton work gloves and a black cap with a long peak. He had a canvas sling bag over his shoulder and pointing to it slipped the guard a hundred rand note and said he was representing a pool maintenance company and he'd like to leave leaflets in each resident's gate. He knew which townhouse belonged to Smit – his name and the number – 12 – were noted on the block of mailboxes, and he headed straight to it. There was a combined intercom/security camera at the gate and well before he got to it, he ducked his head so the camera couldn't clock his face. Instead he held the I.D. which he had taken from Bezuidenhout up to the camera lens, rang the buzzer and when Smit asked who was it, growled in a muffled voice: 'Smit, it's me. Bezuidenhout sent me – we need to talk.' He was buzzed through the gate and was met at the front door by Smit, who had a .357 Ruger revolver at his side.

'Jeez! I never expected to see *you* again. What's the problem?'

The problem was the bayonet the killer pulled from the sheath behind his back and plunged deep into Smit's gut just below his ribcage. And as he pushed it in even deeper, slicing through his lungs and up into his heart, he looked deep into Smit's eyes, where he saw the growing awareness that he no longer had the strength to lift his arm. The arm that held the magnum he thought made him safe from intruders at the front door.

It had only taken two minutes from when the killer had left the front gate to the complex and another thirty seconds to wipe the bayonet clean on Smit's shirt, put it back into the sheath and get back to the main gate. There he asked the guard to let him out again, and laughing, said that he'd forgotten to bring the leaflets and would be back later with them if that was okay? The guard let him out, shaking his head at how stupid white men could be.

The sun was dancing in the wake of a passing waterskier on the stretch of flat water in front of Coetsee's retirement home at Cosmos on Hartebeestpoort Dam. It was an early Tuesday morning and the lone skier belied the flotilla of speed boats and jet skis which normally churned up the placid waters on weekends. Jan Coetsee, ex-Commandant of guards at Pelindaba, and his wife Nikki, had recently moved permanently into what had been the weekend getaway they'd bought when Coetsee had been working at Pelindaba. The house was built in the 1920s just after the dam itself and nestled into the hillside in a lush, semi-tropical garden overlooking the dock where Coetsee had his bass boat moored.

Commandant Coetsee had done well in the new South Africa and instead of, as he had feared, losing his job when they shut down the nuclear arms facility at Pelindaba, he had continued working for Armscor and had somehow ended up as Sales Director for the heavy weapons division. His ex-army rank gave him credibility when demonstrating and selling the various tanks and long-range cannons Armscor designed and built, even though he had been involved in little active duty himself. Life was good with a fat, inflation-linked pension and Coetsee was looking forward to years of doing very little at all. His most important goals were to spend his time cultivating his prize-winning fuchsias and to winkle out one of the big black bass that patrolled the margins around the dam.

The killer had been staking out the Coetsees every day for the past two weeks. He had a good idea of their routine. Most days at about ten in the morning, even on weekends, Mrs. Coetsee would either meet friends from Pretoria at the nearby Village Mall Mugg & Bean or drive to Pretoria and meet them there. She'd get back home in time to prepare a late lunch for her husband and then head out again to meet more friends for either bridge or back to the Mall for tea and cake. Coetsee never joined her. He'd get up well before she did, make breakfast for himself and either potter around the garden, or more often, grab his fishing tackle and head to his boat, and go off fishing. In the weeks the killer had been staking him out, he usually went across the dam to the drop-off where the Magalies River entered it.

For the killer, the best option was to do Coetsee when he was fishing. It would have been easier to kill him when he was gardening but it would be hard to make it look like an accident or a random crime. No, when he was fishing would be better. Today Coetsee was in the garden. Tomorrow he'd most likely fish. So it would be tomorrow.

The killer had spent the last several weeks sleeping rough in the back of his bakkie next to a shack in the poor-white squatter camp *Sonskyn Hoekie* – one of the dozen or so white squatter camps that have sprung up around Pretoria since 1994. He'd paid the *oom* who owned the farm where the displaced, mainly Afrikaners, had thrown up various shanties, two hundred rands to park his bakkie under the sparse shade of a gum tree for a month. He packed up and left the camp at four in the morning before anyone was up, and drove to the Magalies River Resort, parking next to the entrance, eight kilometres from Coetsee's house at Cosmos. He was glad to shake the dust of *Sonskyn Hoekie* off him, found it hard to swallow that so many of the *volk* he had fought for on the border were now such feckless no-hopers.

He walked briskly in the dark. It took the expected one-and-half hours to get to Coetsee's place. The killer was carrying a light fishing rod and had a rucksack on his back, in which was a bottle of brandy, the wheel spanner he had whacked Bezuidenhout with, a thick rope with a pre-prepared noose and the dead Bezuidenhout's 9mm Star parabellum.

He waited in the dark under the large jacaranda at the front of Coetsee's house, his body pressed close against the tree trunk to hide him from any early passing traffic. There was none. Lucky though that he'd made it early, Coetsee was up early too – at first light. He came out of the house carrying a short spinning rod and a large plastic box of bass lures. As he reached the jacaranda the killer stepped out of the darkness and fell into stride with Coetsee.

'*Môre* Jan. Nice day for fishing.'

Coetsee, who nearly had a heart attack when the figure had jumped out from behind the tree, blanched when he realised who it was and then became very frightened when he felt the gun shoved against his earhole.

'What do *you* want?'

'We need to talk and on the lake is best. No-one around. So let's go to your boat and head out. And no shit, or I'll shoot you where you stand.'

There were no problems from Coetsee. The killer kept the gun at his side as they walked the hundred metres to the jetty. There was no-one else around. He ordered Coetsee into the boat first, then jumped in beside him gesturing with the gun, and telling Coetsee to stow the rods and then go to the back to the engine, start it and get going.

Coetsee asked, 'Where to'? And the killer told him, 'Where you've been the last few trips, Magalies River, near the resort.'

It took half-an-hour to get to the Magalies inlet. The sun was a ball of fire on the horizon when they arrived. Coetsee, sitting, steering the motor at the back transom was framed in the rising sun. The killer was on a bench seat just forward. He had the gun in his lap and his hand on the rucksack. He told Coetsee to head slowly towards the willows at the bank and stop, they could talk there. Coetsee obeyed. Just as they got to the bank, the killer half jumped out of his seat, pointing behind Coetsee.

'Jesus Jan, what the fuck's that?'

And when Coetsee turned to look, the killer hit him on the head with the wheel spanner. Not too hard this time. Not like with Bezuidenhout but enough to drop Coetsee, stunned. The 'look at that' trick was the oldest in the book; the killer smirked, but it never failed.

The rest took twenty minutes. When Coetsee had half come round he had his arms roped behind him and he was choking on the harsh brandy that was being forced down his throat. He hadn't come around enough to struggle much, even when the killer dragged him half over the side on the boat and pushed his head underwater and held it there. Then he struggled. But the killer was strong and Coetsee couldn't fight him as he sucked the water into his throat and down his lungs. Brandy and water. *Dop en dam*. Too much of it will kill you.

The killer removed the rope from Coetsee's arms – it had hardly left a mark – and then he pushed the body into the water and, leaving it to float in the shallows, pulled himself and the boat hand-over-hand through the willow branches to the bank. He stowed the rope, wheel spanner and gun in the rucksack and grabbing his fishing rod, jumped onto the bank. The walk to where he'd left the bakkie earlier was only a few hundred metres. He met one other fisherman carrying a rod and wished him luck. The man thanked him.

The killer was home and dry. And he hadn't even got his feet wet.

He didn't need to stalk Pienaar like he had the others. Just phone him. Where he had only met Bezuidenhout, Smit and Coetsee when they were called to a meeting by the Colonel, he and Danie Pienaar were friends from the army days. Or as friendly as two solitary hunters of people could get. Their mutual love of weapons and the differing abilities of various weapons to kill and maim gave them something in common. Sometimes they tried out their new weapons on the hunting trips they shared every now and then – Pienaar had a certificate of exemption from Nature Conservation and was allowed to shoot on his farms all year. So when the killer phoned Pienaar on his home farm, *Springfontein*, in the bushveld just north of Marble Hall and asked him if he still had guineafowl on his game farm, *Draaikraal,* and could he come and try out his new 12-bore on them, Pienaar said sure, come down, how does next week Thursday sound? The killer said Thursday would be perfect, if a little tight, as he had to be in Pretoria early afternoon so could they meet at the gate just after sunrise? He'd bring coffee and rusks and they could shoot at the best time, as the flocks were gathering for their day's scratching in the mielie fields nearby.

Pienaar told Sannie, his wife, the night before the bird shoot not to prepare breakfast for him the next morning as he was leaving for *Draaikraal* early in the morning to meet up with an old pal to shoot guineafowl. Sannie said she'd make up some sandwiches and leave them in the fridge. He told her not to make too many, he'd be back at lunchtime.

The killer was waiting at first light the next morning, leaning against his bakkie at the game farm gate. Pienaar arrived five minutes later and took his own 12-bore out of its carry case. They shook hands and the killer showed off his 'new' gun – a finely-engraved, Spanish-made Aya he'd picked up for a song at a Cape Town auction years ago but had never shown Pienaar. They shared one of the sandwiches and had coffee and a rusk for afters – they ate and drank hurriedly though – the cackling of the guineafowl calling each other for their own breakfast couldn't be ignored.

It was a short walk to the fence between the game farm and the lands. It was a high fence, two metres of barbed wire with a metre of mesh at the bottom. It was designed to keep the buck fenced in and out of the mielie fields and worked for everything except kudu, high jump champions of the animal kingdom.

The killer went through the fence first. Broke his shotgun so it couldn't go off accidently and laid it on the ground, barrel facing away, as an additional safety precaution. Pienaar put his foot on a lower strand of wire and lifted the strand above, making it easier for his pal, who he had noticed was getting a bit thick around the waist, to climb through. The killer thanked him and once through the fence, retrieved his shotgun and, turning his back on Pienaar, loaded it. He turned round. Pienaar was going through the same safety precautions, gun broken, barrel facing away … he was half way through the fence when the killer gave him the right hand full-choke barrel full in the chest. Pienaar died quickly, and hung bloody, caught on the wire. The killer set the scene carefully. He retrieved Pienaar's 12-bore and after loading both barrels, closed the gun and pinting it skywards, pulled the front trigger. Then he carefully positioned the shotgun under his old army buddy hanging in the fence. And left.

They found Pienaar in the early evening after his wife had told a neighbour that she was worried as her husband hadn't returned when he had promised to from shooting guineafowl with a friend. It looked as though the friend had never turned up; there was no sign of anyone else except Pienaar dead on the fence.

The local police were called. The investigating officer took photographs and then quickly examined the scene. It was obvious what had happened – straightforward even – another fool too stupid or too lazy to follow basic safety proceedures. The officer opened the gun. Yes, it was the right barrel that had discharged – it nearly always was – the front trigger, which fired the right barrel, nine times out of ten, the one that hooked itself on the barbed wire.

It looked liked a tragic accident, which surprised everyone. Pienaar was always so careful with firearms.

He left the Colonel for last, admitting to himself he was still shit-scared of him. But as it turned out the Colonel was the easiest of all. The killer hadn't yet figured out how he was going to make the hit when, driving out of town one morning, he noticed the Colonel was in front of him. He'd caught up with him and smashed the smaller vehicle into the donga with his much heavier one. Literally bumped him off. It was too good an opportunity to miss. The Colonel must have gone senile, completely lost his touch, even waved the killer on to overtake. It was disappointing in a way.

The killer switched his mind off and went into the automatic reloading sequence he had learnt was foolproof. Well almost foolproof. First, the most important, the ten steps needed to prepare the brass cases for long-range accuracy. As good as Winchester were in making their brass, the manufacturing process left minute differences in each casing. So each had to be hand-tooled, trimmed, deburred, polished and chamfered, expanded or sized to within one grain of weight to each other. Then the flash hole and primer pockets had to be made uniform on each casing and the primers seated. Then the powder carefully weighed on scales as sensitive as a jeweller's – 40 grains in each shell, no more, no less. And finally the bullet heads, all examined and weighed beforehand, any inconsistency rejected and binned, and carefully seated to the exact same depth in each cartridge and identically crimped in.

'Finished. Twelve perfect bullets. Two Sako magazines-full. Next time I won't miss.'

FOUR

It's your funeral

THEY KEPT CAROLUS IN HOSPITAL over the weekend and on Monday morning Annetjie and I went to fetch him home. As I had hoped, he wasn't seriously wounded but would have a helluva headache for the next few days. The doctor gave him something a lot stronger than aspirin and told him to stay in bed. Annetjie tried to get him to follow the doctor's orders, fussing over him like a mother hen, which, of course, she was, but by the afternoon he was up. He was saddling up to go check on the stock, his head bandaged under an old broad-brimmed felt hat. I noticed he'd cut the inside of the brim so it would fit over the bandages. I told him to wait a couple of minutes as I had something for him and went back into the house. When I got back I handed him Pa's Remington hunting rifle.

'You better take this, I take it you know how to use it?'

'Yes, the boss taught me.'

'That's good enough for me, he taught me too.'

Later that evening I called Chesney and filled him in on

the *kak* we'd had at the farm but also in the hope that he had some news for me. He said he had, but I wouldn't like it much. He told me that Makatini Investments were big players with tentacles into all sorts of things. Mining, banking, the arms industry, you name it. Geo Logical, the prospecting company I'd asked about, was part of them.

Makatini had big money backing them, much of it government, some of it foreign, a lot of it criminal. Their founder and chairman, Sipho Makatini, had started out in the shebeen trade in Soweto, graduating to drugs and prostitution – nothing too out of the ordinary there. But later he'd branched out into illegal gold mining, stolen IDs and passports, and people trafficking:

'You know there's over two million Africans from various countries north living in Jo'burg, all on dodgy papers,' Cook said.

'I wouldn't be surprised,' I replied.

'Well someone supplied them, and Internal Affairs claim it wasn't them.'

Cook went on to tell me that Makatini Investments started seriously coining it when the ANC government took over all the country's underground mineral rights. Most of the whitey companies and individuals who previously owned them, quickly sold out or entered partnerships with newly-formed black empowerment companies, who bought into them on a promise and just about *fokol* else.

'Wouter Van Schalkwyk is one of those Johnny-come-lately partners. He's small fry in the organisation, but one of the token whiteys they use as a front when they're trying to pull the wool over the eyes of you simple Boere. But if they're interested in what's underground on your farm, it's likely to be something big – they don't get involved in chicken feed. Although they'll buy the mineral rights from the government, they'd still have to pay you for the surface rights to set up the mining operation. Those surface rights could be worth a lot of moolah.'

I told him that I wasn't holding my breath that I was about to become the next Harry Oppenheimer and asked him if he'd found out anything more about the men on Pa's list.

'Ja, I have. They're all dead, except for one I can't track down. But that's not all though, they also all had close links to your father. Four were ex-Koevoet – Pienaar, Smit, Bezuidenhout and van Niekerk, and the other one, Coetsee, was his second-in-command at Pelindaba. He took over from him as head of security.'

'Dead? How?'

'Well I checked through the police national data base and it seems that two were accidental deaths, one a random mugging and the other a murder during a house-breaking.'

'Go on,' I said.

'Well, Coetsee drowned at Harties, when he was pissed. Pienaar in a shooting accident at his farm. Bezuidenhout, who was a security guard, was mugged and hit on the head with an iron pipe or crowbar, and Smit answered the door to the wrong person. Stabbed, probably by a burglar, the report said.'

Cook never ceased to amaze me. He obviously had a contact who had hacked into the main police computer. Or knowing him, he probably did it himself.

'It all sounds fishy to me though. Just too much coincidence. Four people, all with links to each other, all on your father's list. There's too much sloppy police work involved – none of the conclusions look right. Especially the Smit killing – to me doesn't look like a burglary. He was lying there with his gun on the floor. Didn't look like anything was stolen and also the killing was too clean – one stab wound, deep – he knew what he was doing.'

'And what about the fifth oke, van Niekerk?'

'Disappeared. Left the army the same time as your father

and gave a forwarding address – a farm in the Karroo near Beaufort West. I phoned, but the person I spoke to, a Mr. Dippenaar, said he was long gone. Packed up in the drought in 2005 and went bust. Also his wife died in a car accident.'

'And no trace of him since?'

'No, Dippenaar thought he was from somewhere in Cape Town, but I haven't been able to trace any van Niekerk here that fits the bill,'

'And you said they had close links to Pa?'

'Ja. I hope you don't mind, but I pulled your father's army file as well. Seems that the four were all in your father's squad and were involved in some very heavy stuff deep in Angola. They were, to put it bluntly, an official death squad. The file, as the Yanks say, had a lot of stuff redacted – blotted out with black ink – but reading between the lines, they took out some important people, and not just in Angola, some of them here.'

'Shit. I'm getting a bad feeling about this van Niekerk person. You're going to have to dig deeper.'

'My thoughts exactly. I'll get back to you shortly.'

I spent the next couple of days helping Carolus with farm things and preparing for the funeral which was set for midday on Friday. Most of the arrangements were in hand but I found some time on both days to drive into Terre'Blanche with an excuse to meet with Mauretia, followed by a late lunch at Steers. I hadn't expected many people for the funeral, just Oom Mackie and his family and maybe a few of the other farmers from the area, and possibly the lawyer, Eloff. I was surprised though at the number of calls I'd got early in the week from old army and hunting buddies of Pa's. Most of them almost forgotten names from the past, all of them asking what time the funeral was and where. Quite a few asked if I could put them up and I thought, why not – Pa would probably have liked them around one last time.

We arranged to meet at the Royal on Thursday evening and they could follow me back to the farm. I got Annetjie to prepare the three spare bedrooms and if more pitched up they could sleep on the stoep. We had plenty of blankets and although they'd all be getting on in years, they were ex-army and used to roughing it.

One call was from Eloff, asking if I had any reply yet for Wouter van Schalkwyk. I told him, no. And another was from the young guy Bolton from the mining prospecting company. He wanted to know if he could come back to the farm to do some further exploration. He'd have to set up camp but would try to stay out of the way. I told him fine, but could he wait until next week. He said that would be perfect.

The killer had been scouting the place for the past four days. Scoping the farmhouse and getting the rhythm of the farm routine. Every morning just after sunrise the old Coloured woman would leave her small house and walk the one hundred metres to the back door of the main farmhouse. The puff of smoke that soon followed told him that her first job was to light the stove. About an hour later, if he was downwind, he could smell coffee and breakfast. The Hotnot, Carolus, who he'd shot, was up and about again. At about 08:00 he'd collect a metal pail from the woman in the kitchen, saddle up and ride out. Every morning doing a complete circuit of the farm, checking on livestock and watering points along the way. The killer noticed that, unlike the day he shot him, he was armed, carrying a hunting rifle in a saddle-holster on the side of the horse. Carolus would return to the farmhouse at 12:30 sharp and would collect another pail of food from the woman who worked in the house. Later in the afternoon he'd ride out again.

At about 09:00, Koekemoer would appear, stand on the stoep and make a couple of calls on his cell – maybe reception's not great in the house. Sometimes he'd head into town, but usually he'd go back into the house until around 12:30 –when he'd come out and have a chat to the Hotnot who'd had just arrived back from his patrol. They'd meet under the pin oak where the horse would be tethered. They were probably talking farm business – he'd never got close enough to listen in, and anyway what they were talking about was unimportant. Today was no different. He put the crosshairs on Koekemoer's head, then moved rapidly to the Hotnot's. Easy.

It was a good time to do it. Just after noon, when the sun was no factor. No shadows to distort the distance. And there was a good field of fire – a slight uphill shot from the donga four hundred metres away. Two quick shots half-a-second apart. If the woman came to see what was happening, he'd shoot her too … but it wasn't really important whether he did or not. She'd never stay on if the men were dead. The escape route was easy too – down the donga to the old picnic spot on the main road. He could leave the bakkie there. Nobody would be chasing him though, he'd make sure of that. Yes, he'd do it tomorrow, Friday. Both of them.

Thursday early evening I headed into town and met up with Pa's pals at the Royal. They made a brave attempt at having a wake, a couple of them already halfway pissed, but they were definitely past it. None of them would see fifty again and a couple would have been closer to Pa's age – in their late sixties. From the talk, it didn't seem that any of them were prospering in the new South Africa. Most of them were scratching a living, doing what they could to keep their heads above water – inflation was killing them. And it was impossible anyway to make ends meet on a military pension. If they were lucky enough to get one.

It was funny. These were Pa's pals, come to see him buried and all of them told me how sorry they were 'for his passing' and swore that 'anything they could do, just ask'. But I felt like an outsider. I realised I had nothing in common with them. Couldn't share in the stories which were stuck in the same record groove from their glory days in the old South Africa.

I couldn't even talk to Fat Face. There was a spotty young guy with a protruding Adam's apple behind the bar and he said that Fat Face, or GT as he called him, was away on a week's leave and he was just standing in.

The talk from the ex-soldiers had progressed to where all such gatherings in South Africa always deteriorate – how shit and corrupt the ANC government was. How the faint hope that Mandela brought of being able to carry forward Archbishop Tutu's Rainbow Nation, had descended into the current President's kleptocracy. Only they didn't use polite words like 'President' or 'kleptocracy'. I switched off and retired into my own head.

I once shook Nelson Mandela's hand. It was maybe fifteen years ago, outside the Sandton Sun in Jo'burg. I was parked outside, working undercover keeping tabs on a crook we were interested in, when the great man walked by. He was no longer President and he was by himself – tall but frail. No security, no police cavalcade with sirens blaring, just Madiba, in the flesh. I got out of my bakkie and said, 'Sir, can I shake your hand'.

He asked me what my name was, and I blurted out, 'Jacobus Koekemoer … I'm a policeman.'

He smiled at me, shook my hand and told me to have a good evening.

I've never been star struck and, in fact, have made a point of never letting on I was in awe of anyone. Mandela was only the second person I'd ever asked to shake hands with. The other was on a plane to Port Elizabeth years earlier. Danie Gerber had just scored three tries in a test match against the English, and they hadn't laid a finger on him.

After a couple of hours of listening to old war stories and complaints about the country, I'd had enough. I collected anyone who wanted to come with me and told them to follow me to the farm. I deposited three of them in the freshly made-up bedrooms and the other two on the stoep to sleep on cushions and mattresses Annetjie had earlier laid out. I told them we had to leave at 11:30 sharp.

Friday at 11:00 the killer was in position. He had arrived half-an-hour before, keeping low, out-of-sight in the bottom of the donga. He had brought a small burlap sack with him which he filled with sand. He laid the filled bag lengthways on the rim of the donga – a perfect benchrest for the rifle. He was taking no chances this time. He rested the rifle on the sandbag and carefully sighted in on the pin oak in the farmhouse yard. He did a quick scan through the telescopic sight, not expecting to see anything out of the ordinary. A fat, elderly man with short-cropped hair and a dark suit walked into the cross hairs and stopped to urinate over the edge of the stoep. He panned the sight a little left. There was another man, this one probably about fifty, doing the same thing. The man zipped up his fly. He was also in a black suit. Shortly the two men were joined by another three and then by Koekemoer. Koekemoer led the group around the house and disappeared out of sight. There was the sound of various vehicles starting up and then a convoy of bakkies drove through the sights which he had moved back on to the pin oak. He could see the Hotnot seated in the front of Koekemoer's bakkie, the old maid between them. He thought of taking the shot but stopped his trigger finger half-way. No time to get both of them.

Shit I should have taken them out yesterday when I had the chance. Without witnesses. Where have they all come from?' Then he realised: 'Fuck, fuck … the funeral. Today must be the day of the Colonel's funeral.'

#VerwoerdMustFall

The funeral had gone off without a hitch. It had been a perfect day for it. A typical summer's day – bright and hot with the promise of a thunderstorm later. The service had been surprisingly well-attended and mercifully short. There were fewer of us at the grave site on the farm. Just me, Oom Mackie, Mauretia, the minister and Pa's ex-warrior buddies, stoically standing at attention during the final prayers, giving no outward signs of the hangovers they must have been fighting off. Most of the mourners had on dark glasses and were dressed in black suits and ties, some even had on the black homburgs that were so popular back in Apartheid government times. It looked like a scene from Godfather II. As Pa's only blood relative, I stood at the head of the grave and watched as the coffin was slowly lowered – the sun glinting off the fake brass handles, muted behind the RayBans I wore. I let a handful of white Kalahari sand trickle slowly onto the coffin in the bottom of the grave and walked away. Mauretia put her hand on my elbow and walked with me. Funerals are a good time to have a woman's support.

The weekend went by in a blur. Friday night, after the funeral, we drank. Pa's comrades came back to the farm with me. So did Mauretia, Oom Mackie and a bunch from town. Someone had brought along a case of beer and a couple of bottles of Klipdrift brandy. Another brought Red Heart rum and several two-litre bottles of Coke. I recall sometime late that night kissing Mauretia – but also that she pushed me away, saying, 'No Jaco, this is not the time nor the place.' I don't remember her leaving shortly afterwards or me going into town on Saturday morning to stock up on more booze. Sometimes it pays not to remember.

Monday morning I woke up fine. Not a trace of a hangover. The crowds had left. One of them had even left a note saying thanks for the best funeral they'd been to in years. You can't say our nation lacks class. I showered long and hard and ate a double-ration of Annetjie's breakfast. And drank a bucket of coffee. I was ready for anything.

There was no reason to call Mauretia anymore but I did anyway. She sounded fine and said nothing about any kiss. Maybe I'd imagined it. We had lunch again, and she said she had the afternoon off and asked me if I would like to see where she lived. I said yes. Apparently it was now the right time to kiss her. And a whole lot more. Later she cooked me supper and also breakfast the next morning.

We promised we'd get together that evening after she was finished at work. I headed home and then later drove back into town to see if Captain Mpanza had learnt anything about Pa's murder. He had. The black paint was a special brand of hammer paint that Toyota's bull bar suppliers used and some of the glass was from the lens of a Toyota Land Cruiser bakkie – an old model from around 1996. There was also news on Carolus's shooting. Witbooi, the tracker, had found two spent bullets from the scene of the sniper's attack. One in the intestines of the big bull, and the other, the one that had grazed Carolus's skull, in the trunk of a tree. Both were damaged – the tips mushrooming on impact – but both were still identifiable as .243 calibre.

Mpanza went on to say that ballistics experts in Pretoria

had written that the .243 was a popular hunting round but not a regulation SADF military sniper's round. But also that it was one of the most accurate long distance, high velocity rounds there was, with an extremely flat trajectory. They also concluded that the bullets found had been something pretty special – Sierra Spitzers, used only by serious handloaders. They had already put out a request to all South African gun dealers for information on all Sierra Spitzer sales in the previous two years. Mpanza asked them to extend that to five.

Mpanza also said they may have had something of a breakthrough of their own. Witbooi told him that he knew of a sniper that used a .243 who sometimes worked with Koevoet in the old days. The sniper was only a youngster at the time but he already had a big reputation – he had killed many people and was expert at it. He was a special forces operative in 32 Battalion, but he could even have been a recce and went by the nickname of *Rooikat*, after the secretive yet vicious lynx that was the bane of South African small stock farmers. He said that, like the animal which would kill an entire flock of sheep in a lust for blood, the human Rooikat would not stop until he had sated his own lust to track and kill his target, and heaven help anyone in the way – they just became 'collateral damage' – innocent or not.

He said he'd never actually served with this Rooikat during his stint in Koevoet but he knew others who had, and as tough as the men in Koevoet were, they were always a little nervous when they spoke about him. As if he might overhear them.

I immediately told Mpanza that Pa was ex-32 Battalion and also, I suspected, linked to Special Services and Koevoet. He whistled.

'Your father was something of a dark horse, as you people sometimes say. I've done some checking on him and he seems to have had some highly suspicious connections.'

I decided to trust Mpanza and to tell him everything I'd so

far learnt reading Pa's files and through Cook's investigations.

'I've been finding out a lot about my father that I didn't know,' I said. 'A lot that I don't really want to know, especially about his army days. But I don't think his murder has any connection with the army, although there is a link. I think it has something to do with his days as head of security at Pelindaba. At the A-bomb research facility.'

Mpanza, wide-eyed said, 'Like what?'

'Like there was some right wing plot going on in the late nineteen eighties that concerned Pa and a small group of his friends. I found a list of names. Four of them were army men who had served under Pa and the other was the man who later took over from him as head of security.

'What names?'

'Jan Pieter Coetsee was the security head, and the soldiers were Gerhardus Tertius van Niekerk, Danie Pienaar, Derrick Smit and Carel (Boet) Bezuidenhout – the last four all 32 Battalion. Oh, and there was also General de la Rey.'

Mpanza, who had been writing down the names I had given him, paused.

'De la Rey? Wasn't he an old Boer War general?'

I told him yes but that it was also the code name for one of the A-bombs the Apartheid government built at Pelindaba. And then it struck me … how could I be so slow?

'*Fok*. I think they were trying to steal an A-bomb!'

Captain Mpanza looked at me as if I was crazy.

'What! It's lucky then that they didn't succeed. Imagine the havoc they could have caused.'

'Imagine.'

Mpanza said he was going to see what Coetsee, van Niekerk, Pienaar, Smit and Bezuidenhout were up to at present. I was just about to tell him not to bother, that they were all dead, except for van Niekerk, when I thought, shit that would be telling him we had somehow hacked into the police computers. But in for a penny. I told him anyway.

'They're all dead in suspicious circumstances. All except for van Niekerk. And he's disappeared from sight. He could be our killer.'

I elaborated on exactly what the suspicious circumstances were and how we weren't able to trace van Niekerk's present whereabouts, when another brainstorm hit me:

'*Fok*. He could be Witbooi's Rooikat!'

On the short drive back to the farm I noticed a lot of activity going on at Verwoerd's Koppie. It looked like a small shanty town had grown up in its shadow and some scaffolding had been erected underneath the giant bust of Verwoerd's head. There were several ant-like figures on the scaffolding and it seemed they were painting the sculpture. I noticed a splash of red at the top and then some blue and yellow below.

When I got back to the farm, Carolus told me the young guy who was doing the survey had returned and that he was setting up camp on the Verwoerd's Koppie boundary of the farm. He told me that it looked as though he was expecting people to join him, as he'd set up three tents and a lean-to attached to the side of a Land Cruiser campervan. He had also towed in a heavy-duty trailer with what appeared to be drilling equipment and a generator. Carolus said he thought they were planning on doing some mining and not just prospecting. I said I'd go out to the camp and see what was happening.

The easiest way to get to get to where Bolton had set up camp was on the back road to Terre'Blanche. Drive past the small koppie where the bushwacker had laid in wait for Carolus and then carry on for nearly two kilometres to Verwoerd's Koppie itself. Once there, I parked at what was once a well-maintained visitors' car park, in the shade of some falling-down, thatch-roofed braai pits that were built at the time the monument head was opened to the public. I got out of the bakkie, to be met by a blast of heat and the teeth-rattling jangle of jackhammers. Every now and then the jackhammers stopped and were replaced by the throbbing of African drums. It was like listening to a head-bangers gig on a building site.

I moved away from where the cacophony was coming from, when mercifully the jackhammers stopped and the drums seemed to fade almost into bearable. The place was deserted and full of rubbish. If the old government had expected throngs of the faithful to make patriotic pilgrimages to view Verwoerd, they must have been disappointed. It became more of a place for the youngsters of the town to gather in the night to drink and generally get up to the things that youngsters driven to terminal boredom in places like Terre'Blanche tend to do. None of it rooted in ideas of patriotism. A short walk from this picnic area, there was an old commando shooting range where you could still find old spent brass *doppies* of a variety of calibres, and what had once been old mine workings – a horizontal shaft that went about a hundred metres into the koppie. These old workings had been a magnet for kids for years. I'd played in them too, looking for pieces of iron pyrites – the fool's gold that had originally driven the early miners deep into the koppie. This had all stopped some years back when the mine had been sealed after some kids were hurt in a rock fall. I remember Pa telling me the entrance had been dynamited shut.

Bolton's camp was only fifty metres from the fence that marked the border of Verwoerd's Koppie and the farm. He had quite a set up. A Land Cruiser campervan and lean-to and three of those new igloo-type tents with ventilation slots along their sides, solar panels that drove lights, and a small generator for what looked like a bar fridge. He had a heavy commercial generator and a couple of jackhammers in a trailer parked off to the side and a heavy red box in the shade under the trailer. He was lounging in a deck chair, beer in hand, and listening to something on his headphones that was leaking heavy base guitar. He didn't even hear me approach and was startled when I tapped him on the shoulder. He offered me a beer though, which was welcome as always. He told me he was waiting for his colleagues who had been prospecting up north somewhere. But that they'd been delayed, so for once he had a bit of time to relax. I asked him how long he thought he'd be around and he said he didn't know, perhaps as long as a month, depending on what they found. He also said that if I heard some blasting, not to worry – they were going to do some seismic testing. But it would be best for me and the farm staff to stay away from the area as it could be dangerous. I said fine but not to blow himself up, and he said he'd try not to and he'd be in touch when he had some results.

As I climbed back through the barbed-wire fence to where I'd parked the bakkie, I thought maybe I should also see what the shanty town and red and blue paint was all about. And the noise. There was a stone-paved path from the car park at the braai area that lead to a viewing platform about chin height to the massive head. As I walked along the path the sound of drums got louder and louder – the bongo player in the bar had probably cloned. The smell of *boom* was also getting stronger. I could see why as I rounded the corner and some haphazard tents came into sight. A mix of teepees and sagging army surplus. This was no neat prospector's camp but more Woodstock-in-the-veld – a haze of smoke from cooking fires and three-blader joints.

Just above the tent town was the scaffolding. This at least looked professional. Or at least I hoped so for the painters' sakes. I saw a burly black guy in a hard hat resting in the shade, a jackhammer next to him. Then I saw the great leader, Thabo Mkhize, in a #VerwoerdMustFall T-shirt, supervising the painters from the bottom level of scaffolding. He had his arm around a very stoned, but pretty, little redhead – the prettiest girls being the main perks of student activists for generations.

I quickly worked out what they were painting – a giant new South African flag. Verwoerd was beginning to look like he'd pulled a pair of multicoloured underpants over his head, balaclava style.

Mkhize noticed me and shouted: 'Policeman! Do you see what we're doing?'

I shouted back: 'Yes. But you've missed the thin strip of white between the red and the green...'

He had the grace to laugh.

'I see you're right. But I don't think anyone will notice.'

'What was that racket I heard earlier?'

'We're drilling holes for the dynamite.' And Mkhize pointed to several places on the edges of the giant bust.

'Holes there, there and there. A couple of sticks in each should bring the whole thing down.'

'But why are you wasting time painting Verwoerd's face then?'

'Because we want him to look his best for the cameras. We're going to film the whole thing at the big rock concert.'

Then in case I didn't get it, shouted: 'Yes a big, big *rock* concert where Verwoerd will be the main attraction. We're going to call it Blow Oppikoppi.'

I shouted back: 'I hope you've got a licence!'

And left as the jackhammer started up again.

FIVE

Cockroaches

THERE IS ALWAYS DODGY MONEY behind liberation movements and the African National Congress was no different. But when the liberation movement takes power, that's when the cockroaches come out of the woodwork. Although in South Africa's case, there were some genuine international companies interested in re-building the country, and some that were buying back those they'd sold to their Apartheid-era South African management. There were also many new entrants scrambling to grab a share of the First World economy built by the previous regime – industries that had flourished with international sanctions as the catalyst. These companies, by and large, were good for the new country. Vital in generating the growth needed to satisfy the aspirations of a long down-trodden population.

South Africa, like most newly-independent African countries had started brightly. Ethics and the rule of law kept graft and corruption at bay. But only for a time. It was not long before the African curse of tribalism, patronage and nepotism began to chip away at the new democracy. And it was not long before wide-boys from around the world sensed there was a new goose to be plucked. Soon every government tender became an invitation for a bribe, with every new Black Economic Empowerment partnership a potential vehicle to spread the spoils.

You could see them laundering these ill-gotten gains in the five star hotels of the Johannesburg satellite town of Sandton. Cheap gangsters in Armani suits with Rolexes on their arms, wining and dining $1 000-a-night whores on $500-a-head crayfish dinners while hungry, newly-enfranchised locals served them – wondering when their own promised post-election BMWs would be delivered by their new government.

If truth be told though, these cockroaches and parasites were no different from those who fed off the old Apartheid government. The crony capitalists who through influence and bribery and corruption grew fat on the proceeds of the perverted ideology, and who now live in the various tax havens of the world bemoaning how 'the blerry blecks' have ruined their country, while sipping Bollinger at their weekend braai. 'Saffer boat people' – fly to Monaco and buy a yacht. A big ocean going boat to park next to their new Eurotrash best friends.

You want to find the next booming third world economy? Follow the Russian hookers – they can smell the opportunity to cash in on freshly-laundered greenbacks quicker than a hungry hyena can a smell a week-old carcass downwind. And from a lot further off.

Khan

Husain Azhar Khan, father of Azhar, Reza and Sabbar, was head of the Khan family in South Africa. Unlike most South Africans of Asian extraction (who were originally brought to the Cape by the Dutch East India Company in the 1700s as slaves from what is now known as Indonesia), the Khans were part of much later emigration of Pashtuns from the borders of the present Pakistan. They were not part of the Hindu and Tamil indentured labour migration to the Natal sugar fields from the Indian sub-continent in the 1860s onwards, but rather 'passenger Indians' – Muslim traders who paid their own way, lured by the riches to be made on the newly opened coal, diamond and gold fields. These merchants soon began to thrive in commerce, especially in northern Natal and the Transvaal Republic – the Khans in particular. They opened their first trading store in the Transvaal soon after Paul Kruger became President in 1883 and by 1899 were one of the most prominent of the five thousand 'Indian' trader families in the Boer Republic. With interests ranging from grocery stores to supplying provisions and equipment to the mining industry and, it is rumoured, even some of the arms later used by the Boers in the second Anglo-Boer war.

But it wasn't easy for traders like the Khans. There were, from the beginning, many racially motivated laws that restricted them from buying property in certain areas and entering certain businesses. Despite their contribution to the prosperity of the Transvaal Republic, they were denied the right to vote and could be expelled from the state with little recourse to the law. These restrictions became even more onerous after the fall of the Boer republics and the return of British rule. However they continued to thrive – in business anyway. The frustrations of success on the one hand and officially sanctioned prejudice on the other, burnt deeply. On the surface most appeared to keep their heads down, going about their business. But many lived a shadow life, active in early resistance movements like the Transvaal Indian Congress. In 1948, when the Afrikaner-dominated National Party regained political power, things became worse and in 1961, when South Africa cut ties with Britain and became a republic, worse still.

Many, now fourth generation South African Indians, left the country altogether. The majority however, had nowhere to go and so had to stay and make the best of what they could under the Apartheid regime. But some, like the Khans, decided to fight. And they did it in the best way they could – by supplying money and arms to banned liberation movements like the ANC and Pan African Congress. They were the perfect conduit to launder foreign funds destined for the movements and, unlike some, scrupulously honest in distributing these funds. Their reward came when Nelson Mandela became president of the new South Africa. As trusted comrades, the Khans made a fortune in the first ten years of independence, expanding their interests into legitimate industries like mining and banking. But as successive governments succumbed to the corruption endemic in newly-independent African countries, new, better-connected black African businessmen, got the front seats on the gravy train. The realisation grew that, if the family were to hold on to their wealth, they would have to expand further afield than the rapidly deteriorating South

African economy. For that they would need serious money – US dollars – not inflation-raddled rands.

So the family began to move their assets and interests overseas. The Middle East was chosen as the place to be. Not just because of religious and family ties, but in recognition that war zones and chaos often provide great opportunities. And the Khans were experts in making money out of war and chaos. Husain Khan's eldest son from his first marriage, Azhar, a chartered accountant, was sent to Riyadh to be close to the Saudi bank where Khan had deposited much of their fortune. The younger son, Reza, to Baghdad, where he headed their honest businesses as well as their more shadowy.

They started slowly – keeping out of the big markets to begin with since there were not enough resources to play with the big boys in Dubai and the Gulf. Their first major deal came through an approach to Reza from a cousin in Baghdad in the mid-1990s. He offered the Khans a share in a deal to supply the Iraqi government with black granite stone for the new presidential palace Saddam Hussein was building. Saddam specified that it should be of the same stone used in the Vietnam Memorial in Washington. The problem was this was only available in three countries – India, Sweden and South Africa. The Indians and the Swedes would not touch any deal to do with Saddam, so it seemed South Africa was the only solution. Could they help?

They could indeed. They had family connections in Belfast in Mpumalanga where the stone was quarried, and had soon bought out two of the local quarries and were in business. Export licenses were quickly granted through their government connections and supplies of the fine black stone were soon on their way to Iraq. This successful transaction led to other orders in other businesses and the big breakthrough came when they were invited to bid on an oil-for-arms swop. The Khans had always been arms traders and the products they now had access to – Kalahari desert-proven South African weapons and vehicles, from small arms to long-range cannons, all-terrain scout vehicles to tanks were, at the time, unmatched anywhere. South Africa was also rapidly growing and the thirst for oil was insatiable, so the family was in a real win-win trading position – sought-after products to export in return for crucially needed oil. They had it made coming and going.

The fall of Saddam was just a blip. They'd already expanded their business into Iran, Pakistan and Afghanistan when another lucrative market opened – the supply of weapons to the new Sunni-dominated resistance movements. Many of these had been joined by people the Khans had done business with before – ex-Saddam army officers, men with ruthless backgrounds and serious ambitions, who turned resistance fighter rabble into substantial forces. These forces, that had at first armed themselves from the vast arsenal of weapons that the Americans had left behind when the Iraqi people were more or less abandoned to their own fate, soon need re-supply. The Khan's were happy to be of service.

They became trusted suppliers to al-Qaeda and what morphed into ISIS, Boko Haram and Al Shabbab – all ever more radical Islamists with even bigger dreams. The principal of which was the re-instatement of a Caliphate in the Middle East, Africa and, later, the world. Something that in recent years had been an ideal close to Husain Azhar Khan's own heart, even though he kept it hidden.

The latest deal, though, was the most dangerous that Khan had ever considered. So dangerous, that he decided that the only member of the family he could trust to become involved was his only son from his second marriage, Sabbar. Although even Sabbar wouldn't be told the full story. But if they could pull it off, it would be the biggest arms trade in history and secure their family future forever.

The deal was to sell a nuclear warhead.

Rooikat

It had all begun with a text message Husain Azhar Khan received one afternoon. The message was from the head of a security firm his company sometimes used when they needed armed guard services and asked if they could meet urgently. They were called Strike First Security and their slogan was, 'We Make Problems Go Away'.

The head of Strike First was a man called Mohamed Aziz who attended the same mosque as the Khans and was rumoured to have been some sort of operative in *uMkhonto we Siswe*, the ANC's military arm. Khan texted back: My house 6pm.

Aziz was punctual. He arrived at Khan's Houghton, Johannesburg home five minutes early and was ushered in immediately. Khan himself met him at the front door and lead him back outside to a small building that wasn't visible from the front gates. Inside was a surprisingly austere office. He'd expected big and plush but instead it was cool and clinical with a bank of screens on one wall, online 24/7 to the world's main stock markets as well as several different news channels.

The two men shook hands in the western way and Khan asked him to sit.

'Mr. Aziz, I'm intrigued why you need to see me so urgently, but before we go on, I asked you to meet here because I know it's secure and no-one will interrupt us. Also there are no bugs. I won't be recording anything.'

Aziz nodded.

'Thank you, Mr. Khan. What I've got to tell you is going to sound like a crazy man's story. But the source it comes from is absolutely reliable. It's a long story though.'

'I'm listening, I have as much time as you need.'

'Thank you. But first, I don't know how much you know about me? You might have heard I'm ex-MK. Well that's only partly true. But my other affiliations can wait until later. Do you know that MK was talking to the Apartheid army long before Mandela was released?'

'I had heard something of the sort.'

'Well it's true. In fact we had a house right in the grounds of the old Defence Force headquarters off Rigel Avenue in Pretoria. That big white building on the right hand side of the highway heading north.'

'Yes, I know it – visited there once or twice myself.'

'Well I was there plenty of times. Believe it or not, we were meeting top army brass about the future after any political settlement. The whole lot – state security, army, Special Forces, even those bastards who ran Koevoet and other such murder squads. They all saw which way the wind was blowing and wanted to know essentially if they had any future.'

'And you told them?'

'Let's say we suggested that it was hoped that the army would keep their oath of allegiance to whatever government was in power.'

'And they bought that?'

'Well look what happened after independence. The only backlash was from those right wing lunatics in the AWB. Everyone else was more interested in keeping their jobs, so they toed the line.'

'So what this got to do with what you want to tell me?'

'Well during the two years of these talks, I met, as I said, all sorts of army people. And when I set up my business once Mandela took over, those contacts proved very useful. In fact I built my business on employing ex-defence force personnel – especially ex-Special Forces men. Let's face it, they were extremely well trained and good at following orders.'

'I suppose they would be.'

'So when one of them came to me and told me that one of his old comrades wanted to see me, I listened. I asked him what this man wanted with me, but he said he couldn't say, as his pal wouldn't tell him. Only that it was something big, and that as an MK operative I'd be very interested. I asked him what his ex-comrade's name was? He said he couldn't tell me that either except that I might know him as Rooikat.'

'Rooikat? What sort of name is that?'

'It's the codename of one of the most ruthless killers of the Apartheid regime, a special forces operative who was responsible for scores of deaths – Cuban, MPLA, ANC, ZANU, MK, even a Russian general once – you name it. Like the wild caracal cat he was named after, this Rooikat was never satisfied with one kill at a time. When the blood lust was up, he just killed and killed until it was sated. We were never able to find out his real name, or to track him down, and after independence he just melted away. No Truth and Reconciliation Commission for him.'

'So did you meet him?'

'Yes, late one night in a lay-by near the N4 East flyover in Pretoria North. It's a good spot to wait for someone, plenty of escape routes and you can see anybody coming from way off. I was deliberately early, and got out of my car and leant back against the door, hands out to each side as he'd instructed. He just suddenly appeared like a ghost. He was carrying what looked like a hunting rifle, but with a camouflaged stock. He told me that I'd been in his sights for the last few minutes and then he laughed and said to me, "You know Mr. Aziz, I never forget a face I've had framed in my telescopic sights and this is the second time with you. The other was long ago, up in the Caprivi at that waterhole just outside Katima."

'I tell you my blood ran cold. I remembered it very well. One of my men had just walked in front of me when his head exploded. We were pinned down for an hour and lost three more men who were stupid enough to raise their heads looking for something to shoot at.'

'And this was the man?'

'Yes, and you know, he didn't look like much. Nondescript, a bit down-at-heel and as if he enjoyed too much brandy and braaivleis. But enough about him, it's his story that's important.'

'So tell me.'

'He said he had an atom bomb for sale.'

'A what?' Khan said incredulously.

'An atom bomb. He said he'd stolen it from Pelindaba twenty-five years ago and he wanted to sell it back to the government. Or to anyone who was prepared to pay for it.'

'And you believed him?'

'Not at first, but then he told me this long story about a Colonel Koekemoer who had been head of security at Pelindaba, and a right wing plot, and getting into Pelindaba late one night with a special Unimog truck. Also he said that the Colonel, who was the leader of the plot, was still alive and lived on a farm near Terre'Blanche in the North West Province and that he used to go to regular meetings there and that once the Colonel showed them a file that he said would one day tell the world their story and that would make them famous. He said the file had a full record of everything and was kept in a filing cabinet in the office on the farm. Or at least it was there when he had last visited a few years back.'

'And you believed that?'

'Not completely, but then I went and got the file, or at least a copy of it. It's one of the perks of owning a security business. I have people who can break into just about anywhere without leaving a trace. It's all there, except for the exact location of the bomb.'

Aziz handed Khan the dossier, which he quickly skimmed through.

'That's quite a story. But I have two questions. Where is this bomb now and why have you come to me?'

Aziz hesitated,

'Well let me answer the last question first. I know that you have a major interest in the arms trade and that you probably are the only person with connections to people who may want to acquire it.'

'And what about the government?'

'No, they'd just take it – probably destroy it on the quiet. Don't forget, they're going for a seat on the UN Security Council and if there was a hint South Africa still had a bomb, that would kill any chance of getting it.'

'And who'd buy it then? North Korea?'

'Sure,' said Aziz. 'But I was thinking one of the Middle East powers … or …'

'And where is this bomb now?'

'Rooikat said he's the only one who knows. Or at least will be once he's got rid of the other conspirators.'

Khan thought for a moment.

'Okay, tell this Rooikat that I may have a buyer for him, but only if he's the sole contractor. I don't want to meet him, I want you to be the only go-between. In the meantime find out everything you can about him including his real name. Offer him five million rands. That will sound like a fortune to him. We'll work out payment details later. Your finder's fee will be twenty per cent of what I sell it for. You are to tell no one else about this and keep no records. Does that sound satisfactory?'

Aziz thought a moment.

Twenty per cent and future Khan family business?'

'That goes without saying,' Khan replied.

The two men shook hands again and Khan watched as Aziz walked back towards his car, buzzing security and telling them to let him out but not to enter any details in their logbook.

As he watched Aziz leave he realised he had forgotten to ask him what he meant when he said he had affiliations other than MK. Didn't matter … he had an e-mail to send. An e-mail that went through ten different re-mailers and a dozen separate encryptions: I have Atomic Bomb available, $20 million. Advise.

The reply came through in less than an hour: We have deposited $5 million into the regular account. Balance on delivery. Instructions to follow.

Fishing at Lamu

Two days later Khan took the early flight to Nairobi and then the shuttle to Lamu Island on the Kenyan coast. Lamu, the most northerly of the Kenyan beach resorts, the string of pearls that begins with Funzi island three hundred kilometres to the south, then Msambweni, Diani, Mombasa, Kilifi, Watamu, Malindi and Lamu heading northwards.

The flight from Johannesburg was four hours, the shuttle to Lamu a short hop of an hour. He was met by his Kenya agent who, on the short drive to Khan's beach house, confirmed that all of his requests had been met: the outboard motors serviced, the fuel tanks topped-up, and that the crew would be ready and waiting at the small boat launch area at dawn. Also that provisions for an overnight fishing trip had been prepared and the staff had cleaned and made ready the house for his arrival.

Khan gave his thanks and said that he would contact his agent when to collect him to take him back to the airport.

The house was an old Arab villa with a flat roof and white crenellated walls. Yunnis, his long-serving Somali major domo, welcomed him at the door. As the agent had told him, the house was, as always, spick and span. The cool cement floors gleamed red with polish, the beds were freshly made and a light lunch of mild fish curry was ready and waiting. Khan, who had declined what South African Airways claimed to be edible, was hungry, and after quickly freshening-up and changing into a just-laundered, lightweight cotton *thawb*, sat down and ate.

Afterwards he walked out on the verandah, a long, iced-lime drink in hand, and savoured the balmy Equatorial air. The tide was out and the local fishing skiffs were resting on the white sand past the sea wall. The sea was flat and turquoise blue. He watched as a kingfish chased a shoal of mullet in the shallows – the small fish scattering like shards of glass in a bomb blast. He felt the surge of excitement he always experienced when he was going fishing. This trip more so than ever, because now he would be fishing not only for marlin and sailfish but venturing into forbidden waters in search of bigger things.

Khan had always been a fisherman – his mother's family had owned fishing shops in Johannesburg and in almost every town on the East Rand, selling the mine owners their trout and big game tackle and the mine workers their bait fishing tackle. His mother's brothers were great fishermen and taught him everything they knew. Bait fishing, lure fishing and, later, flyfishing. He cut his teeth on the little kurper at Hartebeestpoort, soon graduating to black bass and yellowfish in the Vaal and trout in the old Eastern Transvaal. He fished every moment he had spare: rock and surf in Natal, deep sea in Mozambique – everywhere there was family. Every weekend, every holiday, he fished. Sometime during his fishing education he learnt that he had entered a world of true equality. That being a skilled fisherman was not a province of who or what you were, but something inside you. He had, when he was a young man, hungered to have more money to fish wildly exotic places like the men in the fishing magazines, but later when he was himself rich, he realised that money didn't buy better fishing, just easier. And that it didn't matter how wealthy you were, and on how many occasions or places you fished, you would never be as good a fisherman as someone who started fishing at a young age. It was impossible to gain the almost telepathic link between a fish and a boy – the instinctive knowledge that *now* was the moment to strike, when you were older. The synapses in the central nervous system don't exist anymore – they've been lost to the chase after money and women.

In his prime, he had little time to fish, business and family took over. But when he became more successful and could hire other people to do the mundane things and as his wealth and family grew, he made the time. He fished exotic places, for exotic species of fish.

And as many hardcore fishermen do, he became besotted by a single species of fish. Some become addicted to trout, some to salmon, some to giant marlin or tuna, some to tarpon only from the Florida Keys – Khan's fix was sailfish. And it wasn't long before he discovered that the best sailfish fishing of all is off the Kenyan coast. He settled on Lamu as his base. It wasn't the very best fishing in Kenya; further south the resorts of Malindi and Watamu were rated more highly, but he liked Lamu. The fishing wasn't crowded or overrun by tourists, and he felt somehow that he had come home at the old Arab slave trading post.

As the sun set with the brief, vivid twilight of the tropics, a light breeze drifted in from the sea. Not really cooling the air but slowly stirring it. Khan could feel it as it caressed his forehead and gently brushed through his hair. He thought to himself, what am I doing? Why this endless hunt for money and power? Am I really doing it for my sons or just for my own ego? Wouldn't it be better to cash it all in now? There was enough money to last several lifetimes of rich retirement looking out over the sea from this verandah. Watching the movements of the tides and the fish. Always the fish.

And Sabbar? My last and favourite son … shouldn't I let

him go his own way … make his own decisions, his own mistakes, his own money? Certainly I can guide him, help him, but perhaps he should be set free. His mother would have wanted that, beautiful Sabha, who was taken so young. She would have made a difference. It was hard for him bringing up the boy alone. He knew that he had failed. On the surface things appeared well. Sabbar was always respectful, sharing in his interests. He knew he didn't have the same passion for fishing that he did, but at least he pretended to. No, Sabbar was a child of today. With South Africa a liberated country for most of his young life, he had been able to indulge in all the freedoms that Khan himself was not permitted. And he did: fast cars, gambling, and Khan suspected, alcohol and possibly worse. No, he hadn't been good enough as a father, and now his son, he was afraid, was lost to him. Or if not lost, slipping away. This will be the last deal. Time to spend time putting things right. Time for Sabbar, his son.

Woken by the early call to prayer from the Masjid Riyadh, Khan quickly dressed – light cotton trousers and a long-sleeve cotton tunic, wide brim hat, Ray-Bans and, last, the new pair of desert boots that had been brought to his Johannesburg home the day before he left by Aziz the security man. Slipping his satellite mobile phone into his shirt pocket he debated whether to take a gun out of the lock-up – maybe the little .25 baby Browning. He thought better of it. No, where he was going he'd likely be outgunned even if he took an AK along. He walked down to the small boat launching area in the cool of the dawn. His fishing boat skipper, Mahmood, who was an experienced big game fishing captain and very handy with a gaff, and the regular boat boy, Mahmood's nephew, were already there, and Khan's boat *Aisha* was gently bobbing alongside the sea wall. His crew greeted him respectfully.

'Salamu jumbe.'

'Habari ya asubuhi.' Khan replied.

Khan quickly checked through the boat, confirmed the tanks were full and the tackle was ready and rigged. He saw that the new kona heads he had couriered up from Jo'burg had been taken out of their packaging and were already in the big tackle box. Also that Mahmood had brought the cool boxes with food and cold drinks and he'd stowed them in the small cabin.

Satisfied, he pushed the electric starters on the big twin Yamahas and headed out to sea. Rendezvous was at noon sharp and there was a good hour or two to fish before that.

At 12:00 sharp he was at the co-ordinates he'd been told to be – just north of the Kenya-Somalia line and twenty-five kilometres offshore. There was nobody at the rendevous point. The fishing had been mediocre – just one sailfish boated and another broken off. Khan didn't mind that but he didn't like being kept waiting. He was always punctual himself.

Forty-five minutes later a traditional coastal trading dhow, sail billowing, hove into sight. The design probably hadn't changed in a thousand years. Neither had its tardiness – African time keeping. The further north, the worse it got. The routine was practiced. Khan had several such liaisons in the middle of the ocean over the years, usually dealing with the same type of people, trading arms for money. Sometimes he would board the dhow and be carried off to a meeting with the principals of whatever Somali gangsters or radicals he was dealing with at the time. He always did the face-to-face meetings himself, never trusting even his closest lieutenants to get too close to the real powers-that-be.

He pulled up to the side of the dhow and threw one of the sailors a rope. The skipper of the dhow was new to Khan, almost a caricature of a Barbary pirate, swarthy, with lank hair and gold in his teeth. Khan didn't trust him on sight and as he stepped over to the other vessel asked, 'What happened to

Captain Suleiman?'

Gold Teeth smiled. 'Mercenaries shot him when he hijacked the wrong cargo ship up near Aden.'

'Pity, He was a good man. And usually on time.'

The new captain grinned. 'On time for his own funeral.'

And then summonsing one of his men over, again spoke to Khan. 'Okay, you know the drill, hand over your phone, and spread.'

Khan did as he was told and was thoroughly frisked by the crewman.

'He's clean, skipper.'

Gold Teeth nodded and then looked at the iPhone and said 'Pity about this. It looks expensive.'

And he tossed it into the water. Then handing Khan a dirty piece of brown paper with some numbers written on it said, 'Tell your man to meet us at these co-ordinates at noon in six days time. I'll try not to be late.'

Khan did as he was ordered, leaning over to the *Aisha* and handing Mahmood the piece of paper.

'Pick me up in six days, Mahmood. Enter these numbers into the direction finder and throw the paper overboard.'

Mahmood nodded and whispered. 'Watch that one boss. He's dangerous.'

'They all are Mahmood. They all are,' Khan said.

SIX

Mauretia

IT WAS TWO WEEKS since we'd buried Pa. I'd driven back to Lanseria and dropped the hired bakkie back at Tempest – there was a different girl on the counter this time but same tits and teeth. I flew Mango back to Cape Town as the plan was to drive back to Terre'Blanche in my own vehicle – also a Toyota bakkie but a bit more beaten up than the hire one.

While I was there, I helped Chesney with a new case that had come up, like they all do, out of the blue. It was a complicated affair concerning the kidnapping of a gang leader's daughter, half-a-kilo of cocaine, a deranged hitman and a bakkie-loving yellow cobra. *Ja*, I know, you work it out – we certainly couldn't. Eventually, though, it ended as well as it could have. We got the girl back, her father paid up, or at least he promised to – the fee was him lifting the hit he'd put out earlier on Cook and me when we were still on the force. The deranged hitman, who was *bosbefok* infatuated with the gangster's daughter and thought his feelings were reciprocated, was the kidnapper. When he realised that all she wanted was to go home to daddy, he decided to ransom her instead and to stave off the boredom while he waited for his money to arrive, he snorted the whole half-kilo of coke. When we tracked down where he was hiding out and came to take the girl back, over his dead body if necessary, he was so out of it he was sitting *kaalgat* cross legged with a vacant smile on his face singing what sounded like the greatest hits of Justin Bieber. Cook *klapped* him one. He hates Justin Bieber.

And the bakkie-loving snake? When we were taking the girl out to our car to take her back home, we walked past the back of the hitman's vehicle (a modified black Opel bakkie with black tinted windows and all the badges taken off gangster-style) when Cook nearly got bitten by this yellow cobra. It was taking a nap in the heat of the black rubberised load area at the back of the bakkie, and we must have disturbed it. Cook was all for shooting it full of holes, but after his heart stopped racing, decided not to. We were driving off in our own Toyota when I noticed, in the rearview mirror, this scrawny scarecrow clutching clothes in one hand and a 9mm in the other, running after us firing as he went. He was so stoned it's lucky he didn't shoot himself. There was no chance he'd hit us. Still, I put foot, and we got out in a hurry.

Later I heard that the deranged hitman was last seen in his Opel heading north on the N1 through the Hex River Valley. I hoped the cobra wasn't still in the back – it was a long way home from there. Also I really hoped it didn't bite the hitman, it would probably have proved fatal – for the snake.

I took the N7 up the West Coast almost to Namibia, spending the night at Klein Plasie B&B in Springbok. Had a late breakfast before heading east on the N14 through the northern Cape past Pofadder, on to Upington and then into the North-West Province and the back roads to Terre'Blanche. It was nearly twice as long as the drive from Jo'burg to Terre'Blanche and three times as boring. The road was a little better though, especially at the beginning of the journey through the Western Cape where the DA governed and actually did some road maintenance.

I arrived back as thirsty as when I first drove up. But I didn't go straight to the Royal, I stopped off at Avbob to see how Mauretia was. It's what the love of a good woman does to you. Or a bad one, take your pick.

She sounded pleased to see me.

'Look what the dust devil's blown in.'

Then she kissed me long and hard. She whispered that there were cold Castles in her fridge and she'd taken the next two days off starting right now and that she'd see me at home in an hour. I said, 'I missed you some too. But why wait an hour?'

So we left right away. Lucky there were no speed traps on the road to her place or we both would have been caught.

We spent the next twenty-four hours in bed lost in a world populated by just two people. We didn't get up except to raid the fridge for food or grab another beer or bottle of Alto Rouge to take back to bed with us.

We made love and we talked. Made love again and talked some more. Mauretia told me she'd had a boring, normal, but happy childhood. She'd grown up in Somerset West in the Cape. She'd gone to the local Afrikaans primary and high schools and had done well enough in Matric to get into Stellenbosch University to start a BA in social sciences. About the most useless degree there is, she said.

Her father had worked as an estate agent but had retired a few years ago. His name was Pieter le Roux and her mother was Adeline. Her parents were both alive and now lived at Onrus in Hermanus, a couple of roads up from the beach. They were getting on a bit and planning to move into one of the retirement villages nearby at some stage.

'And the Nienaber?' I asked her. 'How long were you married for?'

Mauretia went quiet for a bit and said 'You don't really want to know about it.' I told I wanted to know everything about her, good and bad. She said okay, but it wasn't a very interesting story, just sad.

She'd met Henri at Stellenbosch. He was in the third year doing a BSc. Agriculture, and was something of a big man on campus – tall, dark and handsome and a regular first team rugby player. Everyone knows if you made the Stellenbosch firsts you were something special. Stellenbosch (or Maties as they're known) has produced over a hundred and seventy Springboks and no less that fifteen Springbok captains. This put me and my third team Tukkies rugby into true perspective – compared to ex-husband Henri I was *kak*.

'So what happened?' I asked. Mauretia went quiet.

'We had such high hopes. We got married when Henri graduated. I packed in my useless degree. Our wedding was a big one with lots of guests. We went to the Maldives for the honeymoon. And then moved into the manager's house on Henri's father's big cattle ranch near Ventersdorp.'

'And then?' I asked.

'And then Henri was killed in a stupid road accident.' Mauretia put her hand to her mouth. 'Oh I'm so sorry Jaco, your father …'

'No, please go on, I want to know everything there is about you. How come you do the job you do now?

'I was in a bad way when Henri died. His parents were in an even worse state. And they blamed me. Henri and I had just had our first argument. I can't even remember what it was about, but he stormed off and went to the pub in town and got drunk. He crashed on the way home. There were flowers in the car he'd bought at the garage to say he was sorry to me. The only thing that kept me going was preparing for the funeral and the funeral directors we used were amazing. Kind and efficient. They made a bad time just a little less bad. I asked them for a job once the sadness began to end, perhaps thought I could help make someone else's tragedy more bearable. I'd left the farm anyway, it was kinder on Henri's folks and on me, and I didn't want to go back to the Cape. And after a few years, here I am, running the Avbob Terre'Blanche branch.'

Then she ran her fingers down one of my scars, the one the Coloured gangster gave me with a flick knife I hadn't seen him palm.

'No more about me please, lets talk about you now. How did you get this?' And pointing to another, 'And this?'

I told her about my life as a cop in the last days of the old South Africa and in the years since. Some of cases I'd been involved in and some of the bad people I'd put away. I told her about my own family, gilding over the worst memories. She asked me about the women I'd had in my life. And I told her I'd also been married once. But like most cop marriages it didn't make it past the umpteenth time I missed an important social occasion or a promised night out because work always came first. If you wanted to do the job properly, you couldn't have a life regulated by when to get home. I told her there had been other woman too, but the job and the insecurity of not knowing where I was or whether I'd make it back home that night, or ever, had destroyed the prospects of anything long term.

I don't like talking about myself much, or opening old wounds and was glad when Mauretia said, 'Jaco, let's stop talking about sad things and do what we were doing before.'

Only late the next evening did we get hungry for something more than each other and decided to go out to eat. Mauretia said why not make a real night of it and check out who was playing at the Kraal, the local country music joint on the fringe of town. I said country didn't really do it for me, I get sick at the sound of a slide guitar. But she said not to worry they usually went for the rockier side of country at the Kraal.

We showered and dressed up for the night out. I went and got my suitcase out of the car. It was still packed from Cape Town, and Mauretia went through it and pulled out stuff for me to wear. I didn't mind, I knew it was something women sometimes liked to do. Dress their man. She seemed to have chosen pretty much the same things I would have, black on black – Johnny Cash out on a date. Mauretia then shoved me out of the bedroom door and said she'd be half and hour, and that I must know where the booze was by now and to help myself. I poured a brandy and Coke, added ice and, sipping it slowly, reflected on the last day or so. Life was good. Mauretia had really got to me – I hadn't felt this way about anyone, in years.

'Don't bloody mess this one up,' I said to myself.

I'd just poured a second Klipdrift when Mauretia came out of the bedroom. I'd expected she'd stay with the theme and come out in something a little bit country, a little bit rock and roll – you know the look – Bapsfontein via Nashville. Instead she had on a simple, shiny green, clingy thing that lit up her eyes like emeralds. It was tight in all the right places and I told her she looked beautiful. She came into my arms and for a moment it looked like we weren't going to be going anywhere, but then she laughed and pushed me away.

'Later, Jaco, later.'

The Kraal was done up a little bit country, and the food was much as you'd imagine from the decor. *Boerekos* – but a lot better than you'd expect. Besides the inevitable *potjie* (or Afrikaners burnt stew, as a *rooinek* pal of mine calls it), there was venison pie, chilli from mild to volcanic and, of course, steaks. Any cut you'd like, anyhow you'd like it cooked, as long as it was flame-grilled. You could choose the cut you wanted from a glass-fronted cooler as you went in. I chose a thick rump, done rare with side orders of chips and onion rings and green peppercorn sauce. Mauretia went for a fillet kebab and a side salad. We asked them to bring it as soon as possible as we were starving. The steaks really filled the gap. I lashed out on a bottle of Graceland cabernet – I think the Kraal stocked it for the Elvis connection, but I knew that it was made by the wife of one of Oom Mackie's distant McNaughton relatives down near Stellenbosch, and it was a seriously good wine.

The seriously good wine went well with my seriously good woman. We were comfortable together, as if we'd known each other for years. I'd wanted to know everything about her and, for once, I hadn't been afraid to talk about myself. And I knew both of us liked what we'd heard. So we ate in silence, enjoying the food. But every now and then she gave me a smile that made my knees weak, a secret smile that was all for me.

The band came on stage at around nine for their first set. I hadn't seen them before but I'd heard of them – a country rock band called The Reckoning. I recognised the front man, he was an old-time rocker called Stewie Irving – at one time, the other half of Alter-Irving – Cindy, the Alter part. I saw them at a bar in Jo'burg once, before they went their separate musical ways. They did a version of *Jolene* that brought the house down. The Reckoning didn't disappoint either, they moved from moody to hard rock at the drop of a Stetson and in no time the Kraal was rocking on its foundations. They played covers and a lot of their own stuff. I didn't even get sick when one of the numbers had a slide guitar in the background.

We left the Kraal after midnight and, as often happens, felt that the night shouldn't stop. I asked Mauretia, when we got into the bakkie, if there were any late night quiet places. She laughed.

'Where do you think you are?'

And then with a mischievous look she said,

'I've heard of one place, and I'd never go there on my own.

It's a club on the strip called the Slipped Disc. Apparently they get up to all sorts of things there.'

I felt her blush; it was too dark to see.

'Well in for a penny, in for a pound.' I said.

It actually cost me two R100 bills to get inside the Slipped Disc. It looked like a double story industrial warehouse, which I suppose was exactly what it once had been as I vaguely remembered it as the old BKB wool storage shed. They had a cover charge to keep the rabble out, or so the doorman said. He was standing under a sign boasting 'Where the Elite Meet the Beat'. He saw me looking at it and laughed. 'No, that's an old sign from when we used to be a disco. We're now a classy Jo'burg-type gentleman's club.'

Ja well no fine. Classy if you had a colour-blind hooker as an interior decorator. The L-shaped chrome and glass bar down one side of the room wasn't too bad but didn't quite tone in with the red velvet booths and orange shaggy carpet. But then the elite didn't come for the decor but for the girls that decorated the hanging cages, or who were trying to skewer themselves on two poles on either side of the stage.

It was hot inside. Even though the place was no more than half full the aircon couldn't cope with the smoke or the press of bodies. We sat down at the end of the bar and I ordered and paid for drinks. Back to cold Castle for me while Mauretia had an Amarula Cream. We'd got there just in time for the stage show, which seemed to consist of a scantily dressed lady struggling with a python. The patrons were the usual sort you get in classy Jo'burg gentlemen's clubs – drunken sales reps on expenses, town councillors and officials mixing with the voters, and would-be gangsters who worked as second-hand car salesmen during the day. There were also, because it was Terre'Blanche, several miners and a couple of farmers spending money they had put aside to buy mielie seed for next year's planting. None of them paid much notice to the girl writhing with the snake. In fact the only time they paid any attention at all was when a stray coil wrapped itself round her throat and started to choke her for real. But they lost interest as soon as one of the bouncers stepped in and rescued her.

Most of the men sitting at the tables had women with them – most of them *skelm*, pros or amateurs. The men without women were mostly at the bar. One of them was Fat Face, my talkative barman pal from the Royal. I remembered he said his woman was working here. He was probably waiting for her to get off her perch. I wondered which one she was? The rest were nondescript, mainly locals I guessed. One however stood out. He was dressed flashily, in black like me, but had a gold chain around his neck and a couple of gold rings on his fingers – I saw them glint when he lifted his glass to drink. He finished it and the barman immediately put another in front of him. Looked like whisky, straight. He saw me looking at him and gave me a venomous look back. I ignored it. There was always someone looking for shit in every late night bar I've ever been in.

Mauretia was having fun surreptitiously scanning the tables and then whispering to me the name of one or other pillar of the local community she'd spotted, when she suddenly gripped my arm harder than usual.

'*Yussus* Jaco, it's the Dominee, and I think he saw me.'

I told her not to worry. He wasn't going to tell anyone, as long as she didn't tell anyone about him being there.

I noticed that Fat Face was talking to the flashy oke who'd given me the snake eyes. Fat Face had a hand on his arm like he was restraining him. The guy shot me another look. Fuck, what was his problem? I saw a chick in a long leather coat join them. Fat Face took his hand off the guy's arm and put it around her. His chick I thought. Not a dancer but the girl with the python. I saw him say one last thing to his pal, and then he and his girl made a move to leave. They came toward us at the end of the bar. When they got to where we were sitting, Fat Face stopped to say hello.

'Long time no see.'

'Thought you'd moved to Botswana,' I replied.

'No no, thinking of Durban now. Poppie here is missing the sea and the night life.'

Then he moved closer to me and said quietly so only I could hear, 'Listen, watch yourself, Buks van Tonder over there is after your blood, he's bad news.'

'I don't know any Buks van Tonder and I can't recall any reason why he'd want to cause me problems.'

'It's not you, it's your chick. She gave him the big brush off a while back. He thinks he's God's gift and he's still really pissed off.'

'Fuck him,' I said.

'Well don't say I didn't warn you. See you around. We want an early night.'

It was after one and I was thinking that maybe we should make tracks too, when who should pitch up, but van Schalkwyk. He greeted me like a long lost friend and insisted he bought us a bottle of champagne. I thought, why not, Mauretia seemed still to be enjoying things. He had a fat Indian guy with him who he introduced as Mr. Reddy, and a couple of what looked like Russian hookers in tow. The Indian was as pissed as a lord and not a local. He mixed up his 'v's and 'w's.

'What business are you in, old chap?'

'The refuse business,' I told him.

Van Schalkwyk laughed.

'No, Amichand, this is the gentleman we were talking about earlier.'

'Oh, the one with the farm we're interested in.'

Just then the manager of the Slipped Disc arrived, telling van Schalkwyk his table was ready.

'Yes, but now's not the time for business.'

They left leaving the bottle with Mauretia and me. By the time we had finished it things were getting a little hectic in the Slipped Disc. I noticed that my nemesis, Buks whoever, was no longer at the bar and saw he'd joined van Schalkwyk's table up front. There was a new, very raunchy stripper on show on the stage and the hookers, pro and amateur, were getting pretty close with some of their customers. Mauretia seeing one particular close encounter near us said:

'Jaco, what's she doing?'

'They call it private dancing,' I said.

Mauretia looked on a bit more with a grin slowly spreading across her face. After a bit she whispered in my ear. Suggesting that maybe we should go home so she could show me her own version of private dancing.

I said that would suit me very well, just as an old Bob Seger song went through my head. *Horizontal Bop.*

Forever Italy

The old fort was in a long forgotten wasteland fifty kilometres from nowhere in the Somalia hinterland. Built out of dry mud bricks and stone it was a ruin. It had been put up by the Italian Somaliland Colonial Government in the late 1880s during their ongoing battles against Abyssinian warlords and to protect a little used trading route into the interior. It fell into neglect shortly afterwards when a peace treaty was signed with the Emperor of Ethiopia. It had a brief moment of importance during the 1936 war between the new fascist Italian government and Ethiopia, but was to play little part in the main conflict happening further to the north near the Red Sea. For the next few years it provided a temporary home for the occasional Italian colonial patrol and, when they were not in residence, various bandit gangs on their way to steal cattle from northern Kenya.

It finally became of some military importance in WWII when the British Empire troops, many from southern Africa, drove into Somaliland. There was a brief but bloody battle with the fascist Italian army which was soon over when the combination of South African artillery and Rhodesian Air Force bombs forced a speedy surrender. The survivors were dispatched southward to Kenya and P.O.W. camps, while the main British Empire forces continued with their sweep northwards. But not before the South African sappers had dynamited the remaining walls of the old fort.

With peace, and for many years after, the old fort became almost forgotten, reverting to a stopping off point for ever-bolder marauding bandits on their forays south. Except for a lonely graveyard with the buried bodies of two generations of Italian soldiers, very little remained and what had certainly wouldn't house the headquarters of a boy scout troop, much less the high command of El Shabbab. Or so Khan thought after they'd finally reached the destination.

The journey had been tortuous, the heat almost unbearable. It took nearly two days. First by the dhow to the coast just below the port of Marka, then by rubber duck up one of the shallow creeks that led inland, then by ancient Landrover through the rocky wasteland and heavy sand until they reached the rise that led to the plateau in the middle of the country. They had travelled mostly at night to avoid the heat and the slim chance that they'd be intercepted by Somali government or African Union troops who were, on rare occasions, stirred up enough to leave the safety of their bases and the whores who followed them. The Al Shabbbab fighters had only scorn for them – Aids-infected, black foreigners fighting against their will, waiting for their monthly paychecks which were usually late.

On the trip, Khan's companions, or more accurately guards or even kidnappers, were two taciturn Somali fighters. Throughout the trek they'd communicated to him through the odd word of Swahili, but more often just grunts and hand signals. When they finally reached the fort, the Somalis stopped next to the rock wall which had once been one side to a square parade ground, and motioned to Khan to sit against a low wall of a well, a few metres away. Thankfully in a narrow strip of shade. They threw him an army issue water canteen and motioned him to wait, got back into the Landrover and drove back the way they had come.

Khan waited.

An hour later he was almost nodding off when a man appeared to step directly out of the rock wall across from him. Khan scrambled to his feet and turned to meet him. He was in full military camouflage with a dark turban on his head, wound Afghan-style, long tail hanging down the front of his shoulder. Khan recognised him immediately – it was the captain from the dhow. Late again.

'I'm sorry for the long roundabout trip, Mr. Khan. But we like to show our guests the scenic route – make sure you were not followed. Come this way please.'

Gold Teeth's demeanour had become a little more courteous thought Khan as he followed him back through the opening in the rock wall. Gold Teeth told him to be careful – there was a hole in the ground with a narrow steel ladder. Khan was told to descend while Gold Teeth did something to the wall. Khan heard a rumble and then the sound of boots following him down the ladder. The wall obviously had a door in it. He was met at the bottom of the ladder by the sailor who had frisked him on the dhow and was once again patted down. He nodded again to Gold Teeth who had joined the pair.

'Welcome to our humble home, Mr. Khan.'

He was led down a passage to a large cavern that had been hacked into the bedrock. It was surprisingly well furnished, and quite cool compared to the oven-hot earth above. Gold Teeth ushered Khan to a pair of sofas facing a coffee table and asked him to sit. He poured out two long *jallab* drinks – grape syrup and rose water on ice, so popular in the desert countries of the east. Khan took a sip and nodded in appreciation, then asked Gold Teeth,

'When do we meet your chief?'

Gold Teeth smiled. 'You're looking at him.'

It began to make sense to Khan. He himself always

conducted serious business personally. It was why he was so successful. No subordinates, no middlemen to misinterpret things. He knew that the former head of Al Shabbab had been killed by an American drone, as had his replacement, Gold Teeth could certainly be the new head.

'Shall we get down to business Mr. Khan?'

'Indeed. Do you have a name, captain? We never properly introduced ourselves.'

'My name is not important. You may continue to call me Captain if you wish. Now tell me how I can help you with this bomb you have sold to the Caliphate. Al Zawahiri himself, may Allah protect him, has instructed that I give you any help to procure it.'

'I need three men who will take orders without question to get the bomb from where it is now stored, and out of South Africa.'

'Why not use your own men?'

'I want there to be no chance of a leak about what we are doing.'

'And you don't trust them?'

'It's not that. It's just that I don't want to take any chances at all. I will, however, provide my youngest son as a fourth member. He, I can indeed trust and he will prove very useful. I had an idea about how it could be done on our journey over here.'

'Yes?'

'We take it out of Maputo harbour in the bottom of my fishing boat and meet you outside the twelve mile limit and hand it over there. I noticed you had a crane more than large enough to hoist the bomb and the boat too if necessary.'

'And you have no problem getting it through the border?'

'No, we go back and forth constantly, often with heavy goods and machinery and we have people in our pay at both border posts, South African and Mozambican. They'll turn a blind eye.'

'You'll supply the code sequences to arm the bomb? The PAL as I think they're called?'

'Yes. Once the bomb is safe in your hands and I have been paid the balance of the money, you'll get the Permissive Action Links.'

'You don't trust us to pay your money?'

'It's not a matter of trust, it's a matter of business.'

'And how do we know you'll give us the codes?'

Khan thought a bit and then came to a decision.

'You'll have my son. He has wanted to play a part in the great cause of the Caliphate. This is his opportunity.'

Gold Teeth smiled and reached out to shake Khan's hand.

'It is done then. We just have to work out the details. You will have to start back in the morning but tonight we can celebrate a little on our great deal. And later I have a gift for you, a young girl – fresh from the mission school we took last week.'

SEVEN

Copycat

THE KILLER HAD DECIDED to move from his ambush position in the donga at front of the farm house. It was no longer safe there. The pattern had been broken. Ever since he'd got back, Koekemoer and his foreman had changed their routines day by day. Also Koekemoer himself was a lot jumpier. Sometimes he joined his foreman, sometimes not. Sometimes he followed him, half-a-kilometre back, as though he was shadowing him. Like he knew someone was hiding in ambush. He could see Koekemoer knew something about manhunting. Always moving around, never far from cover. Always watchful, scanning the veld with a pair of high powered binoculars and, when it was dark, night glasses. Never showing enough of himself for the killer to get a clear shot. Pretty impressive for an ex-cop. Also, he noticed that Koekemoer was armed with an R1. Looked like the Colonel's special sniper rifle; he'd seen it in action enough times to recognise it. Shit those 7.62 rounds could do some damage – a lot more than the pisswilly 5.56 round they use today.

No, moving is best. They're bound to spot me here sooner or later.

Maybe back to the ambush position near the koppie at the back of the farm? A double bluff – they won't be expecting me to return there.

The very next day his decision paid off. He'd just settled into his ambush position with the same tree as before as the rifle rest, when Koekemoer and his foreman came riding into view. They were a long way off, too far even for him to be sure of a hit, but they'd move closer. So he waited. Sure enough, they were just about in range and he had the crosshairs right in the centre of Koekemoer's chest and was about to squeeze one off when horse and rider disappeared behind some thick bush. He had just lined up where he expected Koekemoer to reappear when there was a loud bang from a hundred metres along the ridge – followed immediately by the unmistakable sound of a bullet hitting solid flesh. Someone else had taken a shot at Koekemoer! Whoever it was then took a shot at the foreman who had also come into sight, but missed as he dived off his horse into the bush.

The killer watched as the shooter crashed off through the thorn trees down the side of the koppie, bolting hell-for-leather for the boundary fence. 'Jesus, what an amateur', he thought.

Next he saw Koekemoer come round the bush giving chase – he didn't look wounded, so it must have been the horse that was hit. Then he saw Koekemoer's foreman racing off in the opposite direction trying to catch his own horse which had also bolted. It was like a slap-stick comedy. Buggers running in every direction, chickens without their heads.

He saw the shooter attempt to jump the boundary barbed wire fence, straight-on, up and over like an Olympic hurdler, but his back foot caught the top strand and he went down in a cloud of dust. The killer found it hard not to laugh out loud. When the shooter was up again he recognised him. Shit, it was

Buks van Tonder, van Schalkwyk's foreman. Who would have thought van Tonder had it in him, sober.

He saw van Tonder reach the trees at the layby on the road just as Koekemoer reached the fence. Koekemoer was limping; probably twisted his ankle or hurt himself falling off the horse. The killer reckoned he'd never catch van Tonder now. Then he heard a bakkie start up and then the squealing of tyres as it wheelspun off. The bakkie appeared just for a moment through a gap in the trees some three hundred metres off heading north at speed. He watched Koekemoer lift his R1 and stitch a neat row of holes along its side. It was serious shooting – accurate fully automatic marksmanship at long range. The killer hadn't seen many that could match it. But now he reckoned he'd better make tracks too. The place would soon be crawling with cops on the hunt for the gunman. Then the thought went through his mind that maybe he could turn this balls-up to his advantage. Solve the case for the cops and get them off his back. Kill two *mossies* with one stone. Ja, just maybe.

False Spoor

Shit. This time it had been nearly curtains for me. And thank God Carolus didn't get hit again. But my poor bloody horse, it was a good one.

As soon as I got back to the farm house I dialled the emergency police number. Nathi Mpanza and his team took less than half-an-hour to arrive. He'd brought with him the tracker Witbooi, Pieterse, his forensics man, Sergeant Gugu Mayisela and a constable I hadn't met. Mpanza greeted me.

'Morning Mr. Koekemoer. My you certainly bring trouble with you.'

'Morning Captain, sorry to get you out again so soon,' I replied.

While Carolus stayed at the farm house, the police followed my bakkie down the track we'd been riding along when we were shot at. We stopped and got out when we got to where the dead horse lay.

I couldn't fault the way Mpanza and his crew went about the investigation. He was patient and meticulous and went by the book. First he secured the scene as best he could, placing the constable on guard over the dead horse – not to warn gawpers off as would be necessary in town, but to chase off any hyenas or jackals which may have wanted to eat the evidence. Then he gathered us all around and asked me what had happened and I gave him everything I could remember. Mpanza kept quiet as I described being shot at and then chasing after the shooter. He grunted a couple of times when I told him about taking a couple of pot shots at the fleeing ambusher. When I was finished he said that all of us except Witbooi should wait at the scene. He sent the tracker off, telling him to shout for us once he'd done his work and found out what he could. Then he turned to me again.

'This man you shot at, did you hit him?'

'No. I wasn't trying to. But I did make sure that this time, we'd be able to track the bastard down.'

'How so?'

'I shot the back of his bakkie full of holes. Find the bakkie, find the killer.'

'What colour?'

'A white Toyota HiLux.'

'Well that should narrow it down to a few thousand.'

I don't think Mpanza was trying to be sarcastic, but I laughed anyway.

'As few as that?'

He smiled. 'Just so we know, what gun did you shoot at him with?'

'My father's old army R1.'

'Hau! You weren't messing around.'

Mpanza turned to his forensics man who was kneeling beside the horse examining a bullet hole about a hand's width forward of where my knee had been. Close call.

'Sergeant Pieterse, do you think you can get us the bullet?'

'Yes Captain, if it hasn't gone straight through. I'll need some help to roll the horse over though.'

'I've got a winch on the bakkie,' I said.

We rolled the horse over and since there was no sign of an exit wound, rolled it back so Pieterse could get to work. He removed a square of hide with the wound as centre point, exposing the forward ribs. These he sawed through near the spine and then trimmed off and extracted what looked like a rib roast. This exposed the chest cavity and the heart and lungs. The bullet had virtually exploded the heart – no wonder the horse went down instantly. Pieterse rolled up his sleeves and started feeling around inside what was left of it. He gave a grunt of satisfaction as, rooting around at the bottom of the organ, he felt something small and hard, and then pulled out a completely intact rifle bullet. One side of which, having grazed a rib, was a little distorted. Mpanza would have to get ballistics to check, but I'd bet the house on it that it was a .243.

Not too long later, we heard a whistle from the ridge Witbooi had headed towards when he left us – the same ridge the shooter had used in the previous incident. Leaving Sergeant Gugu behind, Mpanza and I went to see what he had found. We joined him at the exact same ambush point as the previous incident.

Witbooi said: 'One of them was here. See there are faint but fresh boot marks. He rested his gun on the same branch as before.'

Both Mpanza and I nodded. Mpanza was quicker on the uptake than me though.

'You say one of them was here. Was there someone else?'

'Yes Captain. And this one wasn't the shooter. Come and check here.'

He took a position up at the tree branch and, pretending he was leaning a rifle against it, pointed to where we had come from.

'He couldn't have been the shooter, you can't see the dead horse from here. The trees down there are in the way.'

We both pretended to aim and sure enough there was no shot from here.

'No, the real shooter was over this way.'

We followed Wibooi hundred metres west along the ridge.

'Here's where he fired from.'

Witbooi led us to a low anthill on the side of the ridge

where there were marks where someone had lain behind it. The top of the anthill had a faint line scored in it where something straight had been rested. The gun we assumed. This line pointed directly at the dead horse lying in the shade of the trees and to Sergeant Gugu and the guard. Mpanza praised his tracker.

'Good work Constable Witbooi. Very good work.'

Mpanza took some photographs of the scene on his cell phone and we went back to join Gugu. We parted company there. Mpanza said he'd let me know soonest what ballistics came up with and if there was any other progress.

Captain Mpanza called the next day. There had been a big break in the case and he wondered if I wanted to come along with him when he made the arrest, 'just as an observer'.

I asked him when and where.

'Now, at van Schalkwyk's farm just out of town, do you know where it is?'

'Yes. Are you arresting van Schalkwyk?'

'No, his foreman, van Tonder.'

'I'm on my way.'

Van Schalkwyk's farm *Elandsfontein* was the other side of town from *Klein Drinkwater* so it would take me at least ten minutes longer to get there than the police, even if I put foot. When I arrived it was all over. Mpanza and his team had van Tonder in handcuffs and Sergeant Gugu was carrying a Musgrave hunting rifle she'd found in the foreman's house. This was about fifty metres from the main homestead that van Schalkwyk used when he was in Terre'Blanche. *Elandsfontein* was no longer seriously farmed but was a weekend hunting retreat; van Schalkwyk's main residence was in Pretoria.

I recognised van Tonder. He was Buks, the man in black, who had given me the evil eye at the Slipped Disc that night with Mauretia. He was dressed in old khaki farm clothes and looked like they'd just woken him up. Eyes bloodshot with drink instead of dark and vicious when I last saw him. He did, though, manage one poisonous glare at me before Mpanza prodded him into the back of the police van.

They'd also found the white Toyota I'd shot up. It was parked in plain sight next to van Tonder's house – the neat stitching of bullet holes filled with what looked like white tile adhesive – *'n boer maak 'n plan* fix if there ever was one. A lazy kind of boer.

The case hadn't been broken by any police work, meticulous or otherwise, there'd been an anonymous tip-off. Sergeant Gugu had taken the call. She said it was a man who'd called, speaking English with an Afrikaans accent but not an accent from around here.

She remembered the message word for word:

'The shooter at the Koekemoer *plaas* was Buks van Tonder, the foreman at *Elandsfontein*.'

She said the caller had immediately hung up. She'd reported it to Captain Mpanza, and after he'd phoned me and rounded up the troops, they'd left for *Elandsfontein*, all sirens blaring.

I said it was a lucky break and that now we would just have to match the bullet we found in the horse with the rifle and the bullets from the first shooting and you've got your man.

'I see it's a .243.'

Something was nagging at me though, something Gugu had said. Then I remembered. The accent.

'Sergeant, can you remember why the accent of the caller was different from the normal way Afrikaners speak English?'

She thought a moment.

'It was the 'R's. He rolled them. Did a funny sort of 'rrrg' whenever he said an 'R', like 'Koekemoerrrgh', and 'shooterrrgh'.

I said, 'Sounds like Western Cape. From the Swartland. They call it the Malmesbury bray. Could be important.'

EIGHT

Call in the cavalry

THE FARM HAD BEEN ATTACKED twice now. Carolus was doubly lucky to be alive and my horse had been shot out from under me. It looked like we'd caught the shooter, van Tonder, but why he'd done it was another problem. Surely it wasn't because of Mauretia and me? Finding Pa's killer was proving much more difficult though.

Also I'd got no further with Pa's riddle of de la Rey being under Verwoerd. If Pa and his pals had got away with stealing an atom bomb (and I was beginning to think it was a big 'if'), did the message mean they'd buried it under Verwoerd in his grave, in Pretoria? I couldn't believe even Pa would have the nerve for that.

I was in trouble, and there was no cavalry to call. Just my pal and business partner (some would say partner in crime), Chesney Cook. A one-man army if there ever was one. Chesney was the most street-wise character I'd ever met. He claimed to have joined the police because 'it was the biggest gang in Lavender Hill', the not-so-fragrant Coloured township on the Cape Flats he grew up in. He reckoned that the cops had the best guns, and the courts on their side. And this was largely true until the international drug gangs moved in on the lucrative post-Apartheid Cape Town market.

With the hordes of tourists and idle rich of the world, came heavy-duty drugs. Organising and using the existing local gangs like the Americans and the 28 as stormtroopers, these mainly Nigerian, Chinese and Russian gangsters soon prospered. What had once been mainly a small-time dagga and pill market for indigent locals and trendy UCT and Technicon students, quickly became a multi-billion rands hypermarket for coke, heroin and crystal meth. The latter, called 'tik' in the townships, quickly became the drug of choice on the local streets.

Together with the heavy-duty drugs came beefed-up weapons. Knives and zip guns making way for revolvers and automatic pistols, which in turn made way for Kalashnikovs and Uzzis. With the sales came the money to hire heavyweight lawyers and bribe even high ranking officials. The cops, after a time, were no longer the boss gang.

Cook fought all the gangs whether local or international, Nigerian, Oriental or European with cold-hearted ferocity. He hated them for what they had done to the happy, laughing people of his home town. He didn't care who they were, who was backing them, he'd fuck them up, lock them up and bring them down any way he could. In return they put a large price on his head. I know, because they put one on mine at the same time. And as far as I know some of the contracts are still out on us, even though we're no longer police.

I called Cook while Mauretia was helping Annetjie with the breakfast. Annetjie had taken to Mauretia from the moment I brought her home. She beamed when Mauretia told her how nice the house looked and even more so when she asked her how she'd got the *roosterkoeks* to rise so perfectly – crisp-crunch on the outside and warm soft bready inside.

Cook made it to *Klein Drinkwater* at breakfast time the next day. He must have left shortly after I'd called him and not stopped for much on the way. He'd taken the same route as I had from Cape Town but hadn't loitered like I did. Driving his Golf GTi non-stop through the heat of the day and then through the night, catching a few hours kip in a layby the other side of Pofadder. The Golf was his only extravagance – he had blown half his severance package just on the deposit. But he said it was worth every cent.

Mauretia had left early to get back to town and work, but said she'd be back in the evening. I'd asked Annetjie the day before to make up one of the spare rooms as we were expecting an important guest. When she saw Cook she looked at him with suspicion. Who was this big, tough-looking, almost copper-coloured person with the blue eyes and the wide smile?

'You must be Annetjie', he said. 'The Captain here says you're the best cook and coffee maker in the old Transvaal. I've been on the road for twenty-four hours. I'm starving.'

Annetjie had made *pannekoek* with fresh farm butter, cream and honey in honour of the 'important guest', and piled a plate high. She watched as Cook, in silence, waded through the first stack, then another. When he was finished she poured him a cup of *moer koffie* in a big enamel mug – I saw it was the one Pa had always kept for himself – added cream and then four spoons of sugar.

Cook leaned over the cup, sniffing in the aroma and then taking a much too hot sip said, 'The Captain lied. You're not the best cook in the old Transvaal, tannie. You're the best in the whole new South Africa and probably the world.'

Annetjie smiled a gap-toothed smile and gave a little curtsy. I thought, hell, she's almost flirting with Cook and she must be close to eighty. Cook is something else, it's the size of him I suppose and the easy going way he has with anybody who wasn't on the wrong side of the law.

But make no mistake, Cook is not just muscle – he has a fine-tuned, suspicious cop's brain. And a nose for a bullshit story. He could tell if suspects were lying or not within seconds of opening their mouths. In a normal country that didn't have the never ending prejudices of South Africans, he would have risen to chief of the whole force. But Cook never really had a chance of that, he was not even close to being white enough to get ahead under the old government, and not nearly black enough in the new. If it worried him, he never let it show. And he never showed any prejudice himself. In his view a crook was a crook whatever his colour. And he gave them the same treatment.

We knuckled down to business right after breakfast. Cook took over and I let him. He turned the office into a police murder room. Even though we kept all our notes on our phones or laptops, Cook liked the feeling of an old-styled investigation. The photos, the Post-it notes stuck up here and there, things to move around and link with each other. There was nothing modern such as a magnetic whiteboard in Pa's office, or even anything old and useful like a blackboard, so Cook used the wall to write on and stick things on.

'Don't moan, You can always paint over it, but I want to *feel* what's what.'

Cook was funny that way – he liked to physically touch any pictures we had of people in our cases. As if by handling their photos, touching their faces, he could get to know them better, their feelings and emotions, than just by looking at them on a screen. Also Cook could never stay still. He said the board helped him think, he could walk up to it and see one thing, or stand back and get the whole picture. I told him you could do the same thing on the computer, just zoom in and out. He said it wasn't the same thing. Funny, he's fifteen years younger than me and sometimes I'm the geek.

He started by sticking a picture of Pa in the centre of the wall about half-way up. It was one of him in his dress uniform receiving the *Honoris Crux* medal from then-Defence Minister P.W. Botha. Cook had cut Botha out of the picture so it only showed Pa. He used a piece off a roll of double-sided tape which he pulled out of a battered document pouch with a zip across the top – the sort low-ranking government officials carry. He grabbed a thick black marker pen from the same bag and neatly printed COLONEL above the picture.

'There, Colonel. You're the centre of our universe.'

I let him carry on, thinking that the ink would take a minimum of three coats of white to hide.

Then, above the picture, Cook put up Pa's deceased comrades – Coetsee, Pienaar, Bezuidenhout and Smit. He had recent pictures of all four; he had gone to each of the surviving families saying he was a much younger comrade and was very sorry to have missed the funeral but could he please have a photograph from the funeral order of service as a treasured keepsake. The last picture he pulled out with something of a flourish and handed it to me.

'And I found one of the mysterious Gerhardus Tertius van Niekerk, the guy you call Rooikat. It's not a very good photo, but at least he has distinctive features. I surfed every place I could think of online, every reference to van Niekerk, Rooikat, Koevoet, Special Services – everything – but found *niks*, not a sniff. It's like he never existed. Then as a last resort I thought of his original army files – everyone was photographed and fingerprinted in the old days, especially if they'd been called up by the government. They were like the fucking Nazi's. And there he is – Rifleman Gerhardus Tertius van Niekerk.'

I took a close look at the photo. It was dark and faded – an old Polaroid they used for I.D. pics before the Polaroid Company joined the sanctions exodus and disinvested. It showed a young, pock-marked individual, with no chin and stick out bat ears. It wasn't clear if the pockmarks were on his face or on the picture surface itself. He'd probably changed a lot, this was him thirty-plus years ago. But almost certainly not the ears or the missing chin. You can't change those easily. I racked my brains trying to think if I'd ever seen such a person, but realised that no, this was a complete stranger, some outsider in the shadows. I handled the polaroid back to Cook and he stuck it up with the others, carefully annotating each one in turn.

The next thing we did was to discuss everything we knew about each and every death and then stuck a short description under each pic and, if we had them, additional photographs of the scenes of the crime. Under Pa we added 'Traffic Accident', an official police file photo of the scene and shots I took of the black scrape on the side of the bakkie. Under Coetsee, 'Drowned at Hartebeestpoort'. Under Pienaar, 'Hunting Accident'. Bezuidenhout, 'Mugged' and Smit, 'Stabbed by Intruder'. Under van Niekerk we put: 'Murdered all of them?' And: 'Tried to make them look like accidents or random killings?'

Something was nagging at the back of my mind. Then I remembered – the code thing. PAL code 1847. I told Cook about it. He wrote the number down and stuck it up. We discussed what it meant and went over my thoughts about it being a bank pin number, or maybe a code for a combination lock, or even a grave site – the number had, after all, been in Pa's files on the piece of paper that had 'de la Rey is under Verwoerd' written on it. We got nowhere. Then Cook said. 'Shit, I'm an idiot. Why not just Google it?' He tapped PAL code 1847 into his laptop. And then whistled.

'Jaco, you're not going to believe this.' He swung round and showed me his screen.

'A PAL code is the code you need to arm an atomic bomb. PAL stands for Permissive Action Link. The bomb's useless without the code. Apparently you could explode a hundred tons of dynamite, or even another A-bomb under an unarmed atomic bomb and it wouldn't go off.' He scrolled down the screen, scanning it with his eyes.

'And you were right about the combination lock idea. That's where the PAL code originated. The early bombs, right up to the nineteen sixties had simple three or four digit combination padlocks on them. A little later they had built-in electronic locks also with four digit codes. It was only much later when computers and hand-held devices took off in the early nineteen nineties that the codes become really complicated with long strings of numbers and commands.' He scrolled down further.

'But I don't see anything here with a reference to the number 1847.' Then he went back to Google and keyed in de la Rey, Verwoerd and the number 1847 and began reading what came up.

'Ag man. It's as simple as that. 1847 is the year de la Rey was born. It must be the PAL code for the bomb your father and his pals pinched!'

Annetjie knocked on the door a couple of times, first to ask if we wanted fresh coffee and later to tell us lunch was on the table. If she saw the mess Cook was making on the walls she didn't react, except for a brief shake of the head. She expected she'd be the one left with it.

The morning turned into lunchtime, the afternoon into beer time. We kept at it. I suggested we added the A-bomb to the centre of the board right next to Pa. It just seemed so central to everything. Cook agreed and drew a cartoon bomb and labelled it de la Rey. Under that he wrote, 'Why Steal it.? To sell? To who?'

Then we added a note, '.243 rifle' then 'Carolus', then 'Jaco and horse'. Under these we wrote: '1st Shooting and 2nd Shooting'. With suspects for each. '1st Buks van Tonder?' '2nd

Buks van Tonder and ANO?'

Cook then pulled off a piece of tape and stuck it across the bottom of the board, writing on the tape, 'de la Rey is buried under Verwoerd', and then a second, '#VerwoerdMustFall'.

We then added a picture of Thabo Mkhize addressing a group of student activists from his #RhodesMustFall days.

We started a sub-section: 'Verwoerd stabbed. Houses of Parliament. Tsafendas. Hero's Acre, Pretoria. Verwoerdburg. Verwoerd's Koppie'. And another headed, 'de la Rey. March through west Transvaal. Never surrendered. Shot by mistake in ambush on the Foster gang'.

At this stage we decided to break and have a beer. When we got back we started a new section headed: 'Klein Drinkwater'. Under this we wrote 'Koekemoer' (again), 'Colonel' (again), and 'platinum, prospecting, offer from van Schalkwyk Makatini via Eloff, big money, Bolton and Geo Logical, prospecting, blasting'.

Lastly we added a To Do list: 'Ballistics (too slow)'; 'Check directors of Makatini Investments'; 'Check directors of Geo Logical'; 'Talk to van Tonder'.

Then we stood back and admired our handiwork. We went over everything again. Then again. Trying to find patterns. Anything. Why steal the bomb? Obviously for a new Boer nation. But why the killings now? Was it payback for the original theft, or was something new happening? The killings themselves had a pattern. This was that there was no pattern – they were deliberately made to look random. But serial killers don't think that way – they stick to one tried and trusted method with minor variations. Don't they? Was Rooikat in fact the killer? We both thought he was. Was he actually the man in the picture? Maybe.

Were the shootings at the farm and the prospecting and platinum riches red herrings? If so, why? Or were they tied in with whatever was going on with the missing bomb. Also maybe. Round and round we went. Gnawing on a piece of information here, worrying a fact there.

We only stopped when Mauretia got back. She was a little late but brought some refreshments back with her – a couple of bottles of that McNaughton wine we liked from the other night, and a corkscrew. Chesney, who was meeting her for the first time, took one look at her and whistled:

'Hell Captain, now I can see why you haven't been thinking straight.'

Arrivals

Letepe Thobela, officer of the Department of Internal Affairs Grade 3, looked up from his immigration desk at Oliver Tambo Airport and took a cursory look at the man who flashed his well-used South African passport at him – a passport in the name of Raafi Saayed Meer . He waved him through thinking, 'Lot of charras on this flight, and they don't look like locals'. It was the SAA Cairo flight so Thobela reckoned if the guy was dodgy they'd pick him up at customs. It was always something of an eye-opener what people thought they could smuggle through, and the customs boys had a great time playing spot the sweating whitey.

The 'charra' that Thobela had waved through – born Mohamed James Faris to a Pakistani father and Scottish mother in Manchester and known as Jihadi Jimmy on a M15 watch list – was unlikely to have any problems with customs. He had been careful there was nothing on him that could be remotely classified as contraband. Except, of course, the passport, which had been bought and paid for and issued under-the-counter by an official in the Pretoria passport office.

Quickly clearing customs through the green lane, Jihadi Jimmy met up with two black, supposed South Africans, who had also travelled on SA passports and who were also on the MI5 watchlist under a variety of aliases. All three were dressed in fashionable casual gear that wouldn't have looked out of place in any capital city of the world. Levis, knock-off Boss or Armani T-shirts and Nikes on their feet. They had been told to wait in the arrivals hall after they'd cleared customs, to be met by a man who would introduce himself as Sabbar. Jihadi Jimmy had been issued with a picture of Sabbar and would recognise him.

They didn't have long to wait before a young guy their age, dressed in a flowing white *thawb*, sandals and Prada sunglasses, approached them.

'*Ahlan wa sahlan*. I'm Sabbar Khan, please come with me.'

Jihadi Jimmy took a long hard long at this traditionally dressed person and thought, 'Jesus Christ, what is this? '

The three followed their guide across the covered bridge into the big parking garage across the street. They each had hand luggage only – their orders were to travel light as everything would be provided in South Africa. Sabbar led them to his car. Jihadi Jimmy whistled in approval.

'BMW X6. Nice motor.'

He looked at Sabbar with new interest – maybe he'd been too quick to judge him. Sabbar opened the boot and told them to put their bags in it. Then he quickly pulled the *thawb* over his head to reveal underneath he was wearing similar clothes to the others, but the genuine articles, not Chinese knock-offs. Kicking off the sandals, he reached into the boot and slipped on a pair of Air Jordans.

'There, that's better. Sorry about that guys, but my father he's old school, he said dress properly, I'd probably be meeting some old-fashioned bearded types, and told me to dress with respect.'

Jihadi Jimmy laughed and stuck out his hand.

'That's not us mate. I'm called Jimmy and these two are Ahmed and Ahmed. They don't speak English, but don't worry, I'm here to translate.'

The three shook hands with Sabbar. He failed to notice that their smiles didn't come close to reaching their eyes.

The drive into Johannesburg took half an hour. Sabbar took them on the direct route on the dual carriageway through the light industrial area, then turning right past the old Bruma Lake shopping centre going through its umpteenth redevelopment. Then another right turn up the hill past Chinatown in Cyrildene and then down the winding route to the wealthy suburb of Houghton. Sabbar told them that Houghton, with its palatial houses, had originally been built by the Randlords who had once owned the gold mines. But that today it was home to people who had become rich in the new South Africa – politicians and businessmen, mostly blacks, but with a fair sprinkling of other races. He pointed out the gates to the mansion where Reza Khan, Shah to all Persia, had spent his exile during the Second World War, dying there in 1944. Jokingly saying, 'He was no relation to my family'.

They drove down the leafy avenue past the house where Nelson Mandela had spent his final years, with uniformed guards standing outside black painted gates. Then two streets down they stopped at another guarded gate – massive, of brass-burnished steel. They were quickly let in, the brick driveway leading to a large white house in the style of the traditional Gulf courtyard house with huge hand carved doors and wind towers that you find in the old Persian Bastakiya district of Dubai. But instead of it built of desert sandstone, the Khan house was white marble. Flanked by date palms it would have been more at home at Jumeirah Island than Johannesburg.

Jihadi Jimmy whistled once again, but this time kept his thoughts to himself. He wondered what sort of man felt at home in a palace like this.

He didn't have long to wait. Sabbar showed the men through to the guest wing which, he told them, was occasionally occupied by family visiting from elsewhere in the country or from overseas. Sometimes though it was used by business acquaintances who wanted to keep a low profile, and were not keen on showing their faces in any of the five star Johannesburg or Sandton hotels.

The guest wing had a sitting room, four bedrooms each with en suite bathrooms, and a small kitchen stocked with luxury snacks and, rare for a Muslim home, a variety of alcoholic drinks. Each of the three men were shown to a room of their own and, while the other two immediately stretched out on their beds ('Always bloody sleeping,' thought Jimmy).

Jimmy had a quick shower, changed to a fresh shirt and helped himself to a can of Boddingtons. It went down just as smoothly as he remembered.

He lounged back in a deep sofa, feet up on the coffee table. 'This is the life,' he thought, 'Christ, you could fit two of the council house shitholes I grew up in back home in this bloody guest suite alone.'

He was just about to pop the tab on another can of the creamy bitter when a flunkey wearing a cotton suit knocked on the door.

'Mr. Khan would like to see you in the office now. Follow me.'

Jimmy, who thought he saw a glimmer of disgust in the black servant's face as he noticed the empty can said, 'Just me?'

'Just you please boss, just you.'

Jimmy liked being called boss and followed the servant.

Khan could have been any rich, Armani-suited, Arab businessman, Jimmy thought on first impression. The kind you see in hotels in Knightsbridge in London. Like one of the marks he used to pickpocket before he joined the Jihadi racket. Easy pickings. You just had to keep a lookout for bodyguards, they often took their jobs seriously. But when he looked at Khan more closely, he realised that there was no way he would have tried it on with this man. Beyond the suit and the thin smile there was something that would make you hesitate, something that said keep away, bodyguard or no. Jimmy prided himself as a good judge of character, and this was a man to be very careful of. He may look fat and prosperous, but there was a savagery underneath – he'd seen it before in the eyes of the True Believers.

He wasn't surprised when Khan got straight down to business.

'You're the one who's called Raafi?'

'Yes sir.'

'Well I suppose one name is as good as another.'

'It's what I say too.'

'The others, I hear, have no English?'

'No they're along for the muscle. My boss told me that there would be a bit of digging. And digging they can do.'

'I saw, at the fort.'

'The boss didn't tell me what we are digging for though. Treasure?'

'Some would call it that. No. A bomb. A big bomb.'

'What? But why would we come all the way here for a bomb. We've got plenty of our own?'

'It's an atomic bomb. You don't have any of those.'

For one of the few times in his life Jimmy was lost for words, but not for long. The thought went through his head that he was about to nick the biggest thing of his life, and then some. But shit! Atomic bombs were bad news. Look at the poor saps the bloody Yanks dropped the bombs on in Japan. Those who died instantly and those who died horrible deaths for years afterwards – thousands and thousands of them – of burns and cancer that ate out their insides. He tried to speak slowly and calmly.

'Aren't those things dangerous?'

'Only if you key in the codes and drop them.'

'No I mean to handle. The radioactivity. The stuff that

makes your nuts shrivel up and kills you years later.'

'No there's little chance of that I'm told.'

'But...?'

'Then you die. For the Caliphate.'

Jimmy thought, 'Shit, this guy is even more dangerous than I thought. He believes in the Caliphate. Next he'll be telling me that dying for the cause will be a pleasure and that seventy-two virgins will be waiting for me in heaven. Christ!'

'Or you can die right here, right now. Not accepting this job is not an option. Running away isn't either James, Mohamed, or is it Mr. Faris?'

Christ! How did he know my real names? *Nobody* knows my real names.

'Am I clear, Raafi?'

'Yes sir.'

'All right. This is how it's going to work.'

Jimmy listened carefully as Khan went through the plan of action in detail. He told him that the team would consist of Jimmy, his two colleagues, Khan's son Sabbar, a man called Bolton who had set up a camp for them and another man he called Rooikat. Khan said that except for this Rooikat, Khan himself, and Jimmy's boss, that Jimmy would be the only other person who would know about the A-bomb – and that only the last three, would know its ultimate destination

He was told that Khan's son Sabbar would be going with them as driver but that he would also help with the work and would later be vital in getting them and the bomb across the border into Mozambique Also that none of them were to leave the camp outside Terre'Blanche where the bomb was hidden or communicate with the outside world except for two texts on a pre-paid cell phone to Khan himself. The first to be sent immediately after they reached the bomb, was to say 'Pay the man'. The second, 'Arriving soon', when they had secured the bomb and loaded it on the truck and were on the way home.

Lastly Khan told Jimmy to be very careful of the man called Rooikat and to do whatever he was asked without hesitation, but to tell him nothing of any further plans about the bomb. And, he said that if Bolton did not cooperate then Jimmy could dispose of him as he saw fit.

'Got all that?' Khan said. ' Good, go and round up the others, Sabbar too, and meet me at the front door.'

A little later Khan led the four young men round to the back of the house and a large, reinforced steel door to a bunker-like concrete outbuilding almost hidden in heavy shrubbery. The door had a sophisticated keypad lock on it which Khan unlocked with a remote control. A second press of the remote opened the sliding steel door. Inside there was a Land Cruiser station wagon with a heavy-duty off-road trailer, both painted in zebra stripes, safari-style. Next to these two vehicles was a deep sea ski boat with a small cabin and twin outboard Mercury 350s on the back.

Neatly piled on a metal trestle table next to them were a selection of olive green overalls in various sizes with 'Geo Logical' embossed on the pockets, four green hard hats with the same logo on the front and several pairs of steel-capped boots in a range of sizes. The four were told to kit themselves out and to take a couple of spare pairs of overalls as the job could take a week or two. There were also two steel boxes, one contained three AK47s and the other, three machine pistols.

Khan called the three jihadis and his son together and made a short speech. He spoke of the importance of the mission they were to undertake. That Raafi was to be leader and they must follow his commands. That they should get an early night as there was a long journey the next day and that if they succeeded in the mission they would go down in the history of the Caliphate as great warriors.

Then he shook the hands of each one of them and wished them well. *Inshallah.*

Later Jihadi Jimmy lay back in bed with the last of a six-pack of Boddingtons in one hand and a Cuban cigar he'd found in the kitchen in the other, and shook his head. Couldn't believe all the bullshit he'd heard that day. Noble cause. Caliphate. And all delivered with the same manic religious intensity that he'd seen in the eyes of Christians he was about to slaughter in Nigeria one time. And shit, those A-bombs were dangerous just to be near – that radioactivity stuff would fry your Jackson Pollock's at fifty yards. Bleeding hell, if he had the sort of dosh Khan had, he'd be doing a lot more interesting things than messing around with the likes of his own boss and the rest of the Al Shabbab madmen.

'But I suppose different strokes for different folks. Me, I'm just in for the kicks and the ganja and the sluts. Fuck, if they could only see me now back home though. They'd be lining up for it.'

Resurrection

Jack Bolton wondered what the hell he was doing out there and what a waste of time it all was. He wished he'd been allowed to do some real prospecting. The geology of the area was really exciting, with some of the oldest igneous rock on earth – in places rich with minerals and untold wealth. Why just a year or so ago they found a diamond the size of a tennis ball just across the border in Botswana.

But he had been told by his boss, Mr. Shaik, to wait for the crew that was going to help him, and when they arrived not to interfere with them. Let them get on with what they were doing. That was three weeks ago and they still hadn't pitched up. He'd also been told not to go into the town, and to tell the farm owner to stay away from the area as he'd be doing some blasting and it could be dangerous. The whole thing had smelled fishy right from the start with the original prospecting trip he'd made, and the supposed samples he took. And especially the report he wrote about the platinum reef ducking under Verwoerd's Koppie onto *Klein Drinkwater* farm. But he'd been told to do it, and was paid handsomely. And heck, if he was going to get paid for sitting on his arse in camp, with a bonus promised on top of it, who was he to complain? It was not what he'd expected when he'd graduated near top of his mining engineering class at the University of the Witwatersrand. However, it was his first big job, a job that in the current economic straights of the mining industry he knew he was lucky to get. So he supposed he'd just have to suck it and see.

If only though. The report may have been pure fiction, but you never know. It *could* be possible.

The four guys arrived dressed in their new Geo Logical overalls and they looked a little hung over. Bolton tried to strike up conversation with them, but soon realised that while one was local and looked like he was probably into the Jo'burg scene, and one of the foreigners seemed to be a Pom, none of them had anything to say to him, so he lay back in his deck chair, put his headphones on, upped the volume and lost himself in Facing the Gallows' album, *Chapter*. Mental, he thought. Seriously rad, and I'm going to see them live on Saturday at Rumours when I'm back in town.

Rooikat, who'd been sussing out the camp from a hideaway on the koppie saw the group arrive. Thinking, '*Fok*, plastic game rangers in a pretty painted zebra 4x4 and matching trailer. I'd better go and see what's what.'

He hitched his machine pistol on his back and stuck the bayonet in its makeshift sheath and sidled his way towards the camp, more like a mamba gliding through long grass than the fat middle-aged Afrikaner he'd become.

Lost in heavy metal dreams, Bolton didn't even notice Rooikat when he walked into the camp, not until he landed on his arse after the deck chair had been kicked out from under him.

'What the hell was that for?' Bolton said as he scrambled to his feet.

'No the question is, who the *fok* are you?' The new arrival said.

'I'm Jack Bolton. I'm a prospector.'

'Prospector's *gat*, where are the other okes?'

'They're having a kip in the tent there. They've just arrived from Jo'burg.'

'*Fok*, are you all half asleep here, or what? Go and wake them up, they're expecting me. Tell them it's Rooikat.'

Bolton went to over to the tent and, after a brief conversation with someone inside, came back.

'They said go away, they'll speak to you later.'

He saw the man called Rooikat narrow his eyes as he strode over to the tent. Now he saw the sub-machine gun strapped to his back, and the razor sharp bayonet that suddenly appeared in Rooikat's hand like a magic trick.

'We'll see about that.'

Rooikat didn't stand on ceremony. He reached the tent and instead of calling out or opening the flap, he slit it straight down the middle so it collapsed inwards, at the same time shouting sergeant-major fashion. '*Op en Wakker*! Get up! Wake-up!'

And then when one of them dived towards the trunk where the Ak47s were, 'Don't even think of it!'

There was a slick, oily, metallic 'clack' as the Uzzi was cocked and then silence all round. The first person to speak was Sabbar, Khan's son.

'You can't talk to us like that, *my* father …'

The last was strangled in his throat as he felt incredible pain in his testicles. Rooikat literally had him by the balls and was crushing them like ripe grapes.

'Fuck your father. And fuck you *laaitie*, I don't talk to childs. Who's the boss here?'

Jihadi Jimmy stepped forward.

'Sorry, sir. That's me, what can I do to help.'

'First you can tell that long drink of water over there, Bolton he says he's called, to get on with his prospecting. Then grab your pals and come with me.'

With Bolton duly dispatched, Rooikat herded the four men ahead of him, pointing the barrel of the Uzzi down the path they should take.

'Walk in front of me, I don't trust you fuckers. Any shit and you're dead meat.'

The path led to Verwoerd's Koppie and the old mine workings. When they reached the boundary fence he told them to climb through it and walk a further fifty metres down the path and stop there. Then he climbed through himself, making sure the barrel of the Uzzi was aimed in their general direction. He then herded them down the path towards the old mine and when they reached it told them to stop again. He pointed at the fallen rocks and boulders that had sealed off what was once the mine opening.

'You're here for one reason only. Work. No drinking, no sleeping, no shooting. No visiting town, no nothing – just digging through this *kak* here to get to what's behind. A big heavy black box. Once you have it my job is over, but until you find it I'm your lord and master. And you do things the way I say. Understood?'

Jimmy translated quickly for the benefit of the two Ahmeds who nodded their heads.

'Understood boss,' he replied.

'Now another thing, the weapons. Lose them. Lock them in the truck. Wear your overalls and hard hats at all times. You're mine workers, not fucking jihadi's now. Get used to it. I was told you're good at digging and that's what you're going to do. We start at first light tomorrow. Bring the tools, all of them, and the big tin of grease and the grease gun – we'll find a place near here to store them. Also bring the red box. It's got dynamite in it so don't drop it. Alright, get the fuck back to camp. Tomorrow. First light. Don't be late.'

Jimmy turned to his two comrades again, who, muttering between themselves, started towards Rooikat. Jimmy spoke to them sharply in Arabic and led them away. He could feel cold eyes focussing on middle of his back as they walked along the path to the fence. Every now and then he glanced back. Rooikat was standing in the centre of the clearing outside the mine entrance still watching. And then he disappeared, into nowhere. Jimmy thought, 'That is a very freaky dude.'

At first light the next morning the four were waiting outside the entrance of the mine. They looked all around them but could see no sign of Rooikat. Then there was a whistle from the hillside just above the rubble-closed mine entrance. They still couldn't see him. Until he waved his arms. There he was, in camouflage battledress, but in plain sight once you knew where to look. Rooikat greeted them.

'You buggers couldn't find your arses if you used both hands. Move the equipment to the side over there and two of you bring up the red box. We're going to start by shifting some rock the easy way.'

It took about an hour for Rooikat to set the charges exactly where he wanted. The plan was to shift the broken rock from the top of the pile and then move it manually out of the mine mouth. Rooikat didn't think it would take that much explosive to do the job. The original rock fall that blocked the mine had been set off by the Colonel and he was an expert demolition man. He wouldn't use a stick more than was needed to bring down more that just enough rubble to seal the entrance.

Rooikat was right. The first series of small explosions did the job. The very top of the mouth of the tunnel was open. The explosions weren't even that loud, and anyway he was sure that people in the area had become accustomed to them, since Bolton had been using small amounts of dynamite in his prospecting the whole of the previous week. Now it was time for real work. Nothing fancy, no heavy equipment, just jackhammers to break up any rocks still too big to manhandle by sheer muscle-power.

Rooikat had to admit that the men worked hard. Especially the three foreigners. The local youngster was a waste of space and soon complained of sore hands. Rooikat told him to carry on or he'd break his balls again. They'd opened half of the entrance by the end of the day and were keen to go into the mine. Rooikat said no, only when they're finished. Two days later, about noon, it was done. Tons of rock had been piled either side of the mine opening and the final rocks moved had revealed rail tracks leading into the tunnel. Rooikat called across to Jihadi Jimmy.

'You, Boss Boy, follow those tracks to the back of the mine. There you'll find a rail cart with the black box. Take a crow bar and check inside and see if the merchandise is still there, then come back.'

About half-an-hour later Jihadi Jimmy re-appeared and nodded to Rooikat.

'It's there.'

'OK. That's my side of the bargain finished. Now you, phone the number.'

'It's a text. I've got to show you the confirmation.'

'OK.'

Jimmy took out the pre-paid cell phone Khan given him and tapped in, 'Pay the man'.

Thirty seconds later there was a bleep – an answer for Rooikat. He told Jimmy to toss the phone to him. He had a look at the confirmation from the bank: To G. T. van Niekerk, Standard Bank Botswana – pay R5 million from H.A. Khan, Absa Johannesburg.

They tried to take him down the second his eyes moved down to read the text. Rooikat was expecting it and was ready. In his line of work you were early dead if you ever lowered your guard. He thought it would be Jimmy or the stupid youngster, but it was the other two. One with a knife, a long, thin, fish filleting knife. The other had one of the pick axes. Jimmy, clutching the crow bar and Sabbar with his blistered hands, looked on, smirks on their faces. These soon changed to open-eyed bemusement as Rooikat, in what appeared to be slow motion, reached out and took the knife from the first jihadi's hand, then twisting him round, broke his arm over his knee. The jihadi with the pick axe fared little better – a kick in the kneecap stopping him in his tracks, a punch to the throat putting him down, gurgling like a baby.

'Stupid *dooses*. Now he'll have to help you push with his left arm. And this oke with one leg.'

Rooikat bade them *totsiens* and walked off. He didn't bother telling them to take the grease into the mine with them to oil the cart's axles – let them find out for themselves. As he ducked under the fence he had one more thought. He must be getting soft in his old age, letting them off so lightly.

Jihadi Jimmy excepted, it was the walking wounded trying to move the cart. The walking wounded, that is, with one hopping. The cart's wheels were frozen solid with muck and rust and one of the wheel bearings had seized. They couldn't do it. Jimmy told Sabbar to come with him and the others to wait and went to get help from Bolton. Bolton, who was stretched out in his deck chair, lost in his headphones, wasn't keen – but Jimmy told him the sooner he did the sooner they'd be out of his hair. So Bolton grudgingly got up and joined them. They drove back in the zebra Land Cruiser, towing the heavy-duty trailer behind them. When Jimmy cut the fence wire to get through, Bolton told him he'd have to fix it on the way back. Jimmy said fine.

Back in the mine, examining the old railway cart with its heavy load, Bolton saw the problem immediately.

'You're not going to move this without greasing these wheels first. They're frozen solid.'

Jimmy remembered that Rooikat had told them to bring the grease when they brought the tools. Bastard didn't bother to remind them.

He fetched the tin and the grease gun from where they'd stored the equipment and Bolton showed them where to apply the grease – to the large, rusted, grease nipples in the centre of each wheel. They rocked the cart backwards and forwards for a few minutes to spread the lubricant and then tried pushing again. Bolton's extra weight helped. Slowly, very slowly, the cart began to move. Soon it began to run smoothly and in minutes they were at the mouth of the tunnel.

It was quite a job getting the heavy steel coffin-shaped box onto the trailer, but in the end, with a bit of help from Bolton's knowledge of levers and brute force, they managed. They were about to drive off when Bolton banged on the back of the tail gate, and shouted, 'Hey guys, stop. Have you seen this?'

They all got out of the vehicle and Jimmy said, 'Seen what?'

And pointing at a three-cornered triangle symbol stamped into the box Bolton said, 'This. It's the old symbol for danger from atomic radiation. I wonder what's in this box? Let's open it.'

Jimmy shot Bolton twice in the chest. He told Sabbar to help dump him in the trailer next to the black box – a body outside a coffin.

Sabbar, in shock, screeched, 'What does he mean, atomic radiation?'

Jimmy told him to shut it and drive.

They buried Bolton in a shallow grave with his boots and his headphones on. They left everything as it was at the camp and headed back to Johannesburg. The sun was beginning to set and it would be a long, difficult drive with a heavy load, right through the night. Sabbar's hands were killing him but he wrapped them in bandages from the first aid kit and kept his mouth shut. And drove. He could still see the surprise on

Bolton's face as Jimmy shot him.

Rooikat, who hadn't left the area watched as the junior jihadis loaded the bomb onto the trailer and saw the one called Jimmy shoot Bolton, the prospector. What a bunch of half-wits. At least that was one thing he wouldn't have to go back and clean up. Bolton had seen his face and knew that he was involved with the four morons, so they'd saved him the hassle. He'd have to trust them though, as well as the charra he'd met setting up the deal. But then he knew more about them than they knew about him so it was to both their benefits not to let anything slip to the wrong people.

He'd lie low in Botswana for a couple of days. Wait to see if they'd got away with it. If they got caught by the authorities on the road back to Jo'burg someone would leak it to the press or TV. In South Africa it would be a miracle if it didn't get leaked. The real test would be whether or not they got it over the border and out of the country, because he was pretty sure they'd have big plans for it. Bigger plans than making a big hole in some South African city. So, so far, so good. His old dead comrades, his new business associates, none of them could hurt him in any way. The first he'd dealt with permanently, the second were too busy with their own plans.

Koekemoer though, was a different kettle of snoek. He was the one oke who could really cause *kak* for him. Lucky he'd been as thick as the local cops. And he was meant to be such a hot-shot detective.

The bomb, code named de la Rey, was on the move again – the journey eastward on virtually the identical route once taken by General de la Rey, 'the Lion of the West', on his epic fight against the British over a century before.

Confrontation

Cook spent an hour before breakfast on his laptop checking out the South African Companies Register. It seemed that both Van Schalkwyk Makatini and Geo Logical were subsidiaries of Makatini Investments but that Makatini Investments was in turn owned by a holding company, Khan Makatini. Makatini and Khan had common shareholdings in all three companies, as well as in numerous others, but van Schalkwyk's sole directorship was in the company that bore his name.

Sipho Makatini was a post-Apartheid personality – a flamboyant character fond of fast cars and Johnny Walker Blue Label and was a poster boy for the successful black entrepreneur. There was little known about Khan though, except that he was extremely wealthy and thought to be the power behind certain high-ranking politicians. Cook hacked into the police computers and could find nothing on Khan, H.A., but there were two arrest dockets on Khan S. Both were for driving under the influence, but neither had been passed on to the State Prosecutor as the breathalyser evidence had 'gone missing'.

The delay over the ballistics was another story. Not being in the Force we no longer had any pull (if we ever had), but Cook thought he might still have one contact that could help out, but we'd have to approach him through the locals.

So after breakfast we went to the police station to see Nathi

Mpanza. I'd rung first to make sure he'd be in, and when we arrived, Sergeant Gugu said he was expecting us and to go right through. Mpanza got up from behind his desk to greet us. I introduced Cook to him. They shook hands and looked each other up and down, both appearing to approve. Mpanza's news was that van Tonder was already out on bail.

'Nothing I could do about it, Mr. Koekemoer. A lawyer called Boshoff drove all the way from Pretoria with a High Court order. He said he was representing van Tonder on behalf of Makatini Investments. You know how well connected they are.'

'That was bloody quick,' I said.

'Very. Look I shouldn't be telling you this, but when I interviewed him, he admitted to poaching and shooting out of season, but says he mistook you and your horse for a kudu and your foreman's for another.'

'Ja,' I said, 'and if my auntie had a dick she'd be my *oom*.'

I asked Mpanza if he'd sent van Tonder's rifle and the bullet from the second shooting to ballistics. He said he'd got Sergeant Gugu to deliver them personally, driving all the way to Pretoria and she'd got back this morning. While she was there she'd asked ballistics if they had anything more on the first shooting, from the sales records search of the various gunshops countrywide, but they said they were sorry, there was a long queue and they were short staffed. Cook asked him who they were dealing with and he said a sergeant called Visagie at the main forensic science lab at Pretoria Central.

Cook said, 'Maybe I can help, Captain, I know Sakkie very well. When I was in the Gauteng force I spent half my life in the Koedoe Building chasing forensics.'

Mpanza nodded. 'I'd appreciate any help from anywhere.' And picked up the phone, 'Sergeant, can you put me through to the ballistics man, Visagie, at Pretoria Central.'

A minute or so later the call was put through to him.

'Hello Sergeant Visagie, this is Captain Mpanza from Terre'Blanche. How is my bullet analysis going? … Next week? Look I have a friend of yours here who is keen to speak to you … a guy called Cook, he's involved in the case, can you speak to him?'

Mpanza handed Cook the phone.

'Sakkie, it's Chesney here. Naw, I'm not back in the force, just helping Captain Mpanza. How are the twins? … Hells bells, Matric already. Listen can you do us a favour and speed things up on the ballistics, that was Jaco Koekemoer they tried to shoot, and his foreman … Great … Tomorrow will be fine … Also the new bullet sample from the second shooting, can you match it to the rifle? I think a Sergeant Gugu delivered it personally to you … Tomorrow as well! Thanks very much Sakkie, I owe you big time … Give my best to Bettie and the family … Ja send it to Captain Mpanza. *Totsiens.*

Mpanza was impressed.

'How did you do that?'

'It's a long story. My friend Sakkie is a good guy but a few years back got into some shit with some Jo'burg gamblers. I got him out. He likes to think he owes me, but I was happy to help a pal and anyway I hate scumbag gamblers.'

For what it was worth we had brought a copy of the old army picture of Rooikat for Mpanza's files. Also to show it to Witbooi the tracker on the off-chance he recognised Rooikat from his Koevoet days, but I wasn't holding my breath. Mpanza got back on the phone to ask Sergeant Gugu if she could find Witbooi and ask him to come into the office for a moment.

The tracker joined us and carefully studied the photo. Then he shook his head and clucking his tongue sorrowfully, told us the photograph wasn't of Rooikat but of a young national service rifleman he thought was called Smit. He was killed in South West Africa an operation against Swapo Witbooi was also on. Witbooi remembered him as a quiet youngster who they had nicknamed *bak oor* after the jackal with stick-out ears. Pity those ears hadn't heard the Russian tank coming over the horizon.

I got tired of waiting. Patience has never been my strong suit. Van Tonder was out on bail and Mpanza couldn't do a thing about it. But I could. I decided it was time Cook and I paid him and his boss a visit. We'd do one of our famous double acts on him. Not the good cop/bad cop routine you often see in the cop shows on TV, but our own version. I lose my temper with the suspect and Cook stands back and tries to gauge the response to my apparent rage.

Just before lunch we drove over to *Elandsfontein*, van Schalkwyk's farm. I stopped in front of the farmhouse stoep and pulled in next to the bullet-riddled white bakkie. Mpanza must have let van Tonder drive home in it when he got bail. I pressed the hooter. Once, twice, half-a dozen long blasts. It was the typical, annoying, Toyota bakkie hooter, a high bleat like a newly castrated sheep. Van Tonder came out, followed by his boss.

'Oh, it's you. Koekemoer.' Coming from van Tonder's mouth my name sounded like a particularly foul swear word.

'Ja, van Tonder, I want to talk to you.'

'Ja? Well I want to *fokken* talk to you, too. Look what you've done to my *fokken* bakkie! Bullet holes everywhere. You could have killed me. And who's going to pay for the damage? Not me.'

'Well you tried to shoot me first. And my foreman, Carolus. Who put you up to it, your boss here, van Schalkwyk?'

'I told that dumb cop Mpanza that it was a mistake.'

'Some mistake. And don't try to tell me the bullshit you told Mpanza … that you thought we were bloody kudu. Nobody shoots kudu in summer.'

He paused as if he was pondering the wrongs and rights

of shooting kudu out of season and then continued right on shitting me out.

'Look I admit shooting your horse and over your man's head but I wasn't trying to kill you. I was just trying to give you a *spook*. If I was aiming at you you'd be dead right now.'

Van Schalkwyk backed him up.

'Ja, Buks here is a crack shot.'

'You van Schalkwyk, you probably put him up to it. And the first shooting. I wouldn't be surprised if you had a hand in Pa's murder too – you've always been a greedy bastard.'

It's funny, I was beginning to calm down a bit and I even half believed van Tonder when he said he wasn't intending to kill me, just give me a fright. Well he succeeded in that. But somebody must have put him up to it and that somebody was standing next to him.

I lost it for real though, when out of the blue, van Tonder took a swing at me. He thought he'd catch me cold, but he telegraphed the punch like a fighter on amateur night. I swotted it away with my left arm and with my right, gave him a good old-fashioned *snot klap*. A flat hand roundhouse on the side of his head. It sounded like I'd hit him with the full face of a cricket bat. Thwaaak! He went down like a sack of mielies, and didn't get up. Then I turned round to give van Schalkwyk a dose of the same. But I stopped myself mid-swipe. Shit Koekemoer, I said to myself, this man you're about to *bliksem* was once a friend of your Pa's and had given you a grudging leg up in the Force. Van Schalkwyk had just stood there, almost happy to be hit, but I fancy I saw a flash of relief when he saw the rage fade out of my eyes.

'Shit, Jaco,' he said, 'you always had a hot temper. It's what made you so good at rugby. But also, it's what made you not good enough to play it at the level you should have. Glad to see you've managed to control it a little.'

Then he walked over to see how his man was. Van Tonder

was sitting on the ground, shaking his head trying to clear the ringing in his ears.

I had been so involved in the altercation with the two of them that I hadn't noticed the arrival of Mpanza, Gugu and the tracker, Witbooi. The Captain greeted us all.

'Good afternoon gentlemen, is everything okay here?'

Van Tonder, now on his feet and despite the vivid red handmark on the side of his face, was still mindlessly belligerent. He poked his finger in Mpanza's chest and shouted, 'Arrest this man, arrest him. You saw him, he assaulted me. *Klapped* me when I wasn't looking.'

Mpanza turned to Cook.

'Did you see what happened?'

'No Captain. One moment they were arguing, the next this oke was on the ground.'

Mpanza turned to Gugu.

'And you Sergeant?'

'I only saw this man, van Tonder, trip and hit his head on the side of the bakkie, Captain.'

'Yes that's what I saw.'

Then to van Tonder he said, 'You should look where you're walking in future, sir.'

Van Tonder was now apoplectic with rage. He turned to van Schalkwyk, almost screaming.

'Boss, boss, you saw it, tell them!'

But van Schalkwyk told him, 'Cool it, Buks. You're in enough shit already.'

And then he said. 'Sorry about the minor disagreement you witnessed Captain, but you must have driven out here for something, can I help you?'

'You can sir. Do you own, or did you own, a nineteen ninety-six model Toyota Landcruiser with a black bull bar?'

'Hell, I don't know, I might have done. Land Cruiser bakkies were very popular back then, still … '

And then we were interrupted by a muffled explosion and a flash of intense white light from about five hundred metres away. It looked like it had come from an old broken down barn just off the farm access road, back towards the main tar. Flames were already licking out of the rusted, corrugated roof. Van Tonder rushed into the farm house and came back lugging a heavy duty fire extinguisher. Van Tonder, Mpanza and I jumped in my bakkie and I put foot. We were there in minutes, just as there was another muffled explosion, this one red and fiery. It blazed intensely for several minutes and then was smothered by the thick acrid smoke of burning rubber. The others arrived in the cop van. We waited until the fire burned down, which didn't take long – concrete, steel T-bars and corrugated iron roofing sheets are not the most combustible materials. But what was still smouldering, was what had once been a white, old model, Cruiser bakkie with black bull bars that had been parked inside the barn. Van Tonder sprayed foam on the few flames still licking on the tyres and the smoke lessened. The stench was overpowering.

Mpanza asked van Schalkwyk again, 'Are you still claiming you don't own or have never owned a nineteen ninety-six Toyota Land Cruiser with a black bull bar?'

'I never owned this one', van Schalkwyk said. 'We always put the farm's brand on the side of our vehicles, for marketing purposes – a big Elandsfontein Stud.'

'Why isn't there one on van Tonder's bakkie then?'

'The one Koekemoer shot up? That's his private vehicle.'

While this conversation was going on, Cook and I had walked round the Land Cruiser. The paint had bubbled on the bull bar so it was impossible to see if it had been scratched in any recent collision. But the left front headlight was broken. Cook got on his knees and checked the ground in front of the headlight and found nothing. No glass. The fire hadn't caused the light to burst, it must have happened elsewhere.

I called Mpanza over and Sergeant Gugu came too. I pointed to the broken headlight.

'Could be the vehicle that ran my father off the road. There's no glass on the ground here. I bet it matches the glass from the scene.'

Mpanza told Gugu to find a screwdriver and to chisel out the remaining shards of the headlight glass and bag them. And then do the same with a scraping of black paint and to head off to Pretoria as soon as they got back to the station and get the samples to the lab 'asap'. He then phoned the station and told them to get the tow truck service to remove the burnt-out bakkie to the vehicle park, also 'asap'.

Mpanza then turned to van Schalkwyk and van Tonder.

'You two had better come in with me and answer some questions.'

Van Schalkwyk tried to argue with him. He said he didn't have a clue how the bakkie had got in the shed – they never parked any bakkie in the old barn, ever. It was only used as a shearing shed once a year and sometimes to hang up the buck after a big hunt. Also he could prove the bakkie was never owned by him or the farm company, his accountant would have records. It all sounded plausible. But I guess Mpanza was a little pissed off by van Schalkwyk and van Tonder.

'Climb in the back of the van, sir, or we'll chuck you in, your choice,' was all he said.

Botswana

Rooikat was alone with his thoughts next to the pool in the house they had rented at Phakalane on the golfing estate outside Gaberone. He was stretched-out in a deckchair similar to the one he'd kicked Bolton out of a few days before. It was only eleven in the morning and he was already on his third brandy and Coke. The chick and the kid were at the nearby shopping mall spending the money that Khan had deposited into the Standard Bank Botswana account.

'Christ, I'm nearly home and dry. Cops are such simple people. They like to tie up things in nice neat packages. Like, if van Tonder was the man that shot at Jaco Koekemoer, he was probably the man who shot at his foreman the week before. If he had such a problem with the Koekemoer family, probably he was responsible for the hit-and-run "accident" that killed Koekemoer's father. It's how most cops' minds work – one prime suspect, pin every crime you can on him.'

It all rolled through his mind. How pissed off he'd been when Buks van Tonder shot at Koekemoer just as he had him in his sights himself, but realising he could use it to his advantage. That van Tonder was using a .243 was a bonus – he could frame the prick for both shootings. The cops, if they were halfway clued-up, would have found spent .243 calibre bullets at both scenes and would put two and two together, and get one – van Tonder. Even if they sent the bullets off to ballistics, it would take weeks, if ever, for any results.

Rooikat also knew there was nothing cops like more than an anonymous tip-off – it means they can make an arrest without actually having to do any work, but also that these days you have to be careful. The cops may be simple but they're not totally stupid. Computers, CCTV and cell phone tracking have made it harder to hide telephone calls in the shadows. Everyone leaves an electronic spoor, or a CCTV picture – the answer is to create a track that leads nowhere, a picture that shows nothing.

Making an untraceable call is not difficult – it just takes pre-planning. You need a burner phone – a cell phone you can use once and chuck, and that can't be tracked to you. The best were out-of-date Nokias bought from a secondhand dealer at somewhere anonymous like the Jo'burg flea market. Buy half a dozen at a time and load each with a ninety-nine cent sim card and the cheapest top-up from an out-of-town supermarket. Use it, wipe it clean and chuck it.

Rooikat went over it again and again. The calls he had made were from the parking lot outside the deserted rugby stadium. He'd cased the place months before and knew there were no security cameras there. And also rugby season was long finished so there'd be no people around, not even a watchman. What was there to steal? Goal posts?

He hadn't even bothered to disguise his voice. Nobody knew him at the local cop shop and he wanted the message to get through loud and clear. And anyway he reckoned one whitey sounded the same as any other to a black police officer. He'd hung up when he was sure the message had been understood, ditched the phones in a stormwater drain and drove out to the crossroads on the main road out of town. The cops had to go past it on the way to van Schalkwyk's farm and he was sitting in the Wimpey having a cheeseburger when they drove by, sirens blaring and lights flashing. Talk about sneaking up on somebody on the quiet.

Rooikat had counted on the cops keeping van Tonder overnight, which would make the second part of his plan that much easier– a second red herring for the police to bite on as readily as they had on the first. That night he rigged up an explosive device in the Toyota Land Cruiser he'd used to ram the Colonel into the donga. Loading his scrambler onto the back, he drove it out to van Schalkwyk's farm and parked it in the old barn near the highway and used the bike back to get back to town.

He wasn't happy he had to lose the bakkie, it had served him well and he wouldn't have had to get rid of it if the bull bar had done its job. He'd expected that there would be some scratch marks on the side of his vehicle that would need touching up, but not for the headlight to smash. The bar should have protected it. So the cops, if they had even done a half-arsed job of the crime scene, would have had some broken glass fragments and a paint scrape on the Colonel's vehicle. That would be enough to make a match on his vehicle if they found it. He knew the bakkie couldn't be traced back to him but why take any chances. Arresting that arsehole van Tonder and van Schalkwyk, his scheming *doos* of a boss, would certainly take off any heat.

The time bomb was a simple trick he'd learnt in special ops – an incendiary device made of white phosphorus flares set off through the pre-set alarm signal of a cell phone. He'd set the phone alarm to go off at 13:00 the next day and phoned the police just before 12:00. This time not bothering to check whether they responded immediately or not, but it would have been nice if the explosion had caught them, or maybe Jaco Koekemoer too if they'd phoned him. They seemed to be getting very pally-pally with him.

'Ja,' Rooikat thought. 'No comeback to me – can't see how there's any comeback to me – I can relax.'

After three days of relaxing, Rooikat was getting sick of it. Botswana wasn't all it was cracked up to be. The diamond mining industry was pretty much a closed shop, not the Wild West he'd thought it would be, but a stitch-up between the Botswana government and De Beers. The five million rands made it more bearable though. He'd bought his girlfriend a big rock, and himself a new bakkie. A Toyota Land Cruiser like the one he'd had to burn, but a much later model. And there was still over four million left in the account.

Even so, Rooikat was getting cabin fever. The chick was getting bored too, and the boy kept whining incessantly for more games for his new Playstation. He made a decision. Thought it through.

'I think I'll give it a day or two more and then take the Cruiser for a test drive back to Terre'Blanche. One final trip back to clean up a few things. Blow up the old mine shaft properly so no-one will ever know what was once inside it. But I have to do it soon. In the next few days. Before that prick Koekemoer works everything out and comes after me.'

NINE

White wolves and other vermin

MANY AFRIKANERS NEVER FORGOT how hard won South Africa had been. Nor were they prepared to give it up. The struggle to leave British rule in the Cape lead to the Great Trek and the wars and skirmishes against the Zulu Kingdom in Natal and the Sothos in the Orange Free State and Transvaal. And, later, the first of the wars against the British who, defeated at Majuba, grudgingly let them go their own way and even establish their own Boer Republics in the north. Until gold was discovered of course. That changed the picture entirely. The British were hell bent on controlling the gold mines of the Transvaal and engineered a second war against the Boers – and put the entire might of the Empire behind it.

Nor was it forgotten that in this second Anglo-Boer War, eighty-eight thousand of their, mainly farmer forebears, fought more than half-a-million regular British troops to a standstill in two-and-a-half years. The Boers only surrendering after a scorched earth policy, when the British shot their cattle and horses as they stood grazing, and torched their farms. And when twenty-eight thousand of their women and children died in the concentration camps set up by the despised Lord Kitchener.

Their heroes were men like Koos de la Rey – a *bittereinder*. He became renowned as the only Boer general who had never given up, never surrendered. Yet he was adamantly against the war right up to the minute it was declared. In parliament, President Kruger of the Transvaal Republic had even accused him of cowardice over his preference for peace. De la Rey's response was that he'd be fighting the British long after Kruger and his friends had given up and fled to safety.

If the hotheads and loudmouths had had their way in South Africa, we'd still be mopping up the blood.

But they tried their best. On 15 November 1988, Barend Strydom, a self-proclaimed 'Wit Wolf' murdered seven black people and wounded fifteen others in Strydom Square, Pretoria.

There were several well-attended marches and rallies in the West Transvaal and Pretoria in the late 1980s and 1990s by the extreme rightwing *Afrikaner Weerstandbeweging*, or AWB as it was universally known. The AWB was led by Eugene Terre'Blanche, whose long-ago ancestor had founded the town that bore his name at the spot where he'd fallen off his horse. (At one memorable rally, the burly, bearded, Eugene fell off his own horse to universal derision – poor horsemanship was obviously in his genes.) The fervour and rhetoric of these rallies became more and more toxic, especially after almost two-thirds of the white population voted YES in the 1992 referendum to allow full, free and fair, all-party, all-race, elections to be held in 1994.

In 1993, the leader of the South African Communist Party, Chris Hani, was murdered by a fascist Polish immigrant – the gun he used was supplied by an extreme right-wing fringe politician. Hani's assassination came close to derailing the peace process. Thankfully, Nelson Mandela, and other wise heads in the ANC who sensed that victory by peaceful means was so close, managed to cool hotheads on their side of the fence.

Then in early 1994, in an effort to derail the elections, the AWB played their final card and attempted a coup in the Apartheid satellite state of Bophuthatswana. This was intended to lead to a national uprising by like-minded rightwingers with the help of the military and police forces. Then there would be a new government formed – a one-party Afrikaner government. Any uprising by the Communists (or indeed anyone of even a pale pink political persuasion) would be put down quickly and mercilessly and South Africa would return to being white and God-fearing.

It never happened. The army and the police remained loyal to the government and the people, and in 1994 the ANC alliance swept into power with a huge majority. There was euphoria in the country. Much talk about Archbishop Desmond Tutu's 'Rainbow Nation', with opportunities for all. Peace and Love and Brotherhood and all that *kak*.

Of course it couldn't last.

Spook and diesel

We might have solved things earlier and prevented a whole lot of grief for a whole lot of people if events hadn't kicked off in Terre'Blanche itself. We were so close to solving not only Pa's murder and the reasons for the shootings on the farm but also the riddle of the missing A-bomb and where its whereabouts. That is, if there was an A-bomb in the first place.

To help us with our investigations and as an aid to clear thinking, the following evening Chesney Cook and I took ourselves off to the Royal for a quiet couple of cold Castles. The pub was far from quiet though. It seemed that every rock-spider in the district had crawled his way into town and was sitting at the bar in the Royal. The pale remnants of the *bittereinder* AWB had heard that the #VerwoerdMustFall students were in Terre'Blanche threatening to blow up Verwoerd's Koppie, and they had come to put a stop to it. And they'd heard there was going to be a rock concert with Facing the Gallows, the heavy metal band from Jo'burg desecrating the sacred site. This they considered devil's work in a musical wilderness that had, until recently, been broken only by the *sakkie-sakkie* sounds of concertina, mouth organ and *blik* guitar. It was to be a final showdown between the old and new South Africa. One last stand of the brandy-sodden Boers against the dagga-raddled *Kommunis* students.

The *Kommunis* agitators in the guise of an already half-pissed Thabo Mkhize and his coterie of pretty students and assorted bongo-players, were sitting at their usual tables across the room. There was a lot of staring going on, but it was totally one-sided. The AWB members would take a *sluk* of their *dop en dam* or *spook and diesel* and stare ferociously at the students. The students would smile back sweetly through a haze of dope.

Cook went to look for a table and I bellied up to the bar. There was yet another barman there – this time a scrawny old buzzard with Elvis sideburns. He was a member of the taciturn barman society. I ordered the Castles and I asked him if Fat Face, or Gerrie, as I thought he was called, was around. The new barman said, 'Gone.'

'Where to?'

'Fuck knows.'

And then bent down to reach under the counter into the bar fridge for the Castles. He banged them down on the counter and walked off to take another order.

I grabbed them – they were as cold as ever – and took them back to Cook who'd found a table. It had already been taken, but he'd lifted the sole occupant, a comatose student, and gently sat him down in a spare seat at one of the other student tables. We needed the chair in case Mauretia joined us, although she'd said it was unlikely she could as she had a double funeral to prepare for at a farm fifty kilometres away.

We had our beers and then three or four more each. The pub was filling up, but not with anybody you'd ever want to drink with. More glazed-eyed students and *windgat* AWB wannabees with mullet hairstyles and automatics with hair triggers, stuck in fast draw holsters down their butt cracks. Mixed with the rotgut brandy they were drinking it was a lethal combination, often for themselves. (I was once having a piss in a bar in Dullstroom, Mpumalanga, when a *dronkgat* joker pulled out his 9mm to show it to me, and shot an extra hole between his buttocks.)

It was getting noisier too. And we had gone on to harder stuff – the cop's drink, *spook and diesel* (cane and coke if you want to be polite). Thabo Mkhize had left his crowd and bringing the little redhead with him sat down with us.

'Howzit policeman, you here on riot patrol?'

'No we're here for protection.'

'Protection of who?'

'Protecting these fine specimens of Afrikanerdom from being corrupted by radical students such as yourself.'

Mkhize laughed and we started talking bullshit together. He knew Cape Town well and many of the same places and even some of the people as Cook and I. Although totally up his own arse, Mkhize was actually quite interesting and told us that far from being from the humble township background that his publicity machine claimed, he came from a wealthy Jo'burg business family, and the redhead he was with was a friend of his sister's who had gone to Jo'burg's finest girls' school. He went to an equally prestigious boys' boarding school in the Eastern Cape, and had only just got pipped at the post for a Rhodes Scholarship to Oxford. His extremely pissed-off reaction was to join the #RhodesMustFall movement. When this movement began to wane after the UCT council caved in and Oxford wouldn't, he searched around for a similar cause, and when someone alerted him to the giant bust on the Terre'Blanche koppie, #VerwoerdMustFall was born. Surprised at the immediate publicity, he knew he was on to a winner and the best way he could think of keeping in the limelight and having a ball. At the same time furthering his budding political career. He didn't want to end up the oldest student on campus like most radical 'youth league' activists, but was angling for a place on the national parliament candidate list once the current president retired. Sooner rather than later, he hoped.

I said I'd drink to that, and did, after fetching another round from the bar. We were back on beer, but drinking them as chasers to flaming Sambucas. Mkhize asked me what it was like being a cop and always hassling people. I said I liked it. Except that I was no longer a cop having teamed up with Cook to start our incredibly successful private detective venture. He asked me for a card just in case he ever needed our services (he was extremely pissed at this stage) and Cook gave him one of his – our special politically-correct affirmative action business card – Cook first, followed by Koekemoer in fancy, flowery script. Mkhize said they had to make tracks, he had an early start, and with the redhead in tow, weaved his way back to his student pals who were making moves to leave. Two of them were dragging one of their comatose friends out of the pub by his heels, the rest following.

The noise levels in the bar quietened for a moment or two and then swelled again as the students were replaced by a late shift of miners who'd arrived already tanked up from a church braai dance. They'd brought their wives and girlfriends with them. Some of the women looked rougher than the miners.

The crowd had spilled all around us. One of the miners asked if he and his girlfriend could use the spare chairs at our table. We said sure be our guests. I recognised him as the oke I'd seen sprawled unconscious across the table the day I'd first arrived in town. His girlfriend was a big blonde who could have shotput at the Olympics and was now matching him drinking brandy, shot for shot.

Now that the students had left, the AWB guys switched their animosity towards the miners and to us. One arsehole started mocking Cook in particular – I guess it was because of his blue eyes. He started out with the usual *platteland* wit that, in some circles, passes as humour: 'What are you doing up here in God's own country where men are men and sheep are scared,' and all the rest of the bullshit. He progressed to calling Cook names we'd been taught in official police force sensitivity training not to use any more as they might cause offense to the Cape coloured 'clients' we used to call criminals. Capie, hotnot, klonkie … and worse … you name it.

Cook, who is relaxed about this sort of thing and who'd failed sensitivity training anyway, told the miner in his best Afrikaans, 'Your mother had obviously birthed you out of the incorrect orifice', and then told him to fuck off. The AWB guy was too pissed and too stupid to realise that Cook was being just about as polite as he could – like with the Sambucas it would take just one match to light his fuse. This came a moment later when another particularly drunk AWB gent stumbled over Cook and knocked his drink over his lap. Cook got up and *moered* him. Didn't say please or thank you or excuse me *oom*, just *klapped* him. And for seconds, he *klapped* the guy who'd been insulting him. Cook's got a very slow fuse but a big charge behind it.

Thanks to this slight over-reaction by Cook, every AWB member in the bar, who was still sober enough to stand, made a bee-line towards Cook and me. They were brandishing beer bottles and bar stools and had blue murder in their eyes. Fortunately the miners and their female folk came to our rescue. Miners love a good rumble, especially after a church social. The first wave of AWBs were beaten off with the help of our new friends sharing our table. Piet and Pixie they were called. Piet took out two of the farmers with one swipe of his massive hand while Pixie asphyxiated another by sitting on his face until his legs stopped twitching. The second wave that hit us was more serious. It felt like the Blue Bulls A team that once went over me in a loose scrum in a trial match. We were saved by a pack of our own – a dozen miners who illegally joined the scrum from the side and rolled over the AWBs. The melee descended into what could have been an old-time third division Transvaal club match between Diggers and Roodepoort. Ball forgotten, players rolling around on the floor, biting, kicking, punching and eye-gouging. Rugby as it used to be before they brought in the new sissie rules.

In the end, I didn't get to see who actually won this match. Half way through I needed a rest and a pee break, so I headed off to the piss house. I was just coming out again when the lights went out.

I woke up with a head that felt like it had been hit with a pickaxe handle. And that, Cook told me later, was exactly what had happened. He also said that I'd missed the best part of the evening, when the police finally arrived and shot a couple of AWBs with the new tasers they'd been issued. Apparently one of them had called Captain Mpanza a Zulu *doos*. Cook reckoned that Mpanza must have failed sensitivity training too.

Suffering a three Grandpa Headache Powder *babelas,* I came to the realisation that I was much too old for a pub crawl, much less a pub brawl.

The battle of Verwoerd's Koppie

In the morning, Cook and I took our hangovers and sore heads in to the police station. I apologised to Captain Mpanza for the night before and said I was sorry if I had caused him any trouble. He said that as I was unconscious when he and his men arrived, I was no trouble at all. And what could he do for me today? Cup of coffee? Aspros?

I told him no thanks to both; I had already filled up on coffee and headache powders but was wondering whether there was any progress with forensics? He said there was and that Cook's pal, Sakkie, had got back to him that very morning. And that there was good news. And bad.

The bad was that it seemed we were back to square one in the hunt for the killer. While ballistics had proved that the bullet taken out of my horse at the scene of the second ambush did, indeed, come from the .243 rifle found at van Schalkwyk's farm, and the fingerprints on the rifle were Buks van Tonder's, they were not a match for the .243 bullets of the first shooting. This meant that they came from a different rifle.

Also, the police lab had finally completed the DNA analysis on the sample of spit that Mpanza had collected at the first shooting and it didn't match van Tonder's. So the original ambusher could not have been him.

The burnt-out Land Cruiser bakkie, however, was in all

likelihood the vehicle that had run Pa off the road. Although they still didn't have a definitive paint match since, in a drive for new efficiency and cost savings, the police hierarchy had contracted out much of the scientific analysis to a private firm. This meant that all tests now took over a month longer than when they were done in-house. If they were done at all. The fact that the new commissioner's brother-in-law had recently set up this private company by poaching the one remaining, overworked, paint and chemicals technician from the CSIR, apparently had nothing to do with awarding them the multi-million rands contract. Noooo.

Sakkie, however, had come up trumps again despite the lack of in-house resources. He said that while the outside company still had to do a scientific match on the glass Sergeant Gugu had brought in, he was ninety-nine point nine per cent certain that the glass was the same as that found at the scene of the crime. He had come to this conclusion through the very scientific test of matching the glass Gugu had brought in that morning with some of the glass picked up at the crime scene, by simply fitting it together like a jigsaw puzzle.

Mpanza said that it was proving next to impossible to pin ownership of the vehicle on either van Tonder or van Schalkwyk. The national motor vehicle register had it listed as owned by someone called Smit from Bellville in the Cape. But also that it had been reported stolen nearly a year previously.

The worst news of all though, was that Mpanza had been told to put the case on the back burner. The powers-that-be in Pretoria insisted there were other things he'd been neglecting that were much higher priority – in particular what was going on at Verwoerd's Koppie and the fight in Terre'Blanche between the #VerwoerdMustFall 'heroes' and the right-wing AWB scum.

Headquarters had advised him that there was information from reliable sources that the rightwingers intended to disrupt the rock concert Thabo Mkhize was planning to hold and that every effort should be made to ensure the safely of both Mkhize and his group of #VerwoerdMustFall activists. The bosses feared that any trouble could escalate to an international newsworthy event following the increasingly prominent reporting in the local newspapers in the last day or two, and then last night on TV1 news.

Mpanza said he'd told the brass in Pretoria that the fight was actually between drunk AWB members and equally drunk miners, and that it had been sorted out quickly with little damage to anyone. But that's not what Mkhize, the #VerwoerdMustFall head, had told the press. According to him it had been a full scale pitched battle where valiant, outnumbered, students had bravely held off a heavily armed militia bent on perpetrating a new Sharpeville massacre. The police chiefs, while not actually buying this version, said that there was no choice – their political overlords were getting extremely itchy and didn't want any confrontation at all in the country at the moment. They'd had to swallow the bad results of the recent local elections which had been difficult for a neo-Marxist party that considered it had a right to govern in perpetuity. And they didn't want anyone, especially from the growing popular populist left like Mkhize, to get any more good publicity. But they certainly didn't want the negative publicity of him getting killed by a bunch of right-wing lunatics either. So, as the man on the spot, it was Mpanza's job to make sure nothing bad happened to either Mkhize or his #VerwoerdMustFall rabble (er … heroes). Failure to do this would lead to a far worse career move than his current posting to Terre-Blanche and could include a permanent assignment tracking motorists who avoided paying the Johannesburg highway toll fees.

Mpanza told us that he had to assemble his officers and tell them the happy news that they were going on riot patrol. The riot gear would be broken out and the fight would begin over who got a protective vest that fitted. Most of those issued were either designed for nine feet tall, skinny people or the four feet tall obese. There were also a couple that fitted the average size cop and these had often been marked with indelible ink with the initials of the last person in the squad who had wore it. This was always ignored in the next scramble for kit.

Cook and I had been through it all before and Mpanza and crew were welcome to it. I told him to be especially careful at the monument itself as I had been there when the #VerwoerdMustFall lot were planting the explosives and that their understanding of how to set dynamite charges looked a little rudimentary. And they'd probably bring the whole koppie down as well as the statue. With that, we said good luck and goodbye, and headed off to see for ourselves what was happening.

Thabo Mkhize and the #VerwoerdMustFall crowd had certainly been busy. The tent town had sprouted and birthed a host of new teepees, yurts and space pods. The scaffolding in front of the massive head of Verwoerd had been removed to reveal him in the multi-coloured glory of the new South African flag. A stage had been erected with the vast psychedelic bust as a backdrop. A laser light show and smoke and fireworks were awaiting the arrival of the Johannesburg death metal rock band, Facing The Gallows. Similar to Disaster Area, the fictional rock band made famous in *Hitchhiker's Guide to the Galaxy*, who were best heard from an underground concrete bunker thirty-seven miles from the stage, Facing The Gallows were at their acoustic finest when playing at low levels from the province next to the one next door. In this case, KwaZulu-Natal. However, at Verwoerd's Koppie the audience would be hearing them full blast from ten paces away. It was standing room only and strung-out students from every university in the country spread out from the tent town to the cliff face, on the edge of a hundred metre fall.

At the moment the crowd was sparse and only modestly smoked up. Two bongo players and a guy on a penny whistle were sitting cross-legged, playing in the middle of the stage. The roadies from the band were chatting up students, male and female, and checking that the fireworks would head towards the heavens and not into the back of the base player's head as had happened at one memorable Cape Town gig. The band, with their new base player, was only due on stage at around ten o'clock that evening.

Mkhize was supervising it all and came over to see what we wanted.

'I hear you got caught up in the *kak* at the Royal last night, policeman.'

'Ja, we should have left when you did.'

'Are you coming to the big event tonight? You're welcome to.'

'What have you got planned?'

'Like I said, we're going to blow up Verwoerd. But first we're going to party.'

'And the AWB? Aren't you worried they're going to gatecrash your big show?'

'They're welcome to, the more the merrier, and anyway we've got protection.'

He pointed across to where a group of young black guys in red overalls and matching berets were drinking beer in the sun.

'Julius has lent us some of his supporters.'

'You better tell them to hold off on the beer then, they'll be too pissed by tonight to fight anyone.'

'And anyway, we've got the numbers. We'll be thousands strong.'

'You might need to be, good luck.'

Cook and I decided to come back later when the fun started. I'd never been to a heavy metal concert before and I reckon Mauretia hadn't either. We headed back to the farm and I called her to see if she wanted to come.

'What do you wear to a to a heavy metal concert?' Was the first thing she asked.

'I don't know. But whatever you decide make sure it goes with hiking boots, it's going to be tough on the feet on the koppie.'

'Alright, what time?'

'We should leave the farm about nine, so come out when you're ready and we'll go from here, after something to eat.'

'Okay, see you later.'

Mauretia arrived at about eight wearing the slinky green outfit she'd worn on our first big night out. It looked a little peculiar with her Hi-Tec boots and sheepskin jacket. But if anyone could carry it off, she could. I reckoned she could wear a mielie sack and look stunning. We had a light meal of cold meats and fresh baked farm bread that Annetjie had laid out, and fortified ourselves with some dark red wine – Tassenberg. Might as well get in the student vibe again. It was summer, but nights could get cold on the highveld.

We took the back road to the koppie – the three of us in the cab of the 4x4. I drove past a row of parked bakkies and what looked like a bunch of farmers having a braai at the side of the road. It was a group of AWBs in khaki with three-legged 'bastard' swastikas on the shoulders. They had lamb chops and *wors* on a grid and were drinking what was probably homemade peach brandy from gallon jugs.

Further on at the entrance to the Verwoerd's Koppie parking lot, there was a police van with its blue light flashing. An elderly white police reservist with a flashlight flagged me down and asked where I was going.

'To the concert, officer.'

'Sorry you can't go through. Only students and other such *betogers*.'

'We have an invitation.'

'Doesn't matter, the boss says no-one is to enter or leave.'

Just then the boss, Captain Mpanza, stepped out of the shadows and asked the old cop what was going on. Then he noticed us.

'Mr. Koekemoer. What are you doing here?'

'We've been invited by Thabo Mkhize himself. Thought it would be educational.'

Mpanza shook his head and then told the constable to let us through.

'Just stay out of it if there's any trouble.'

I'd noticed that in the shadows there were three Casspir riot vehicles and about forty policemen in full riot gear.

'Well you look ready for anything. But watch yourself, those AWBs can be dangerous when they're drunk enough,' I said to Mpanza.

'We can deal with them,' Mpanza said dismissively.

I drove through the gate and down the dirt road to the parking area. It looked like a scrapyard for old Volkswagen microbuses and other assorted badly-painted buses and surfer vans. How some of them had made it all the way to Terre'Blanche was a miracle. There were one or two students sitting on the bumpers of the vans smoking dope. And one of the vans was creaking rhythmically on its axles as we walked by. Mauretia said to me, 'Hell, Jaco, you do take me to some very classy places.'

Cook laughed.

The path to Verwoerd's monument was lit with blazing torches. The smell of paraffin mixed with the dagga, but failed to make much impression. We followed the lights and headed to the brightly lit sky ahead, moving towards the babbling of a thousand people at a party about to kick off. The whole place was illuminated like a giant TV studio and a crew was already in place, set to film both the entire concert and Mkhize's grand finale when he blew Verwoerd's head off. We found a perch just above and on the fringe of the heaving crowd. We'd got there at exactly the right time, just as the band appeared on stage, materialising through a thick fog of smoke machines pierced by razor-sharp shards of laser light. They stood on the stage for a moment, their shadows gigantic against the daylight bright backdrop of the flag-coloured granite head of ex-Prime Minister, Hendrik Frensch Verwoerd.

Facing The Gallows looked like unkempt bearded monks in cast-off clothing that they'd found in a Transylvanian dungeon. Christ, they were loud. But good. You could, through the wall of sound that could have been made by a thousand swarms of enraged African bees, even make out the odd individual mangled chord. What key they played in appeared to be a random decision – during their big hit song *Filth* each guitarist seemed to be making it up as they went along. And the bass sounded like the cavern of hell was opening up to swallow everyone, with the lead singer croaking death and destruction heavily amplified in a language only he could understand. But everyone was enjoying it with the rapture of empty heads whose brains had been totally sucked out and replaced with a train crash of exploded guitar chords. It certainly wasn't singalong. More where do I queue for a head transplant? My leg started twitching involuntarily. Shit, it was getting to me. Mauretia was in a trance, and Cook, who'd scored a joint from a dude next to him, was hopping up and down, the corks on an Aussie hat he'd scored somewhere, jiggling up and down in unison with the tits of a little blonde student chick perched on his shoulders.

Time car-crashed by. I though I heard heavy machinegun fire coming from below the koppie but it could have been the drummer beating out a particularly frenzied rhythm. Then the music stopped. Dead. One last thunderous chord and silence. The crowd roared like I'd last heard at Ellis Park when the Boks scored against the All Blacks, and when the roar died down, Mhkise appeared on stage. He had a tough act to follow. But if he thought so he didn't show it.

He shouted into a mike: 'Comrades, now for the moment we've all worked so long for – the moment that Verwoerd Must Fall!'

The crowd began to chant: 'Verwoerd Must Fall. Verwoerd Must Fall...'

One of the minders in a red boiler suit brought a dynamite blasting box onto the stage and Mkhize put both hands on the plunger. He began to count.

'Ten … nine … eight …'

The crowd joined in at, 'Three … two … one … zero'.

Mkhize pressed the plunger and … not much happened

One small charge went off at the top, and to the side, of Verwoerd's giant head. A large sheet of rock fractured and broke, falling off and taking out one leg of the stage. It left a large crack down Verwoerd's left cheek that looked as if he had a Prussian duelling scar. His face had also dropped a couple of metres giving him a lopsided grin.

Mkhize pressed the plunger again, and again. But except for the stage wobbling with each plunge … nothing. Not a puff of a Christmas cracker. The crowd started laughing and was still laughing when Captain Mpanza and his riot squad arrived.

Mkhize then tried to set off the dynamite charges one by one in the three remaining drill holes, ordering his special effects man to re-rig the blasting box to each charge individually. The first went off okay and took out half of Verwoerd's forehead and another leg of the stage, almost bringing both stage and Mkhize down with it. The crowd, the band, the police, Cook Mauretia and me, all were covered with dust and debris but

Verwoerd remained defiantly unmoved.

Luckily no-one was killed. The climax to the film Mkhize had commissioned was, instead of Verwoerd's head tumbling into the valley, his own crestfallen face in close-up, covered in white Kalahari dust face powder. He'd never live it down.

The police got to him as his henchman was trying to wire-up the third dynamite hole. Most of the crowd was beginning to disperse and head back to the car park by this stage. Mkhize was on the mike shouting, 'Come back! Come back comrades! The band is about to play again! Come back!'

The crowd ignored him. The concert was over. Not even a heavy metal death wish band like Facing the Gallows, issued with hard hats, would perform on a rickety stage underneath an overhanging sculpted rock-face with two charges of dynamite still primed to go off.

The riot police rapidly herded everyone off the koppie, worried it was about to come down. Most of the revellers were still in party mood but went peaceably enough, if rowdily. One of the band was last seen crowd surfing a li-lo that was riding a sea of hands before he was dispatched over the cliff into the trees below, fortunately to a soft landing.

Thabo Mhkise though, refused to budge. He continued to rant and shout for everyone to come back, the main event wasn't over. And then, when Mpanza had Sergeant Gugu slap the handcuffs on him, he snarled, 'Do you know who I am.?'

Mpanza replied, 'Are you related to the president?'

'No.'

'Well then shut up. You're under arrest.'

Mkhize shut up. Neither of them realised, however, that the mike on the stage was still live and the cameras were rolling, and this last bit of their heated exchange was what appeared on the world's TV stations and became an instant YouTube sensation.

Mkhize was frog-marched down the koppie to where those

revellers who were so drunk or stoned they were incapable of leaving, were being loaded into police vehicles to be taken to town to sleep it off in the cells overnight. The police bomb disposal squad was finally able to move in and recover the remaining dynamite charges and the koppie returned to peace and quiet.

Captain Mpanza told me later that it had indeed been machinegun fire I'd heard from down the valley during the concert. And that at one stage it had been touch and go with the AWBs who had pitched up at the gates to the reserve after their roadside braai, demanding to be allowed in to attend the concert.

'This is the new South Africa. We're free to go where we want.' One of them shouted at the old cop who had let us in.

The cop told them he had orders not to let them in. And that they were to stop immediately.

'Stop us? You and whose army?'

The cop turned his torch on to Mpanza and the waiting riot squad standing in the shadows in front of the path leading to the koppie.

'That army.'

A couple of the AWBs were pissed enough, and stupid enough, not to give a fuck for the consequences and cocked their rifles and turned towards the massed police. Mpanza said he signalled to two of the waiting Casspirs who switched on their high intensity searchlights and pointed them directly into the eyes of the AWBs. Then both vehicles fired long bursts of Browning .50 calibre machinegun fire over their heads while the riot squad tossed thunderflash stun grenades under their feet.

To a man the half-blind, completely deafened AWBs lowered their guns, laid them on the ground and put their hands up. Mpanza had his squad take down each of their names and their guns from them, and told them to go back to their vehicles, put the braai fires out and go home. They could fetch their weapons in the morning on presentation of legal gun licences. He said the AWBs left timidly. Their leader even said, 'Thank you Captain, we didn't mean any harm. Thank you.'

What became known as the battle of Verwoerd's Koppie was over almost before it began. Not a single person was hurt – only Mkhize's ego, and that soon healed.

TEN

Double-cross

THE DRIVE FROM TERRE'BLANCHE to Jo'burg had been uneventful. The traffic was light and, for a change, well behaved. By the time they arrived, just as the sun was coming up, Sabbar's hands were bleeding. He didn't complain. His father helped him put cure-all Zambuk ointment on them and wrapped them in clean cotton gauze. They were a lot better after a fresh application and repeat dressings, and a day and night's healing time. It was Friday and a good time to leave for Mozambique.

The four 'South African fishermen' left after an early breakfast to avoid the worst of the rush hour, but the road was still busy – South Africans were, more and more, turning every weekend into a long weekend and Friday had become something of an optional day off work. The drive from Jo'burg on the N4, skirting the East Rand mining towns, then past Nelspruit, was no picnic. The first two hundred kilometres on the old R22 had continuous roadworks – but fortunately the traffic eased a little after the Belfast turnoff in Mpumalanga, when some of it headed towards the mountains and the northern gates of the Kruger Park. And once they hit the toll road a few kilometres further on, it was plain sailing. It took the men six hours to reach Nelspruit from Johannesburg instead of the more usual four – roadworks and toll gates slowing them down at all too frequent intervals. Another hour took them to the Komati Oasis on the South African side of the border. There they topped up with petrol and bought cool drinks, snacks and cigarettes. There was no hassle at the South African border post – palms had been greased well in advance so they went through with out a hitch – the formalities, such as temporary export permits for the vehicle and boat, and customs declarations had already been filled in and pre-stamped.

The Mozambique side was a little slower. There were minor irritations: the government had introduced a new export form the week before, and the local police had introduced a special tax for some extra pocket money. Sabbar was used to the ins and outs of African officialdom and despite knowing that most of the border staff were already on hefty monthly retainers, paid up the few extra rands with a smile. The important thing was that customs officials on both sides of the border had simply waved them through, without even an inquisitive glance through the windows of the Cruiser or under the boat's tarpaulin – much to the chagrin of another group of ski boat fishermen who had been waiting for hours while customs officials went through every lure in their tackle boxes, and inspected every reel and rod in minute detail.

From the border it took just over an hour-and-a-half to Maputo, the city that once resembled a mini Lisbon, its buildings gleaming white with red tiled roofs. Now those same buildings were grey and run down, looking as shabby as the beggars in the streets they passed through. They drove on to the small boat harbour and parked outside one of the few buildings with a fresh coat of bright, school bus yellow paint, and bought a permit from a man in a ragged peaked cap who said he was the fisheries officer. Who knows if he actually was? He showed no interest in anything. Not the long black box in the bottom of the boat, not the fishing tackle or the other metal boxes that looked so heavy. Nothing except getting his *bonsella* – a generous tip.

He did, however, for an additional hand-out, help them launch their boat at the crumbling cement ramp. And, the twin motors starting up first time, they headed through light traffic out to sea. It was late afternoon. They'd given their destination as Inhaca Island, but instead took the north passage out of the great bay the city was built on and motored ten miles out to sea, anchoring on the flats just beyond the sand bar, fishing rods out. They didn't have long to wait – a great Arab dhow, running on a soot-snorting diesel engine, hove into sight, slowed down, and anchored next to them. The crewmen helped them fasten straps under the bow and stern of the ski boat which was hoisted aboard.

The dhow spread its massive triangular lanteen sail and, taking advantage of the regular southeaster trade wind which blows in summer, ploughed its way northwards against the swirling, erratic Mozambique current. The dhow bucked and strained against the vagaries of the current, flying fish taking wing under the heavy wooden prow splitting the choppy sea. It was a sight that hadn't changed for a thousand years. The great trading ships of Arabia and the Indian sub-continent heading south carrying beads and beaten metal goods and then north again with spices, gold and slaves. And this time with a cargo like no other.

Sabbar was pleased. The whole exercise, digging out the mine entrance, finding the bomb, getting it to Johannesburg, and hiding it in the bottom of the ski boat and then smuggling it through the border and on to the dhow, couldn't have gone better. He hadn't liked it when they had killed and buried Bolton though. But he supposed that was what war was about, there were always casualties. Maybe they should have taken more time burying him – they'd only dug a shallow grave and animals would quickly find and dig up his body. They should have packed it down with more and heavier stones, there were enough of them. But Jimmy had been in a hurry and Sabbar knew now that no-one argued with Jimmy. Not if they wanted to stay alive. Jimmy's laid-back, let's have fun, couldn't care less manner masked what Sabbar realised was a grade one psychopath. Even so, not as scary as that Dutchman, Rooikat. He gave an involuntary shudder. Fuck, he'd never met a maniac like Rooikat. He hope he'd never meet him again.

But Sabbar was sure his father would be proud of him. It was important to keep on the right side of the old man. And, important to his own bank account. He had an expensive lifestyle to fund, and some even more expensive habits. Sabbar drifted off to sleep with a smile, excited with what the new day would bring.

The dhow had made good time during the night. And, just after ten in the morning, it had reached a point opposite the headland at Inhambane, where Sabbar and his father had taken the ski boat the year before for a two week fishing trip. The Dhow was only a couple of kilometres off shore and was running smoothly at ten knots through long swells, the wind blowing fair from almost directly aft. They had prospected these same waters, mornings and evenings, with feather jigs and Rapalas, his father disappointed that they caught no sailfish. But Sabbar was happy enough with the many sierra and albacore and the lone wahoo that came to his trolled lures.

The next day was hot, the dying and now-erratic breeze shifting to due east – blowing its hot breath across the deck. The night was even hotter, too muggy to sleep. The following day, no better. The first thrill of being at sea in the same kind of ship that his ancestors had probably used to carry their trade goods had, by now, completely worn off.

Despite his protests the captain of the dhow had taken his iPhone from him shortly after they had loaded the cargo. He was not the skipper with the gold teeth that his father had told him was the leader of the fighters he would be joining, but a short, rank-smelling, Bangladeshi who had demanded the phone in grunts that Sabbar realised was language. The Bangladeshi hadn't noticed Sabbar's new generation Apple Watch though. But although he tried, he couldn't access any communications at sea and even the faint signal was too erratic for picking up his e-mails, much less surfing the Net.

That evening they had to use the diesel engine again as the wind had petered out completely, and the fumes rolling across the deck had made him sick. He was exhausted and turned in early after refusing the meal of goat curry and rice the sailors seemed to think was as good as a Big Mac and fries. It was night three of what Sabbar reckoned would be a long week's journey.

They came for him at dawn.

While the two Ahmeds held him down, Jimmy slipped Sabbar's Apple watch off his wrist and strapped it on his own. He'd wanted it the first time he saw it, even though it would be next to useless in the Somali back-of-beyond – no fucking broadband anywhere. But he didn't plan to stay there forever – just until he made a decent score. Then, as Sabbar came out of his deep sleep and started to struggle realising something was very wrong, Jimmy cut his throat. And watched as Sabbar put his hands to his neck, smirking when he saw the quizzical look flash across Sabbar's face as he saw his life blood pool into his palms. They dragged the body onto the deck and slipped it over the side into the water. Shark food. The two seamen who saw them, turned away. They knew it wasn't worth their own lives to show the slightest bit of interest.

Jimmy felt nothing. The leader had told them to leave no loose ends and Sabbar was a very loose end. And anyway he wanted the watch.

In Somalia, Gold Teeth, who was at the underground fortress supervising the digging of a new chamber to house the bomb, received confirmation the next day that all was on track and the loose end dealt with. The message, which had passed by radio phone from the dhow to a base receiver in Mogadishu, then through various servers in East Africa and back, had finally reached him by ancient, untraceable, camel courier. He was pleased. There were only a few witnesses to get rid of now. Khan senior, the most important, but he could wait until he eventually came back to Somalia looking for his son who, he would assume, was now a jihadi. The two Ahmeds and Jimmy he could probably rely on to keep quiet, but he trusted nobody – they would all be given suicide missions. Soon, only he and the ultimate leader would know about the bomb. But only he would know where it was, and that would make him all powerful.

Gold Teeth was not to know that a day after Sabbar Khan was murdered there would be a tremor under the sea a hundred kilometres east of where his body floated in the gentle swells. A tremor that would start the undersea landslide that would cause the tsunami. Not a devastating Thailand-type wave of 2004, but more a superfast storm surge.

Like a giant ripple-ring in a pond, this surge sped to all corners of the Indian Ocean. When it reached the body of Sabbar Khan, floating face down on the surface as if he was goggling for fish below, it picked him up and carried him off. The Tsunami carried the macabre body surfer for nearly seventy kilometres until, finally losing force, it almost gently deposited Sabbar just above the high water mark on the long sandy beach at Macuti lighthouse, Beira.

The body was found the next day and reported to the local police. It was naked except for a pair of cut-off jeans. In the back pocket of the jeans that Jimmy hadn't bothered to go through, was a South African passport in the name of Sabbar Khan. This was not a fake passport, it had been genuinely issued by the Department of Internal Affairs, Pretoria.

Braaivleis

It was Oom Mackie's birthday and half the town and most of the local farmers had taken the day off for his annual bash. The braai fires were lit in the early afternoon and guests were welcome any time from midday to around midnight, when Mackie had stumbled to his bed under the effects of his homemade *mampoer*. It was also school holiday time and Mackie's birthday had become something of a family event – the kids stuffed themselves on the best braai in the district, and the men did likewise on Mackie's copious booze supply, while their wives looked after both kids and men and made sure they didn't totally disgrace the family.

Oom Mackie was a popular host and always did his guests proud. There were two sheep on spits, piles of T-bone steaks and dozens of 'puff adders' – flat, coiled lengths of *boerewors* made to the old Jagter family recipe, sizzling in braai grids on a massive braaivleis fire. There were large iron pots of *stywe pap* and *sous*, and yellow mielies and just-baked *roosterkoek* with lashings of farm butter melting into them. The booze supplied was ample, if limited to Mackie's personal taste – a choice of Castle Lager in ice-filled tubs, Klipdrift brandy and coke, and later for the brave, shots of the special peach brandy that Mackie made himself. If you wanted anything else you had to bring it yourself.

Ma's sister, Oom Mackie's wife, Tannie Hester, planned the whole event. She and Mackie's eldest son and farm partner, Stefan, and his wife Sanette, did a lot of the preparation and work during the day.

Tannie Hester was famous in the district for her baking and she herself was a walking advertisement of the fruits of her endeavours. Where my mother had been slim and pretty, with bright eyes and a quick, always-looking-for-excitement way about her, Tannie Hester was soft and well-padded and content with life. At the annual braai she was the officer-in-charge. Overseeing Sanette who ran the kitchen and at the same time supervising Mackie's foreman and braai master, Petrus, and Petrus's two sons who were in charge of turning the sheep on the spits and making sure the braai meat didn't burn – and also that they remained sober until the guests had eaten.

Cook, me, Mauretia, Carolus and Annetjie got there early and helped out where we could. Carolus joined the men at the fires and Cook and I got involved with the important work; helping Stefan, who was on bar duty, bring out the booze and glasses and fill the tubs with beer and ice. Mauretia and Annetjie disappeared into the kitchen to help Sanette where later, as happens at all country braais, the women would congregate for a party of their own, while the men stood around outside at the fires drinking and talking bullshit, getting louder and louder as the day and night wore on. The kids would run around until they were exhausted and eventually, when their parents were about to leave, would be slowly rounded up from wherever they'd crashed.

I was surprised when Captain Mpanza arrived with Sergeant Gugu, but not so much. Race relations in South Africa have come a long way since Independence even in the depths of formerly hardline right wing country areas and, especially, among the younger generation. And anyway,

Mackie had always been the leftie in the district. One of the early Democratic Party supporters, he'd even stood for the old Apartheid parliament for the Progressive Party a couple of times against the local National Party candidate, losing his deposit both times. Mackie pointed Sergeant Gugu towards the kitchen and the women, and brought Mpanza round to the braai fires where he introduced him. He was made welcome. Word had spread quickly how effectively and bloodlessly he had handled the trouble at Verwoerd's Koppie and had overnight gained local respect amongst the farming community for not shooting the bunch of AWB idiots. Especially as they probably deserved it. Even a couple of the farmers present who had moonlighted as AWB warriors and had been at the 'battle' sheepishly shook his hand.

Chesney, in the meantime, had gathered round him a group of the unattached young women who hadn't joined the coven in the kitchen, and was chatting them up en masse. They'd never seen anyone quite like him in the district and he was telling them the story about how he had got his surname. I'd heard it a dozen times and still enjoyed the reaction it got.

He claimed that he was quite possibly, even probably, the direct descendent of the famous explorer Captain Cook. He said that the story was passed down through the family that the family name had come about when one of his female ancestors, a beautiful Indonesian slave girl (and here he always batted his big blue eyes when telling the story), was sneaked aboard the captain's ship, *Resolution*, one night in 1776. The ship was moored in Cape Town harbour on what was Cook's third and last voyage, waiting for the rest of the fleet to catch up. The captain had been wandering about the town when the slave girl caught his eye and, nine months later, when the captain had long sailed away, a blue-eye boy was born. This boy was known as Cook as was his own family thereafter.

He went on to say that one branch of the family didn't

believe this particular story, but that it had been not Cook himself who had sired the boy, but most certainly one of his crew. Cook always ended the story by saying:

'Of course it all could be total bullshit. It's even more likely that it wasn't Captain Cook or anyone from his ship, but some bloody ordinary ship's cook from God know's where.'

At about three o'clock the food was ready and everyone was summonsed by the clank-a-clank clang of the old cracked farm bell to the long wooden trestle tables that had been set up on the lawn next to the braai fires. The tables groaned with food, and, as this was an extra special birthday for Oom Mackie (his 65th), gallon jugs of red wine. Everyone was talking about what they were calling The Battle of Verwoerd's Koppie as well as the rock concert afterwards, and when they heard that Cook, Mauretia and I, had actually been there, wanted to know the details blow for blow. We naturally embellished it all, especially the part where Captain Mpanza had told Mkhize, the #VerwoerdMustFall leader, to shut up. Mpanza sat there shaking his head.

I'd brought with me the gun that Pa had left in his will to Oom Mackie. I'd put it in a new leather gun case and wrapped it in fancy gift paper. Mauretia had helped with the ribbons and bows. Once everyone had finished their first plate of food, I got up, called for silence and, after a short speech, presented it to Oom Mackie. I'd told the assembled company, (who all knew Pa) that the gun was Pa's prize possession and he had willed it to his best friend, Oom Mackie. I told them that the gun was an antique, full-stock model 1903 Mannlicher-Schoenauer 6.5x54mm rifle, that Ma's grandfather Jacobus had bought as new. And who used to say that if only it had come out a few years earlier, and he'd been able to carry it in the second Anglo-Boer War, the Boers would have won. It had been lovingly looked after and carefully maintained but it was not of great commercial value as its barrel had been replaced a couple of times during its long history because of the thousands of rounds that had been shot through it. Light-weight and reckoned to be the most popular hunting weapon in Africa up to WWII, it was bolt action, weighed three kilograms, had very little recoil, a flat 'butter knife' bolt and double-set trigger.

Mackie was almost overcome with sentiment – I didn't think the tears that welled up in the corners of his eyes were solely the result of what he had already had to drink. He replied with some recollections of the hunting trips he had made with Pa and what a fine shot Pa was – nearly as fine as Mackie himself. He said he'd always coveted the Mannlicher and that we should, as soon as everyone had second or third helpings of braai and Tannie Hester's pudding, go and fire off some rounds to see if it still shot as well as Pa claimed it did. Mackie sent one of his staff to the back of the farm to set up some makeshift targets. But, half-an-hour later, just as we got up from the tables to test out the gun on the targets, a thunderstorm blew up, and the thunder and lightning drove us inside. Night had fallen by the time the storm was over and by then we were a little too tanked up to shoot, even if we could see anything.

It's spooky how big events can turn on small axles – I didn't know it at the time, but that thunderstorm saved my life.

Brainstorm

It came to me in a flash when I woke up back home the next morning. *Fok*, how could I have been so slow? All the *kak* going on at the koppie must have addled my brains. Or least taken my mind off what was really important. *De la Rey is buried under Verwoerd.* It's been staring me in the face since the moment I arrived here. Verwoerd is the koppie … not the man … or the man lying in his grave in the Hero's Acre in Pretoria. The bomb must be hidden somewhere in or around the koppie. It's just the sort of thing Pa would have cooked up – hide an atom bomb right next to his doorstep. In plain sight.

But where the hell on the koppie could they hide a bomb that size? Shit, I am stupid. It *has* to be the old mine. And then … Christ! Bolton and his pals were camped there right now. What if they weren't prospecting at all? What if they were looking for the bomb too? What if they'd found the cursed thing? What if they're already gone?

I jumped out of bed and quickly dressed. Then I woke Cook and told him what I'd worked out. There was no time to lose, the bomb could still be in the mine.

I opened the gun safe and handed Cook Pa's R1 and a couple of clips of ammo. I grabbed the 9mm and holster and checked to see if it was loaded before I stuck it behind my belt. We took the bakkie and I put foot for Verwoerd's Koppie.

I stopped in a cloud of dust next to the fence between the koppie and the farm border. We hopped over the fence and headed for Bolton's camp. Thank fuck it was still there. The Land Cruiser Campervan was parked in the same place. The three igloo-type tents were there too. I noticed one of them had been slashed open – it looked like by a panga. The generator and tools were still there, even Bolton's lean-to and his beach lounger. What was missing was the red box with the explosives – maybe he'd been busy prospecting and used them all up.

The camp however was deserted. Cook pointed to heavy tyre tracks in the sand. Somebody had recently been hauling something in or, possibly, out. A heavy load.

There was no sign of anyone. It was dead still. But then a vulture flapped overhead and landed fifty metres away. It flapped up into the air again as a jackal drove it away from whatever it was eating. Cook and I went to investigate. The jackal ran off carrying what looked like a hand. A human hand.

We'd found the prospector. He was lying half-buried in a hasty grave. There was a foul buzzing of flies and the once-smelled, never-forgotten, stench of rotting human flesh. He'd been dead for a couple of days. I said to Cook: 'Well, I guess we've found Bolton.'

But there was no sign of any of the workers – alive or dead – who were supposedly joining him. Just the tyre tracks.

'Fuck, they've found the bomb already and are gone. Shot Bolton when they left. They could be anywhere. Maybe even out of the country by now.'

I gave Cook the bakkie keys and told him to hurry into town and bring Mpanza back right away. He'd need to see this. Obviously. Meantime I headed towards the koppie and the mine workings to see if I could find anything.

Cook drove off and I scrambled up to the entrance to the

old mine. It was no longer sealed shut with rocks and rubble, but gaped open. Looked like I was too late. It was difficult to climb through – an old mine cart on rail tracks was blocking the entrance. I noticed heavy drag marks leading to the same type of tyre tracks we'd seen at Bolton's camp. Something heavy had been off-loaded from the cart onto another vehicle. I squeezed past the cart and into the mine shaft itself and walked right to the end. It was pitch black and I couldn't see much by the light of my cell phone. I should have brought a torch. But in the dim light there was no sign of any bomb. The shaft was completely empty. Fuck. It *is* gone.

I stumbled back to the entrance, blinking in the sun, then made my way back to Bolton's camp.

I'd walked about ten paces down the hill towards the fence when the first shot hit me in the shoulder, spinning me around. Jesus! I'd been shot once before and the pain is excruciating. But what you don't reckon with though, is the fear. The realisation that you might already be dead but don't know it yet.

The second shot hit me in the back of the knee, smashing the kneecap on the way out. The shock and pain knocking me flat. I fell like a poleaxed steer into the gully running next to the path, the third shot missing my head by millimetres, chips of rock from the ricochet pockmarking my face. I was safe for the moment, hidden from the shooter.

A red mist curtained my eyes. I was about to pass out. I mustn't pass out. I'd be dead if I did. Through the agony, with my good arm, I reached behind my belt for the 9mm. Fuck, I'd left it in the bakkie. Taken it off before I sat down in the driver's seat and stowed it in the cubbyhole. I hadn't been expecting trouble like this. I heard the slither of boots approaching down the gravel track … and then as if from far away, a voice.

'Koekemoer. Glad you could come. I thought you would.

I'm just here to tidy up – and you're part of the mess.'

It was Fat Face the barman from the Royal.

Then through the pain, I finally twigged. 'You're Rooikat? Or should I say, van Niekerk? But you look nothing like your army photo. But then you switched that, didn't you?'

He laughed. 'That was easy enough to do, just slipped into the old personnel archives in Pretoria headquarters one night and swopped photos with a poor *poephol* who died on the border. Smit, I think his name was.'

Then another revelation, shit, I really was slow. The accent. A hint of a Malmesbury bray.

'And the bakkie with the bull bar? You planted that too. Then phoned the cops?'

'Ja, just a spur of the moment plan. And it worked good.'

The pain was getting worse and worse but I knew I had to keep talking.

'And my Pa? Why did you kill him. And the others – Coetsee, Pienaar, Smit and, what's his name? Bezuidenhout?'

'You think the Colonel and the others would have let me sell the bomb to a bunch of outsiders? Ha! That'd be the day. That bomb belonged to the Volk. Your Pa, now he was a true patriot, and the others were under his thumb.'

Van Niekerk spat, took out a smoke, lit it and took a drag. I was drifting in and out of consciousness. The pain was coming in waves of agony. I almost wished the bastard would put an end to everything but something kept me going.

'But you weren't?'

'Weren't what?'

'A true patriot.'

'No I'm a new South African. A paid-up member of the Rainbow Nation. I'd sell it to anyone who had the money.'

'So who did you sell it to?'

'You haven't guessed? Van Niekerk laughed. 'I sold it to a bunch of terrorist ragheads. Al Shabbab they call themselves.'

'Are you *fokken* mad? They're crazy enough to use it – on England or Israel or Kenya, maybe even us! They'll kill hundreds of thousands of innocent people.'

Van Niekerk laughed again. 'Do I look like I give a fuck. They're nothing to me. I'll be sipping a brandy and coke on a beach somewhere far away.'

Van Niekerk took another pull on his smoke. I knew I was dead when he finished it. Then he flicked it away and lifted his rifle and aimed it at my head.

'Anyway, that's enough talking *kak*. It's time to say *totsiens*. Give my regards to your …'

I heard the distant crack of a rifle and flinched as a bullet split the air over my head.

Why wasn't I dead? How had van Niekerk missed? Or was he just toying with me?

I looked up and saw van Niekerk swaying on his feet – there was a neat, red, hole drilled right between his eyes. He was dead on his feet and after taking a half step, collapsed in a heap. I got in the final word as I watched him give a last couple of kicks:

'You should have read the health warning on the pack – smoking will kill you.'

Then I passed out, but only for a moment. When I came to, nothing was moving except for the breeze in the grass and van Niekerk's cigarette. I watched as it was blown along and over the edge of the ridge he had been standing and on. I saw it pick up speed and then come to a stop against a long thin green snake that zig-zagged toward the mine tunnel. I hadn't noticed the snake before. I saw the tip of the cigarette glow as the breeze picked up and was surprised when the snake burst into pretty sparks – like the ones a kid's sparkler makes at Guy Fawkes. I suddenly realised what was happening.

'*Fok*, that isn't a snake, that's a fuse! A fuse that probably leads to a stick or six of dynamite.'

I hadn't seen any dynamite when I was in the tunnel, but that's not what I'd been looking for.

Somehow I had to move quick and get to the fuse and put it out. I tried, I really tried. My shoulder was agony but it still worked, my leg though just wouldn't take my weight, and the pain made me puke when I tried to drag it behind me. I did the best I could in the circumstances, and made myself small in the bottom of the gully, pressing my face into the ground with my hands cradled over the back of my head, like we'd been trained to do during an artillery barrage. Bend down, put your head between your knees, and kiss your arse goodbye, was how the instructor had explained it.

There was an almighty bang and then a storm of falling rock. This explosion was followed by a massive earthquake – the ground shuddering and heaving and roaring. It seemed to go on for minutes, I'd never heard or felt anything like it.

It was the mine cart that saved my life. The mine cart and Oom Mackie. The dynamite had been hidden under the cart at the mouth of the tunnel, and when it exploded, had blown the heavy cart metres into the air and on top of me. Luckily its ends wedging tight into the sides of the gully before it crushed me flat. It had acted as a solid steel roof when half the mountain came down on top of me.

Everything was hazy after that. The pain was something else. I remember Oom Mackie urging a couple of workers:

'C'mon *mense*, put your backs in it.'

And then the ambulance crew was strapping me to a board and sticking a brace around my neck. I heard Captain Mpanza saying: 'No, wait. I have to talk to him first.'

And then leaning close to my head: 'What happened Koekemoer?'

I told him through the pain: 'They've got the bomb. Rooikat was here.' Then someone stuck a needle in me and almost immediately I felt no pain. My one last thought was that if this was death, I'd felt worse.

I woke up in hospital. It felt like days had passed but they told me it was only one night. Mauretia was sitting in a chair on one side of my bed and Chesney on the other. They were just finishing the last of the grapes she'd brought for me when she noticed my eyes had opened. Her smile of relief and happiness was worth getting shot for. Cook gave a little nod hello.

Captain Mpanza was my next visitor. He didn't bring any grapes, just a whole heap of questions. The surgeon who'd patched me up had said that except for the bullet wounds, one of which had gone straight through my shoulder without hitting anything important, and one that took off half my kneecap, I had suffered remarkably little damage. He'd told Mpanza that there was nothing wrong with my vocal chords but he should talk to me quickly, before shock or post-operative pain kicked in to when I needed heavy duty pain relief. The surgeon reckoned that I'd probably be able to talk for an hour and no more. I think I laughed at him.

I told Mpanza everything I could remember and everything I knew about Pa, the bomb, the right-wing plot and Rooikat, selling the bomb to Al Shabbab. I thought it was possible the bomb was still in the country, although unlikely – but maybe he should tell Pretoria the whole story and see if they could intercept it, either in the country or outside. I told him about Bolton and his links to Makatini and van Schalkwyk and their links to some shadowy, and probably shady, Indian businessmen, and one in particular, called Khan. The Captain kept silent through this, taking it all down in an old-fashioned wirebound notepad. When we were finished I told Cook to go with Mpanza out to the farm and take him through all our own investigation notes and 'murder room' and also show him the documents in Pa's filing cabinet, the key to which was hidden on top of the stuffed kudu head on the wall.

By the time we were about finished, I realised the surgeon wasn't bullshitting – it was beginning to feel like someone was pushing red-hot pokers through my knee and shoulder. The Captain saw me wince and got up to leave.

'Don't leave town anytime soon,' was his parting shot.

Mercifully, a nurse was standing by with a drip and some serious happy juice. They kept me half-out for the next three or four days with some very strong dope. When I came round again, Mauretia was still sitting in the chair next to me and still eating grapes. Not Cook though. Mauretia said he'd had to go back to Cape Town as a new case had come up and the hospital bills weren't going to get paid if we were both sitting on our arses relaxing.

I was feeling semi-normal again and they were letting me see visitors. Captain Mpanza came back and, a little afterwards, Oom Mackie.

Mpanza told me that Mackie had shot van Niekerk (aka Rooikat), with the antique Mannlicher-Schoenauer I'd presented him with at the braai. He shot him from four hundred metres away and that it was a helluva shot with such an old gun and open sights. And that I owed my life to my uncle's prowess.

Mpanza said he thought van Niekerk had come back to reseal the mouth of the mine shaft with the dynamite he had packed under the rail cart. Probably dynamite that had been left over at Bolton's camp. And I had arrived just as he was about to set it off. His shooting me was probably not pre-planned but a chance encounter. An unlucky chance encounter on van Niekerk's part. When Mackie had shot him instead, van Niekerk's cigarette had set off the explosion which caused not only a major rockfall in the mine shaft but had the snowball effect of Verwoerd's head, already weakened from Mkhize's efforts, to crash into the valley. It was the 'earthquake' I had felt.

They'd found van Niekerk's body too. They'd had to dig him out with earthmoving equipment. He was hardly recognisable as human but Cook's pal Sakkie had come up trumps again and identified him through army dental records. DNA also matched him as the first shooter. And they were going to make double sure that it was really him by doing a further DNA match through his young son who was with his mother in Botswana. They'd also dug up his rifle and, mangled as it was, Constanble Witbooi said that it was the same as the one Rooikat had carried. So he was positive we no longer had a killer on the loose.

Mpanza also said that he had reported my findings about the bomb, and our hypothesis on the sale of the bomb to Islamic terrorists, to the high-ups in Pretoria police headquarters the day I after I'd been shot. However, he'd heard nothing back from them so far. Not even a request for further information.

Oom Mackie brought more grapes – this time I actually managed to eat a few before Mauretia got to them. He told me that because the thunderstorm had interrupted his intention to test the old Mannlicher on the improvised targets at the farm, he might as well do the job properly and shoot proper targets at the old shooting range next to the koppie. Sighting in the rifle, at correctly measured-out distances, he had just set up the paper targets and was preparing to fire when he'd heard the shots from a little way off and saw me dive or fall into the donga. He'd recognised me by my shock of white-blonde hair. He said he hadn't recognised the shooter from that distance but when he saw him walk up to where I'd fallen, light a cigarette and start talking to me, he knew I was still alive. But when the shooter lifted his rifle Mackie said he reckoned he better shoot quick himself.

Mackie told me it was a stroke of luck that he had been there – he'd planned to drive round to my place and thank me for the rifle but he decided to try it out first. I said that was indeed a stroke of luck, like his fluke shot hitting van Niekerk between the eyes from four hundred metres.

Oom Mackie snorted.

'Fluke? Rubbish! When I saw van Niekerk raise his rifle I zeroed in on him instead of the targets I'd set up. And I shot him. I tell you, I've never seen anything like it. I shot him and then I ran towards where he'd been standing over you. I had about a hundred metres to go when and the mountain fell down! I thought you were dead for sure this time, buried under tons of rock. But if it's one thing I know about you Jaco, you're a lucky bastard. Me and the cops dug you out with some old shovels we found nearby. That bloody cart saved your life.'

'And you Oom Mackie. And you.'

Oom Mackie left ten minutes later still muttering about his 'fluke' shot and ignorant, ungrateful nephews.

ELEVEN

Return to the fort

IT WAS BARELY A WEEK since Khan had learnt of the murder of his son. He and the six-man US army ranger team were strapped into the nylon hanging seats of the Sikorsky MH60 Blackhawk as it skimmed silently over the southern Somali semi-desert. Their field of vision was restricted to the two gunners' windows but it didn't mean much. It was night and the only things they saw were the occasional flash of lights from an isolated settlement or lonely cattle herder's camp fire. They were flying blind, guided only by GPS and radar. Khan didn't know it, but the chopper he was riding was one of those used in the raid against Osama bin Laden back in 2012. Its twin engines and special four blade rotor sounded more like the whispering-death of a black mamba streaking through tall grass, than any chopper he'd ever heard.

They'd taken off from the northern Kenya army base in Mandera County – heading north-west of Uxdur, Somalia. Destination the old fort at the coordinates Khan had taken on his last visit.

It had all happened so quickly. From the notification by the local police that the Mozambican authorities feared that the body they'd found washed up on the shore was his son Sabbar, to this bizarre flight in the dead of the African night – all was a blur. The confirmation at the run-down shack of a mortuary in Beira, the flight home with his son's body, the simple Muslim funeral, it had all gone by in a flash. The first meeting with the American ambassador, the several follow-ups with shadowy CIA operatives, the last with an older man who had flown in specially from Washington, he could hardly remember.

His friends and business colleagues worried about him. He overheard one old friend at the funeral saying that no-one should be so calm in the face of such overwhelming grief. But he didn't tell his friend that his grief was spent the moment he saw his youngest son's body and that what he had felt since was rage. Ice-cold rage that focused him on the single-minded goal of revenge. Revenge on the bastard who had murdered Sabbar. Revenge on Al Shabbab, on al-Qaeda, on the world. But most of all revenge on himself.

The security man, Aziz, had got him the appointment with the Americans. His hidden 'affiliations' were strong enough to get him in to see the ambassador himself. They met at the embassy in Pretoria. Aziz as chauffeur, drove him straight past the security guards at the gates and into the underground car park used only by senior embassy staff. They were ushered to a bay near the lifts and met by two large US Marine guards with stripes on their sleeves. The guards frisked both of them and ran a metal detector over their suits. The meeting was held in the Ambassador's office and the only people attending were Khan and Aziz, the Ambassador, and two young men who were like caricatures of government agents, with crew cut hair and black suits. Both had American flag badges pinned on their lapels.

At first the Americans didn't believe what Khan had to say. He began with the theft of the South African atom bomb back in 1989, and then he told them about buying the bomb from an ex-Apartheid regime operative and then selling it on and delivering it. The story took some time to tell and Khan saw the Americans' eyes glaze over. One of them asked him sceptically, 'And who did you deliver it to Mr. Khan? And where?'

'To a ship's captain who works for Al Shabbab. At sea off the port of Maputo.'

The agent perked up a little.

'Al Shabbab? Huh, and who was this captain guy?'

'I thought at first he just worked for Al Shabbab but later I realised he was much more – one of their top leaders. I'd met him a couple of times, once before off the coast of Kenya, and the second, at an old fort in Somalia when we put the deal together.'

'And what was this guy's name, Mr. Khan?'

'He didn't give me a name.'

'He didn't give you a name! Well can you describe him then?'

Khan described the ship's captain as best as he could – the nose, the dark skin, the gold teeth. The second agent tapped this information into his laptop and then showed Khan thumbnails of a dozen faces.

'Is he one of these?'

Khan went through each thumbnail carefully, most were somewhat indistinct but one in particular caught his eye.

'It could be him. Can you blow the photograph up a little?'

The agent did as he was asked.

'Yes. Not the greatest picture, but yes. That's the man I met.'

'His name is Saqr. We've been looking for him for a long time. He's near the top of our watch list. So do you know where this guy is now, Mr. Khan? And this A-bomb of yours, where is it now?'

Khan winced as he heard his name drawled out as 'can' but didn't let it show.

'I assume both are at the fort. The whole thing is underground. We met in a cave they'd dug out under the fort's old walls.'

'And where exactly is this fort?'

Khan reached into his pocket and held out a slip of paper. 'These are the co-ordinates.'

The American looked at the paper and tapped into his laptop again.

'Holy moly! That's the old fort north of Xudur – in the middle of nowhere. That's been flattened though. Hardly anything left.'

Khan said, 'Not underground. It looked like you could hide an army there. I didn't get to see much more than the room we met in and the room I slept in, but I sensed there was space for a lot more people.'

'And why are you telling us this Mr. Khan,' the first agent butted in.

'I have my reasons but I don't want to go into them now.' Khan folded his arms.

The young man frowned and said: 'Thank you Mr. Khan. We'll get back to you.'

Khan and Aziz got up and left.

'That was a waste of time, they didn't believe a thing,' Khan said as they got into the car.

'Be patient,' Aziz replied: 'I know these guys, they're not the decision makers. They'll report back to Washington and be back to us within forty-eight hours, possibly even sooner.'

Aziz was right. In was late the next day when he called Khan to tell him the Embassy wanted to see him the next morning and he'd pick Khan up at ten sharp. They went through the same security rigmarole but this time, instead of meeting the Ambassador, they were ushered into a conference room. Seated at a boardroom table were the two agents who'd questioned Khan two days before, and an older man Khan thought he recognised – maybe from TV news or a news magazine story.

One of the young men got up. 'Mr. Khan, Mr. Aziz, please meet Mr. Armstrong. He's the director of the agency for the Middle East and Africa.'

Armstrong looked a lot like the younger men, with a crew cut and black suit, but thirty years older. He had bags under his eyes. Khan thought, probably from the result of the weight of the world he carried on his shoulders. That, and the long overnight flight from Joint Base Andrews, Washington DC.

Armstrong spoke. 'Mr. Khan, would you please repeat the story you told my colleagues the day before yesterday.'

Khan obliged. Covering the exact same ground as he had before. When he was finished Armstrong thanked him.

'I needed to hear it directly from you. It's quite a story. I think I just about buy most of it, and satellite surveillance pictures we took yesterday also confirm much of what you say. We took infrared shots and radioactive readings and they don't lie. There's definitely a whole warren of tunnels and larger spaces under the fort. And the heat readings say maybe even a whole bunch of people. And even some signs of radioactivity in one of the spaces. But …'

'But?' Khan's face hardened.

'I find the part about the bomb hard to swallow. I checked with our guy at the International Atomic Energy Agency and he said the bomb part was impossible. He'd been part of the team that supervised the Apartheid government's destruction of their nukes and said there was no way one could have slipped through.'

At this point Aziz spoke up:

'Sir, I can corroborate there was a bomb, but whether Saqr has it or not, you have to believe Mr. Khan.'

'Okay, okay. What is important is stopping this Saqr guy. And if he actually has a bomb … Christ Almighty, we better stop him, and quickly. But tell me Mr. Khan, if you actually sold this terrorist an A-bomb why shouldn't I grab your sorry ass and ship it to Gitmo?'

'Gitmo?'

'Guantanamo Bay, where we put the bad guys.'

Khan answered. 'Because you want Saqr nearly as much as I do. Because he murdered my son. I want to look into his eyes as he realises he is about to die. For that last pleasure and for my son I'm happy to die too.'

'But I could just order in the jets and bomb the shit out of his hideaway with or without you.'

'You could, Mr. Armstrong but how could you be sure you got Saqr? He might not be at home when your F16s come knocking. But I, and only I, can guarantee it.'

Armstrong was sceptical. 'Guarantee it, how?'

Khan tapped his forehead. 'I've got the code sequence to arm the A-bomb. He doesn't. Without the codes the bomb is just about useless and he knows it.'

Armstrong shrugged. 'Yeah, that's if there's really a bomb. So what's your plan?'

Khan laid out the cold-blooded plan he had so carefully worked out over the past several days. Armstrong thought it was audacious but still had his doubts.

'Sounds like it could work, but I'll be honest with you Mr. Khan. I don't trust you. I think it would be better to take our chances that we catch Saqr in his hole and if he's not there, too bad. And as you said, if there is a bomb there, without the codes it's next to useless. We'll get him sooner or later. Sorry, I can't call out a strike on a …'

Khan interrupted him. 'I have something else for you that

may change your mind. But I'm prepared to talk to you only.'

Armstrong, who had got to his feet and was about to leave, hesitated.

'Okay, I've flown all this way I might as well hear you out. You two guys – can you get yourselves lost for a while? And take Mr. Aziz with you.'

The young agents escorted Aziz out of the room. Armstrong turned back to Khan.

'Okay My Khan, shoot. I'm all ears.'

Khan had spent a lifetime in hard bargaining. He had, early in his career, learnt the value of not showing all his cards in any negotiation. This was the most important one of his life and he had not changed his philosophy.

'I can give you Ayman al-Zawahiri too.'

Armstrong was silent for a moment but Khan could guess what was going through his head. Something like: 'Jesus, this raghead in an expensive suit can lead me to the most wanted man in the world. Bin Laden's replacement. Now what would President Trump think about that – he'd be "so, so happy" he'd probably invite me round for a selfie in front of those gold doors of his. And make me director of the whole damned agency!'

Armstrong's face was expressionless. 'And how would you do that Mr. Khan?'

'Who do you think paid me twenty million dollars for the bomb, some gold toothed barbarian in Somalia? I can give the bank transaction paths and also my links on how to contact al-Zawahiri direct.'

Armstrong didn't hesitate for an instant.

'Okay Mr. Khan. You've got a deal.'

The Blackhawk hovered just above the valley floor two low mountain ranges away from the fort. The six US Army Rangers and Khan were dressed in desert camouflage. The rangers were carrying M4 assault rifles, Khan was unarmed. All had small backpacks, the rangers' contained two days' emergency rations and water, Khan's had only a change of clothing. The mission was expected to last just twelve hours and Khan wasn't planning on coming back. The group dropped out of the chopper, bracing their knees to absorb the metre or so fall. They were already on the move when the chopper rose and set off back to base camp in Kenya.

The men spread out in the usual fire-team formation, Khan closely shadowing the second man in from the right flank. There was no talking. There had been none on the chopper either. Anything they had needed to say was said at the pre-operations briefing back at base. The rangers had each memorised the route in intensive pre-mission training and although they all had maps of the terrain there was no need to consult them. Even the miniscule glow of a shaded, red-lensed penlight could give them away.

They had about a two kilometre trek in the darkness but half the night to make it in, so there was no hurry. They moved slowly and silently up the slope of hill, scanning with night glasses the second valley they reached. They moved on only when they were sure there were no surprises waiting for them below. Nobody waiting in ambush, no sheep or cattle or wild animals that would give away their position to flush out. They crossed the valley floor and began the ascent up the next hill. This was much steeper than the first and when one of them kicked a rock which rolled noisily down the hill they all froze instantly. And waited in position for a full half hour in case there was any reaction to the noise.

When they reached the crest of the hill they ducked down – they weren't the only combatants that carried night glasses. Slowly, slowly, they fanned out along the ridge, the point man risking a quick scan of the fort nearly a kilometre away. There was nothing moving there, nothing that would give away that there was anyone there, or ever had been. The point man put away the glasses and like the others waited for dawn.

In the half darkness just before the sun broke the horizon, the point man moved back to where Khan was lying next to his minder. When he saw that Khan was awake he pointed to his watch and nodded that it was time to move. Khan reached into his backpack and took out what appeared to be the full dress robes of a middle eastern potentate. Flowing silk robes with a coiled gold rope desert *agal* on his head. This he pulled over his camouflage gear. If the ranger thought this garb didn't go with combat boots, he didn't show it, instead he gave Khan's sleeve a brief tug and held out his hand. Khan looked at him and smiled, then fulfilled his side of the bargain and handed over the memory stick with the information on al-Zawahiri he'd promised to Armstrong. The point man nodded again and went back to his position.

Khan slowly and carefully began to pick his way down the slope towards the fort. It was full dawn when he reached the flat bottom of the small plateau. In the quickening sunlight he looked almost biblical as he strode across the white sands, a slight heat shimmer already rising from the ground. It took Khan nearly an hour to reach the fort; the plateau which looked flat from a distance, was rough and rocky with shallow depressions carved-out by flash flooding during thunderstorm season.

The only living creatures that Khan saw were a couple of desert lizards that scurried away from under his feet and one lone dassie that was already out sunning itself on the edge of one of the deeper dongas. The silence was deafening, broken only occasionally by the distant cackle of guineafowl and the sliding scales of a pair of courting mourning doves. The ground was, however, crisscrossed with tracks of small rodents and lizards and, here and there, the long hosepipe impressions of hunting snakes – a tapestry of the eternal life and death struggle of the night before. He thought that he should keep a close look where he was walking. Now was not the time to step on a puff adder, or heaven forbid, stumble into the path of a homeward bound Egyptian cobra or, worse, a black mamba.

Khan finally reached the fort and walked to the well in the centre of the ruined parade ground and sat down as he had done so before, back against the low wall. And waited.

It took four hours before Saqr's men arrived. It was hot and Khan was sweating beneath the long robes. He was beginning to wish he'd brought more water, the canteen he had was nearly empty. He' had assumed that they'd follow the same routine as before and that someone would appear almost miraculously from the wall in front of him. But it wasn't like that. The first he knew he was not alone was when he heard the click of a gun cocking behind him. He slowly got to his feet and turned, palms raised to shoulder level. He started to say that he had come in peace, when he was hit on the side of the head with a rifle butt.

When Khan came round he was tied, naked, to a chair. His Arab finery, camo gear and boots were piled roughly on the table in front of him. He recognised the room. It was where he and Gold Teeth had met before, plotting the best way to get the bomb to him, where they'd feasted and drank that night and where the young girls were brought in and paraded before them. He remembered the one he'd picked. She was barely more than a child but with eyes that were already dead. He took her to the sleeping quarters and told her to lie down. She obeyed him and lay there like a zombie. He didn't touch her. He wondered what had happened to her – they'd taken her away the next morning when he left.

He wondered how long Gold Teeth would make him wait. Or even if he was at the fort. Maybe he'd already left, moving the bomb to God knows where. Maybe his great plans of revenge would come to nothing and the men who'd knocked him out were not Al Shabbab at all, but merely passing bandits. How the hell was he going to stamp the left boot on the ground which would switch the GPS off and signal the Americans to strike when he was tied up and the boot out of reach? The thoughts made his head hurt and he closed his eyes and drifted back into unconsciousness.

He woke again when they threw a bucket of water into his face. Now Gold Teeth was sitting across the table from him, and next to him was the English fighter he knew as Raafi Saayed Meer and who MI5 called Jihadi Jimmy. He waited until Gold Teeth spoke:

'Mr. Khan, what are you doing here and how did you find us?'

Khan needed desperately to play for time, but even more desperately needed somehow to get hold of his left desert boot which was still on the table. The boot with the direction finder in it.

'Captain, or is it Mr. Saqr? I'm here to give you the codes you need to arm the bomb and I just followed the direction finder to the co-ordinates that I took the last time I was here.'

Gold Teeth didn't blink an eye hearing Khan address him with his real name. Or, at least, the name that was as real as any of the others he went by.

'You took a GPS position? How?'

'Never mind that. I'm here in good faith, at your request, so why am I being treated like this? And I want to see my son.' And then turning to Jihadi Jimmy, 'Raafi, can you tell Sabbar I'm here.'

Jihadi Jimmy opened his mouth to speak but was cut off by Gold Teeth.

'I'm afraid I have bad news for you about your son. He was killed in an attack on a Kenyan military base last week.'

Khan feigned shock and bent his head as if in prayer, then he lifted his head and said, 'He died in the cause of the

Caliphate. *Allahuh Akbar.*'

'*Allahuh Akbar.*'

'*Allahuh Akbar.*' Echoed Jihadi Jimmy and Gold Teeth who continued, 'Mr. Khan, now I want you to tell me how you took our GPS position. And if you passed it on to anyone else.'

Khan nodded his head towards the table.

'In the left boot. In the heel.'

Gold Teeth turned to Jihadi Jimmy. 'Take a look, Raafi.'

Jihadi Jimmy grabbed the left boot and examined it. There was nothing to see on the surface. He took out a lethal-looking hunting knife and poked the tip into the seal between the heel and the sole of the boot and twisted. The heel came off. He picked it up and shook it into his left palm. A small square, flat metal box with a USB port on one end and a car keyring-type on/off button on the other fell into it.

Jimmy looked closely at the device nestled in his palm and said, 'I've seen one like this before, but a bit bigger. It's German and it's accurate to within ten centimetres. This is the best money can buy.'

Khan strained against the tape that bound him, in the vain hope of grabbing the device when Jihadi Jimmy continued 'You switch it off here.'

And then he pushed the button switching it off.

Khan could hardly believe it and hid the sudden flash of triumph that surged through his body.

Captain Bob Lassiter of the United States nuclear-powered SSGN class submarine *Ohio,* and Rear-Admiral David L. Jones Jnr., of the aircraft carrier *Ronald Reagan*, reacted the moment the GPS they were tracking was deactivated. They were parked inside the main sea lane just outside Somali territorial waters and were triangulated one hundred kilometres apart with the western point of the triangle the old fort north of Xudur, four hundred and sixty-five kilometres away. The strike was carefully coordinated. First to be launched, from the submarine, were four satellite-guided Block 4 Tomahawk cruise missiles armed with three 500lb bunker buster warheads flying at just over eight hundred kilometres per hour, E.T.A. approximately thirty-four point nine minutes. Five minutes later, at five minute intervals, sixteen Navy F/A-18 Hornets would take off from the *Ronald Reagan*. E.T.A. five minutes after the last Tomahawk strike. Each Hornet armed with four BLU 2 000lb Bunker Busters.

While these expensive pieces of US military hardware speeded towards the fort, Khan continued his final negotiation. He knew that there were less than thirty-five minutes left in his life, but that he must do everything possible to stay alive during that time. He *had to* live long enough to see the fear in Gold Teeth's eyes when he realised what was about to happen to him.

'Saqr, I have come all this way to give you the codes to arm the bomb.'

Gold Teeth ignored him. Khan spoke more firmly.

'Saqr. I said I've come all this way to give you the codes.'

Gold Teeth turned to Khan and looked at him as if he was less than a cockroach.

'They are irrelevant. I don't need them.'

Khan feigned surprise. 'How so? Without them there is no chain reaction. Without a chain reaction there is no explosion. No Tel Aviv or London obliterated.'

Saqr sneered: 'We have come up with a better plan than wiping out one miserable infidel city in the name of Islam.'

Khan, still not understanding. 'What, use the bomb as a bargaining chip? You'd still need the codes.'

'We don't bargain with unbelievers. No, we destroy them.'

'I still don't see how …'

'We don't want the bomb, we want what's inside it. The

nuclear material. We can make many bombs … dirty bombs that will make uninhabitable dozens of cities, in many countries. We're moving the bomb to Port Merca tomorrow. A Pakistani scientist is going to cut into the outer shell and get the nuclear material out for us. So you see Mr. Khan, you're of no use to us anymore.'

Khan laughed in Saqr's face. 'Tomorrow is too late.'

Gold Teeth bristled. 'What do you mean?'

'The Americans are coming.'

Gold Teeth laughed. 'You think those six puny Americans you came with will save you? You think we didn't see them? We've been watching you since the helicopter dropped you off. We will sweep them up tomorrow morning on our way to Merca. Killing them will be an amusing diversion.'

Khan shook his head 'I told you Saqr. Tomorrow is too late.'

Khan could see he was getting to Gold Teeth so he pushed the needle in further. 'Don't you want to know who's coming? How you're going to die? Or even why?'

Gold Teeth rolled his eyes. 'Go on tell me, I'm shaking in my boots.'

'You murdered my son.' Khan spat out. 'And now I'm murdering you.'

Gold Teeth spoke to Khan as if he was a child.

'I told you. Your son died in Kenya, in the service of the Caliphate. Raafi was with him, he saw it happen.'

Khan replied in a similar patronising tone. 'My son died when you or one of your sons of whores cut his throat on the dhow. Your mistake was not to weigh the body down. It washed up on the beach at Beira.'

Gold Teeth was tiring of the cat and mouse game, 'Your son was excess baggage. And now so are you.' And turning to Jihadi Jimmy, 'Raafi, round up the new recruits, it's time they see the consequences for traitors to the Caliphate.'

It took twenty-five minutes to round them up. Jihadi Jimmy had changed into the black executioner garb so familiar from TV news. He was masked, but Khan could tell it was Jimmy by his posture and walk. The recruits were a motley bunch – some barely in their teens. Children, killers in training. There were a small group of Westerners too. Sunburnt faces and eyes glazed on a mixture of *khat* and strong Somali weed. Come for the adventure and excitement of slaughtering unbelievers in the name of Allah, having deeply studied Islam via social media, and honed their fighting skills playing *Mortal Combat* or *Soldier of Fortune*. Khan scanned their faces. Most were deadpan, but he could see a few that were pinched and afraid, and several that looked like wolf cubs about to savour their first taste of blood.

As Jihadi Jimmy drew a long curved bladed knife and moved to stand over Khan, Gold Teeth stood up and loudly addressed the recruits.

'*Mujahadeen*, I have gathered you here so you can witness the punishment of someone who betrays our brotherhood. A man who defecates on the flag of the Caliphate. Who has spat in the face of Al Shabbab, who has defiled our very …'

Khan knew he was seconds away from death and loudly interrupted Gold Teeth's flow:

'The tracking device.'

Gold Teeth turned to Khan.

'What about the tracking device?'

'The tracking device will call in the bombers.'

'The device is useless.' Gold Teeth spat. 'Raafi here switched it off.'

'Switching it off was the signal.'

Khan could see the sudden fear in Gold Teeth's eyes as he scrabbled around on the table for the tracking device and, when he finally had it in hand, began to prod frantically at the on/off button.

'The signal for your death. They are coming for you Saqr, fire and thunder from the sky. Shock and awe, total annihil …'

There was a blinding flash of light as the first cruise missile struck at a thousand kilometres an hour, straight down the staircase. It exploded in a massive fireball. Causing the almost complete and instant obliteration of everyone in the room. No time to run. No time to duck. Or dive. Or react in any way. Khan had just a micro-second of thought.

'*Allahu Akbar*. Unlike Gold Teeth, the Americans were punctual.'

The six American rangers sat on the hilltop and watched as first the cruise missiles, and then wave after wave of Navy Hornets bombed the old fort and everything under it, into oblivion. All that was left was a deep crater, smoking like a volcano after an eruption. When it was over, the point man gathered the others around him in preparation for the trek back to their pick-up point. Before they left they took one last look at the crater.

'That raghead, whoever he was, was one brave mother,' the point man, spitting in the sand, said finally.

The others grunted in agreement as they moved out.

TWELVE

Loose ends

THEY KEPT ME IN HOSPITAL for another week and it was over a month before I could walk without crutches. The shoulder healed quickly, but the knee had needed a second op. The physio said I wouldn't have a permanent limp but I'd still got a long way to go before I pulled on a rugby jersey again. I told her those days were over long before I was shot.

I'd been recuperating at the farm. A bear with a sore head, useless with a leg that doesn't work. Mauretia, when she wasn't tired of my grouchiness, was there to coax and cajole me into doing the painful exercises the torturer who called herself a physio had devised for me. She lent me her shoulder and her strength and picked me up when I fell. Then one day she left and didn't come back. My meanness and self-pity had driven her away.

For a week I hid myself in a bottle. When I climbed out of it I still felt shit, but a little better quality of shit. Booze had never been a solution for me, no matter how hard I tried to make it one. Over the next few days I pulled myself together. I wouldn't take no from my leg and forced it to bend and work. I pulled myself up when I fell. Often at first, and then less and less as I got stronger.

Cook was back in the Cape, and bugging me to get my arse down there – something about Chinese gangsters and drugs and *perlemoen* poaching. I needed a new case like a hole in the head, which, if truth be told, I was lucky not to have got from Rooikat.

The local TV news was full of the story that a well-known South African Indian businessman, Husain Azhar Khan, father of the Sabbar Khan whose body had recently been found washed up on a beach near Beira in Mozambique, was missing and presumed dead. Khan, who was head of a wealthy and influential Muslim family in South Africa had, the report said, been kidnapped by Al Shabbab radicals in Somalia and may have been caught up in a fight between Al Shabbab and United States-backed East African forces at a fort west of Mogadishu. The report went on to give a pen picture of Khan's business empire and his work for charities and other good causes. Nowhere was there any mention of atom bombs or gun running to various terrorist organisations in the Middle East and Africa.

The news was an overnight sensation with no follow-up stories. It was dropped like a hot potato and disappeared from both national and commercial TV and radio stations, and most of the mainstream press. It was if it had been censored the way it is in banana republics like Zimbabwe. The way press freedom in South Africa was going recently, I wouldn't be surprised if it had been.

Nathi Mpanza drove out to the farm one day to let me know he was leaving Terre'Blanche and that he'd been posted to Pietermaritzburg as chief of police. I gave him my congratulations and asked him how this turn of events had happened. I told him I'd heard through the police grapevine that he'd been blacklisted for life by the President's lackeys over the Pietersburg highway incident with the President's nephew.

He said it was thanks to Cook and me, and our help, that he'd been re-instated. Seems he had been summonsed to the head of police, General Sipho Tshabalala's, office in Pretoria. The man known throughout the service as The Snake. He assumed that he was finally going to be told what actions had been taken over his report about an atom bomb hidden near Terre'Blanche and the likelihood that it was stolen and sold to a radical Islamist terrorist group. He said that he even expected to be given a pat on the back, but he really went there out of curiosity. Instead he was made to wait outside the General's office for an hour. He said he got tired of waiting and told the secretary to tell the General to see him right now or he was leaving.

When Mpanza was finally ushered into the office it was as he'd imagined a court martial in the army would be like – there was General Tshabalala, the commissioner for Gauteng, the Pretoria chief of police and, surprisingly, his old superior for Kwazulu-Natal, General Nkomo, who had signed the order transferring him to Terre-Blanche. They were sitting in a row behind a long table and he was told to sit down on a lone chair placed facing them.

General Tshabalala opened the proceedings, telling Mpanza he was there because of gross dereliction of duty and that the officers in the room were gathered to hear what he had to say and then judge him and decide his fate. He was warned that he faced dismissal from the force at the very least and possibly even criminal charges.

'I tell you Mr. Koekemoer, for a moment I thought I was asleep and in the middle of a nightmare. My old boss Nkomo was grinning at me like a jackal, with spit dripping out of the sides of his mouth.'

'What happened next? What dereliction of duty?'

'Then the General gives me this story that it had come to his notice that there had been an ex-Apartheid agent operating in the Terre'Blanche area called Rooikat, and he had not only committed murder, but apparently had stolen an atom bomb, the whereabouts of which, if it ever existed, was a mystery. And my dereliction of duty was that I was so incompetent that I didn't bother to report it to my senior officers. I protested that I had reported it – to him and to two of the other senior officers currently sitting in the room. And that also I had urgently advised that the bomb was probably being smuggled out of the country at that very moment and that an immediate all-points bulletin should be issued and the border police advised. He started shouting at me, that was a lie, and that they would add lying to superior officers to the charges. He never received any communication from me and nor did any other officer in the room.

'I was just about to answer when the phone on the table rang and General Tshabalala picked it up and crossly yelled that he was busy and to tell whoever it was to damn well phone later.

So loud and angry was the voice at the other end of the phone that if the General had aimed the earpiece of the phone at the wall it would have set the fire-proof curtains alight. The General had by this stage got to his feet and was standing at attention like he was on parade and was saying, "Yes, Mr. President. No, Mr. President. Yes Mr. President. I will Mr. President. Right away Mr. President. You have my word Mr. President. Yes Mr. President … no Mr. …"

Then realising there was no-one at the other end of the line any more he put the phone down and returned to me.

'"You see what you've done Mpanza, It looks like your bomb has been found. By the Americans. In a fort they bombed in Somalia. They're going to return it to us. The President is furious that neither he nor state security were informed about anything. You should have reported this as soon as you knew about it. You are sacked with immediate effect."'

'So they actually sacked you then?' I asked Mpanza.

'They wanted to, Mr. Koekemoer. They *really* wanted to – but I persuaded them there was a better way to handle things.'

Mpanza said it had been hard to hold in his temper but he knew he had to keep ice cool. So he told the General:

'If that's what you really want to do General, that's okay. But you know and I know that you received a detailed report about the stolen bomb, and an urgent recommendation to alert state security and the border service and neighbouring countries services if necessary. I'm sure the President is not going to like reading about it in tomorrow's newspapers. I sent it high priority not only by e-mail but sent hard copies by courier and through registered post.'

Mpanza went on to say the General had blustered and told him that nobody would believe a junior cop who just got fired for incompetence. And it was then that he pulled out the dossier he had prepared for the meeting.

'They will believe this,' he said to the General. 'Verified copies of every e-mail I sent to every address and copies of the full report. Also all acknowledgements from you and the other gentlemen and the records of receipt straight off the official police computer. I have copies prepared to send to the President's office, the press and TV, and state security.'

Mpanza said that it the General's face went a shade of purple and then grey. The other officers were frowning and looking everywhere but at him. Then the General hissed at him, just like his nickname, and asked him what would it take to keep quiet?

Mpanza said he told the General, ''Maritzburg.'

And the General said, 'You want a transfer back to Pietermaritzburg?'

So Mpanza said exactly that, but as head officer at the

'Maritzburg station.

He said the General looked at Mpanza's ex-boss General Nkomo and told him to organise it immediately and Nkomo said he would.

'But there is more Mr. Koekemoer, I then said to the General that also, when Nkomo retires in two years time I want his job as chief of police for all KwaZulu-Natal.'

Mpanza said that really shook his ex-boss up who snorted that he had no plans to retire in two years time, no plans at all.

'So what did you say to that?' I asked.

Mpanza said he just repeated what he wanted. The General's job as chief of police of KwaZulu-Natal in two years time. And at that Tshabalala looked at him and then at Nkomo and then back at Mpanza and said, 'It is done. *Major* Mpanza.'

I thought I wouldn't like to be in the shoes of the cops at the Pietermaritzburg station when Mpanza got there. He had murkier depths than I had realised and I asked him how he'd learnt to play so rough. He smiled.

'When you sleep with cobras you better have a bite like a mamba.'

'Is that an old Zulu proverb?' I asked.

'No, just thought of it now.'

We laughed. It's funny, Mpanza and I came from two different worlds, but we knew the police force and we understood how things worked. I hoped our paths would cross again one day and I had no doubt at all that, sooner rather than later, Mpanza would be the top cop in the whole country. Then, as we Afrikaners say, *die poppies gaan dans.*

Van Schalkwyk also came to see me. He told me that he was sorry but he was withdrawing his offer for *Klein Drinkwater.*

'My partners are not interested in game farming any more,' was what he said. I just laughed.

'Your partners discovered that there is no platinum under

Klein Drinkwater, is what you really mean. I knew that ages ago and was just stringing you along. Your partners never told you what they were really after did they?'

'You're right there …'

'Well let's just say it was something that was indeed underground but not platinum. It's got something to do with your missing partner, Husain Khan, and Somalia. It was all on TV. And all the prospecting and test blasting was only a ruse to keep me away from the area while they collected what they were looking for. And you, van Schalkwyk, were just a stupid fall guy.'

Van Schalkwyk took the opportunity to play the victim, and said he'd been lied to as well. He didn't know it was all a con. He said there were rumours floating about that his partners may have been involved with some Arab terrorists and if he'd known this he wouldn't have tried to take over the farm. He thought it was all a regular business deal.

I didn't let him wriggle off the hook that easily.

'Yes, you bastard. You thought you had inside information that there was a king's ransom in platinum and you could steal the farm off me for a fraction of what it was worth.'

He didn't even have the grace to blush or even look uncomfortable.

'Ag Koekemoer, it was only business, man.'

Then he put out his hand. I shook it, hopefully for the last time, again counting my fingers when he left.

The day before I planned to go back to Cape Town and whatever trouble Cook had got me into, I phoned Eloff and asked him if he had drawn up the papers I had asked him to. He said he had.

'Could you bring them out to the farm this afternoon at about two.'

Eloff arrived on time, just as Carolus and I were due to

ride out for one final inspection of the farm's borders and to check over the calves that had been born. I took the envelope from the lawyer and quickly scanned through the contents. He'd done the job as requested, leaving blanks where I asked him to. I borrowed Eloff's pen and wrote in the percentages and signed it.

Satisfied I said, 'Send the account to the farm. Carolus here will forward it to me in the Cape.'

Eloff said he would, and that it was nice to do business with me and he hoped that I wasn't too angry with him about the deal with van Schalkwyk going sour. I told him that I wouldn't be doing business with him if I was.

Carolus and I rode down the farm track past the koppie where the ambushers had lain in wait. Both of us, I think, felt a prickle at the back of our necks as we rode by. We stopped at the place the big bull had kicked its last. A cow broke out of the thorn bushes nearby, a lanky, brown and white male calf lolloping along at its side. Shortie's son and heir. It was a good time to give Carolus the envelope. I watched as he read it. First frowning in concentration and then looking up at me, smiling.

I said, 'Partners, 50/50. I know no better farmer than you Carolus, you deserve every bit of it. The farm must stay in the family.'

'Thank you boss.'

I shook his hand and said, 'No more of the boss. It's Jaco. We're partners now.'

That night I had to made a difficult but very important phone call. So important I even showered and shaved before I made it. It helps to look your best when you have to phone someone you really care about and explain and apologise to her for being such a total *doos.* Mauretia and I talked for a long time, said things that we probably should have said before. At the end of the call I asked her if she'd come to Cape Town with me. She said she'd think about it. We left it at that.

The next morning the bakkie was packed and I was saying *totsiens* to Carolus and Annetjie and promising to return soon. Annetjie had packed enough *padkos* and coffee for five people. I climbed into the driver's seat and had just turned the ignition when I saw a dust cloud coming up the farm road towards us. The car got closer – it was Mauretia. She was coming to say goodbye. She pulled up under Ouma's pin oak and got out and then opened the boot. She walked towards me, heavy suitcase in hand.

'Do you still want me to come to Cape Town?'

We headed for Terre'Blanche and the turn-off to the national road to Upington, Springbok and the Cape. Mauretia and I smiled at each other as we passed the sign that read 'Welcome to/*Welkom in* Terre'Blanche' in two of the official languages, over which had been spray-painted, in dayglo orange: #VerwoerdMustFall! We drove through town quickly. What a beautiful day it was. A fine day for driving.

As we climbed up the mountain pass I took one last look in the rear view mirror. One final look at Terre'Blanche. It was still there, sitting squat in the sun. Waiting for better days.

Aftermath

The woman had waited for a month, wondering when he was coming back. He'd never been away this long. The police had come and taken a DNA swab from her son. She realised what it was for. Her man wasn't coming back, ever. There was still around four million rands in the account at Standard Bank Botswana and she had joint signing power. She realised with relief that she had no ties now. And she had money. She'd released the python in the rocky veld a few miles outside Gaberone and wished it well. The boy she had sent down to Parow to stay with her mother. She had been planning to leave the man anyway but had been afraid to. Now she could go anywhere, wash the dust of godforsaken Botswana out of her hair forever. Maybe find a tropical island somewhere, really work on her tan. Or maybe Durban.

* * *

Suleiman Abbas was pleased with his farewell gift from the Great Leader – a nearly-new MacBook Pro. He had been given it at dawn when the leader had left and he couldn't wait until his shift came to an end and he could get online. Its battery was said to be second to none and he had a lot to catch up on. He wondered if al-Zawahiri (may Allah protect him) had reached the new hideout yet. It was good he was gone – there were a lot of dangers here now and he would be safer in the new place.

It had taken only four hours for the new Midas supercomputer at Quantico to follow and track the final destination of the e-mail Khan had sent to the head of al-Qaeda. It took less than a day to get the military hardware in place for a quick, surgical strike.

At over 25 000ft the drone was invisible. It had been circling the compound west of Bannu in the mountains of north Waziristan in long elliptical loops for over six hours. Waiting, waiting. It had several days fuel left to circle if necessary and a drone never got impatient. The signal would come through at one time or another. It circled for yet another loop when … there it was … the laptop had been switched on and the user was online. The drone immediately locked in on the target … two hellfire missiles a heartbeat later were sent streaking down. Suleiman Abbas was dead seventeen seconds after he'd switched on his new MacBook. Mission accomplished Mr. President. You would have thought the Buffalo Bills had scored a touchdown in the Superbowl – the whoops and hollers could be heard right down the corridor outside the operations centre in the White House basement.

***

There were no survivors from the air attack on the fort in Somalia but from the many body fragments found, it looked as though at least two hundred Al Shabbab fighters had been killed there. Two weeks after the bombing raid a US Army team of engineers began sifting and combing through a mountain of rubble – how the terrorists had build such a warren of caves and tunnels, and by hand, was hard to believe. Even with the most modern equipment, it would have taken months, if not years. They finally found General de la Rey six weeks later, at home in his steel black coffin, the box bent and twisted and scorched as if by the fires of hell. His sleep had been undisturbed by the bombing, his nuclear heart intact. Eventually, they took him home and removed this heart and laid it to rest with those of his comrades at the nuclear waste facility at Vaalputs in the dusty, dry Northern Cape.

That night, Technician 1st Class Timunye was jolted out of half-sleep when the warning buzzer alerted him to a surge of radioactivity in the central storage vault. He watched as the needle that showed the increase slowly rose to danger level, and was about to sound the alarm, when it returned to 'normal safe'. He leaned back and closed his eyes again. 'No problem, not worth the hours of paperwork if I report it.'

Perhaps it was only the six generals, Meijer, Kruitzinger, Hertzog, de Wet, Joubert and Cronje, one by one, bidding welcome to their lost comrade, de la Rey.

GLOSSARY

ag	*(Afrikaans)* oh come on
agal	*(Arabic)* black cord ring to keep headdress in place
Ahlan wa sahlan	*(Arabic)* welcome
Allahu Akbar	*(Arabic)* God (is) the greatest
AWB	Afrikaner resistance movement (*Weerstandsbeweging*)
babelas	hangover
bak oor	stick-out ears
bakkie	pick-up truck, ute
BEE	Black Economic Empowerment
betoger	protester
bittereinder	someone who will fight to the end
blik	tin can
bliksem	(lit) lightning, 'beat up'
Boer	South African of Dutch, German or French Huguenot descent
boer/e	farmer/s
boerekos	(lit) 'farmers food' Afrikaans cuisine
boeremusiek	(lit) 'farmers music' *(*the principal instrument is the accordion)
boerperd	(lit) 'farmer's horse', South African horse breed
boerseun	son of a farmer, a true Afrikaner
boerewors	(lit) 'farmers sausage' made with coarsely minced beef with minced pork, lamb, or both) and toasted coriander seed, black pepper
bokmakierie	S.A. songbird of the thrush family
boom	marijuana
bosbefok	bush happy, crazy like a soldier who

	has spent too long on active duty
braai/braaivleis	barbecue
brak	mongrel
broekie	panty
BSAP	British South Africa Police (Rhodesia)
charra	slang for a South African of Indian extraction (from curry)
dassie	rock hyrax
die	the
donga	deep gully
doos	(lit) box, (silly) c**t,
dop en dam	brandy and water (literally dam water)
doppies	spent brass cartridge shells
drinkwater	drinking water
dronk	drunk
dronkgat	drunkard
Dutchman	Afrikaner
fok	fuck
fokol	nothing
ganja	marijuana
gat	hole, arsehole
habari ya asubuhi	(Swahili) good morning
hau!	(Zulu) cripes!
HEU	Highly Enriched Uranium
Hotnot	abbr. Hottentot, derogatory for Cape Coloured

ja	yes
jagter	hunter
Jihad	(Arabic) war against unbelievers
kaalgat	naked
kaaskop	cheese head, blonde, also derogatory name for a Hollander
kak	shit
khat	plant drug stimulant from the Horn of Africa ingested by chewing
Khoikhoi	With the bushmen, the original indigenous inhabitants of Southern Africa. The Khoikhoi were also called 'hottentots' by the early white settlers
klap	hit, slap
klein	little
kleinbaas	young boss
klonkie	a Cape Coloured boy
koevoet	crowbar
koeksisters	syrup-infused twisted fried donut
Kommunis	Communist. In the old S.A., anyone left of Attila the Hun
koppie	(lit) small head, hillock
kraal	traditional African village of huts
laaitie	youngster
magtig	my God!
mampoer	(also *witblits)* Moonshine often made with peaches
melktert	milk tart
meneer	mister

mense	people
moer	beat up
moer koffee	a blend of coffee and chicory
môre	morning
morsdood	as dead as a dodo
mossie	sparrow
Mujahadeen	*(Arabic)* Plural of 'one involved in *Jihad*'
'n boer maak 'n plan	a farmer makes a plan, (usually a Heath Robinson one)
Ngiyabonga	*(Zulu)* thank you
niks	nothing
oke	chap, guy
onder	under
oom	oom
oubaas	old boss, term of respect
ouma	grandma
oupa	grandpa
padkos	food for the road
PAL	Permissive Action Link, an electronic device that prevents arming the nuclear weapon unless the correct codes are inserted into it
pampoen	pumpkin
panga	machete
pannekoek	pancakes
perlemoen	abalone
plaas	farm
platteland	back country
poephol	arsehole

pomp	pump
poppies	dolls '*die poppies gaan dans*' (lit) the dolls will dance, there will be big trouble
potjie	iron pot to cook stew on an open fire, also the stew itself
riempie	leather strip
rooikat	caracal (African lynx)
rooinek	(lit) 'red neck', derogatory term for an Englishman
roosterkoek	bread rolls made over open coals
sakkie-sakkie	Afrikaner dance music
salamu jumbe	(Swahili) peace/greetings boss
seun	son
sies	yuck
skelm	dodgy, crooked, suspect, not their own wives
sluk	swallow
snot klap	open hand smack to side of face
Sonskyn Hoekie	sunshine corner
sous	a onion/tomato/chilli sauce good with pap and braai meat
spook	fright, ghost
spook and diesel	cane (white spirits) and coke
stywe	stiff
stywe pap	stiff mielie meal porridge
swart	black
tannie	auntie
thawb	ankle length Arab robe with long sleeves
totsiens	goodbye, till we meet again

Tukkies	Pretoria University
UCT	University of Cape Town
uMkhonto we Siswe	'The Spear of the Nation' – ANC's military wing, usually 'MK'
Unisa	University of South Africa, distance learning university
vleis	meat
volk	people
wakis	wagon trunk
windgat	braggart
windpomp	windmill
withaak	white thorn
wit wolf	white wolf
Wits	University of the Witwatersrand, Johannesburg
wors	sausage
yussus	jeez